Michelle Kenney is a firm believe[...]
to other worlds can always be fc[...]
She is also a hopeless scribbleho[...]
devices, likes nothing better than to daydream about these
worlds in the back of a dog-eared notebook. When not
scribbling, Michelle can usually be found beachcombing with
her family or rescuing Ted, their loopy Labrador, from himself.
Michelle is the author of the bestselling Book of Fire trilogy,
and a graduate of the Curtis Brown Writing for Children Novel
Course 2015. She also has a LLB (Hons) Degree in Law, an APD
in Public Relations, and an unhealthy obsession with all things
Regency - Doctors say they're unlikely to find a cure any time
soon.

facebook.com/307701063035009
x.com/MKenneyPR
instagram.com/mich_kenneybooks
tiktok.com/@michkenneyauthor

Also by Michelle Kenney

Storm of Ash

City of Dust

Book of Fire

THE MISMATCH OF THE SEASON

MICHELLE KENNEY

ONE MORE CHAPTER

One More Chapter
a division of HarperCollins*Publishers* Ltd
1 London Bridge Street
London SE1 9GF
www.harpercollins.co.uk
HarperCollins*Publishers*
Macken House, 39/40 Mayor Street Upper,
Dublin 1, D01 C9W8, Ireland

This paperback edition 2025
1
First published in Great Britain in ebook format
by HarperCollins*Publishers* 2025
Copyright © Michelle Kenney 2025
Michelle Kenney asserts the moral right to
be identified as the author of this work

A catalogue record of this book is available from the British Library

ISBN: 978-0-00-868490-7

Printed and bound in the UK using 100% Renewable Electricity
by CPI Group (UK) Ltd

For my sisters

Chapter One

Three months until the wedding

I t was the perfect morning for a duel.

Or, at least it would have been had Miss Phoebe Fairfax lived between the covers of a novel where the heroine actually *did* things, as opposed to watching her brothers do them all instead.

The chief offender among them was undoubtedly her eldest sibling, Lord Thomas Fairfax, currently snoring in his bedchamber after the devil's own luck at the races, followed by an even worse run at faro. Which only made her own betrothal all the more vexing. To be betrothed by one's eldest brother was bad enough. To find oneself promised to a gout-ridden old goat more than twice one's age, and without so much as a by-your-leave, a downright outrage.

All of which had left her little choice but to embark on her current course of action – a dramatic yet highly essential dawn flight through the misted grounds of Knightswood Manor.

'Papa wanted this match and you're in no position to object, I'm head of this family now.'

A ready scowl descended as she hastened through the frost-bitten grass of her childhood home. Head of the family or not, it seemed Lord Thomas Fairfax, twelve years her senior, and her legal guardian for the last two, had little regard for anyone or anything, except washing his gambling hands of his siblings as fast as possible.

'The earl is an old family friend, and the match will help to re-establish the Fairfaxes among the ton. Even you have to see that there is no discussion to be had; you will be the Countess of Cumberland in the spring and make the best of it!'

In truth, while becoming a countess didn't *sound* too terrible, she would challenge any young lady to remain in the same room as the crusty old earl for longer than two minutes without concluding it to be the very worst fate to be inflicted on anyone at all.

Phoebe conjured the image of his overstuffed waistcoat and moist, purple lips before shuddering. Quite apart from the fact that he couldn't recall her name, their first meeting last week had only confirmed all the reasons why she should never become a countess.

'Step forward into the light girl! Where I can see you!

'Well, well, your brother could do with feeding you up a bit, but you'll do… Nothing worse than a skinny countess, I say!'

She shuddered again, recalling the way his gaze had rested on her, making her feel the best prize calf her brother could offer after a long, hard winter. Except she had always been the Fairfax least expected to marry, let alone marry well.

Not that she couldn't understand Thomas's perspective, of course. No one had expected Papa's sudden demise from a pernicious toe the year before and, despite being a veteran of the Napoleonic Wars, Thomas was still only thirty years of age himself. Mama used to refer to it as *a gentleman's dangerous age*, the time when he either married, drank himself into oblivion, or became a confirmed rake. Since Thomas had never made any mention of entering into domestic bliss, Phoebe could only assume he intended to embrace one of the latter two options, while subjecting the rest of his long-suffering brothers and sisters to his *Monstrous Marriage Master Plan*, as her sister Sophie put it.

Phoebe stole a glance back at her bedchamber window, just visible in the pale clutch of dawn, and suppressed her rising guilt. Sophie was more than capable of keeping an eye on the Fairfax brood for three months, and she needed this time. She might not be able to escape Thomas's master plan forever, but she could escape it for three months. *Three precious months* in which to live a lifetime of dreams; it was ambitious enough for any heroine.

She drew a steadying breath and hurried onto the carriageway through Knightswood's famous avenue of oaks.

Thomas's Monstrous Marriage Master Plan had begun the moment they lay dear Papa to rest. Phoebe's four brothers didn't feature of course, they were all in varying stages of education, and would have as much freedom as they wished, leaving all of Thomas's unwanted attention directed at herself and their three sisters: Sophie, seventeen, Josephine, sixteen – and Matilda, twelve, who was already on her third governess this year.

Phoebe frowned at a burst of hopeful snowdrops, trying to escape the frost.

Even if Papa's will *had* contained a request for his first-born daughter to make a match with his closest friend, the Earl of Cumberland – who was nearing sixty and alarmingly purple – it was a brother's duty to protect her from such a fate, wasn't it?

Or at least, give her a fighting chance.

Instead, he seemed more than happy to write off a London season as an expensive and unnecessary prelude, and go straight to the main marital event, which seemed just a little unfair when her younger sisters would have ample time to find suitors of a less gout-prone age.

Indeed, the more she'd thought on it, the more it seemed she'd been dealt the largest slice of ill luck since she'd won the hoopla at Knightswood Fair and Alfred, her second-eldest brother, made off with the candy floss. Yet, it was her fate all the same, unless she did something about it. And since she couldn't imagine any of her favourite literary heroines marrying a crusty old earl without a dramatic adventure or two to sustain them for the rest of their days, she really had little choice but to embark on her current course of action.

A flicker of a smile flitted across Phoebe's face – if only Fred could see her now, stealing away from Knightswood Manor in his old frock coat, breeches and boots, her dark copper tresses pinned up beneath a rotund country hat that had seen so many better days. Not that Fred's lack of fashion bothered her. She was quite certain that the more *bourgeois* her appearance, the less likely she would be to attract attention and the sooner she would be mistress of her own destiny. Plus, she was quite certain breeches could be the work of actual goddesses, and was in no mind to trade them for a skirt any time soon.

She paused as the bushes ahead rustled suddenly, and a juvenile doe stepped out on the path. They locked eyes briefly, before the doe bolted towards the rest of the herd in the park. Wistfully, Phoebe watched her darting path through the silver grass towards a waiting buck, his majestic antlers glinting in the amber light. She sighed. Papa used to tell stories about their elusive herd granting wishes, yet none of her siblings had ever been stolen away by moorland fae, leaving her little choice but to conclude that, at best, they were unreliable indeed.

Resolutely, she pushed on, drawing comfort from the sway of her reticule beneath her frock coat. She wasn't such a ninnyhammer as to keep all of her pin money in one of her marvellous new pockets, now that she'd decided to board the common stage, and she still planned to write to dear Fred about a loan the moment she reached London.

A brief smile flitted across her face.

Dear Fred was the least vexing of all her brothers, as well as the one least likely to squeal to Thomas about her whereabouts once he knew the truth; plus he still owed her from the Hexworthy Races two years before. Briefly, she recalled the traditional Dartmoor horse race Fred had dreaded, while filling every bone of her defiant body with envy. Ladies weren't permitted to compete, of course, but with the aid of his riding shirt and breeches – as well as another miraculous hat – she'd not only managed a very credible pass, but also brought home a highly coveted third place in his name. And now he could return the favour.

Phoebe inhaled brightly. She'd never travelled by stage before and was considerably excited by the prospect. Her old governess used to mutter about springs and padding for days after a journey, but she also had a taste for hogs pudding, which Phoebe found most suspicious. Besides which, she really had very little choice; the mail coach would be the very first place Thomas looked, and she could hardly take the Fairfax family chaise, or his favourite racing phaeton to London – there were some things even she wouldn't do.

Humming, Phoebe diverted off the carriageway, and headed towards a discreet estate gate. On reflection, she was quite satisfied she'd managed things reasonably well enough for any girl hoping for a heroic adventure or two. She'd even settle for *marginally unheroic* if it didn't involve being told exactly what to do and think, by someone who'd been absent for most of her life. She would be as free as any of her brothers, or favourite fictional heroines – and even if the latter had rather more important matters to consider than clean stays and lodgings, she was certain her many years imagining adventures with her siblings would stand her in good stead.

'I'm not sure a headless ghost would escape in a chintz curtain, Phoebs – what about the settle throw instead?'

A faint smile flickered across her face. Fairfax Theatrical Company had been a part of their family for as long as she could remember, as well as her only reprieve from a life of corsets and cotillion practice. She never once thought she'd ever actually escape, and yet somehow, at this very moment, she was embarking on a *real* adventure. She had a change of clothing, coin enough to secure a private bedchamber, and she was more than certain she could imitate dear Fred's gentle manner when it came to ordering luncheon, or some such similar refreshment. There was, after all, nothing worse than an empty stomach – it got in the way of plain, sensible thinking. This was a sentiment that had proven quite the bone of contention for her poor, deceased mama, who had given up on her eldest daughter ever contenting herself with just one slice of cake, when Cook had clearly intended her to eat three.

Phoebe's smile widened as she climbed the estate gate, quite certain that breeches were a male conspiracy, too. For years, she'd been inched and cinched into suffocating layers of petticoats, creating a rise of heat she could only equate to one of Cook's rice puddings, and even Sophie had to admit that a hoop and petticoats were a positive disadvantage when it came to *that time* of the month, which must never be mentioned in polite company.

By contrast, Fred's attire felt like utter freedom, and she was never more convinced that ladies' clothing had been designed with canaries in mind, which only fuelled the importance of the next three months. She had this one utterly unique chance to forego all the rules and chase every dream she'd ever had – which was so much more inviting than Sophie's parting accusation.

Briefly, her sister's words echoed through her head. But the more she considered them, the more she was persuaded she wasn't actually running *away*, but rather *towards* the opportunity to discover her own inner heroine.

Because everyone had one of those deep down inside – didn't they?

She was also more than certain she had to have at least one bareback-horseracing-at-midnight kind of adventure waiting for her, despite Sophie's considerable doubts. Why else would she have been blessed with such a lively imagination and, as Mama would say, *hoydenish ways*, if there wasn't some master plan at work?

She nodded briskly at a chirruping robin before turning into the country lane. It had ever been the same. Most of the young ladies of her acquaintance seemed as prone to fits of the vapours, as she was to ravenous hunger; and it was certainly one of Mama's greatest regrets, that she had the most practical head, when needed.

'Really Phoebe, you have the fortitude of an ox!' she complained, the day Phoebe dragged Matilda from Knightswood lake after a skating incident.

From this, Phoebe could only conclude it would have been far more ladylike to let her younger sister drown while she herself expired from shock, which felt a stretch – even for Mama. And while she had nothing against oxen in particular, they did seem quite banal creatures when all was said and done.

Still, Mama had always been somewhat of a stickler when it came to matters of propriety.

'*A young lady needs a certain air of … fragility about her person*,' she would say reprovingly, whenever Phoebe was sighted scaling one of the many trees around the park.

'*Not ruddy cheeks and splinters!*'

Considering an air of fragility seemed synonymous with a life of impressive dullness, Phoebe was certain she would never meet Mama's exacting expectations. It was one of the reasons she'd escape on Misty whenever she could. On the moor, she could ride until she believed she really was Mary

Queen of Scots; or a time traveller from some distant, trouser-wearing age that finally treated men and women as equals – if such a thing were ever *really* possible.

She sighed. For the most part, she also knew better than to rely on any sibling support, despite being considered an all-round *good egg* when it came to quarrels. She no more ratted on the brother who snuck off to a prize fight, than the sister who spent all her pin money on ribbons; and while this loyalty had earned her admiration and reproof in equal measure, there was no lack of genuine affection between them all.

She had *still tried* to call on these affections when challenging Thomas's Monstrous Marriage Master Plan, but as he controlled the purse strings, and therefore every whim and wish of the Fairfax brood, they'd fallen to the wayside quicker than even she'd expected.

'*You've got to see it from our perspective, Phoebs,*' Fred pleaded, after Thomas threatened to cut off his allowance. '*Tom has us over a barrel until we come of age. And the old earl isn't that bad really… You'll have a fine house, your own carriage … and just think of all the climbing trees in his grounds.*'

Phoebe's face darkened as she strode down the last section of country lane. Fred could try to placate her as much as he liked, but how he, or any of her brothers and sisters, could expect her to willingly tie her life to an old man who made her feel like a skinny pullet trussed for the Sunday roast, was beyond her. Let alone the fact that when he walked, a decided scent of onions wafted about his person.

Onions! Phoebe wrinkled her nose just thinking about it.

Matilda was first to notice, and had levelled the accusation when Phoebe refused to buy her a second macaroon on a village outing. But her youthful nose had a sound point, and it was one of the reasons Phoebe knew she had to act – that and the *unfortunate incident*.

Phoebe closed her eyes briefly. In truth, if it wasn't for the *unfortunate incident*, Thomas probably wouldn't have felt quite so compelled to enact phase one of his Monstrous Marriage Master Plan. But Sophie had laid a wager and Thomas, above all people, should have known a wager was a matter of honour.

'*I cannot believe Knightswood's church organist intended to create a scandal with Miss Kettering,*' Sophie had mused. '*In fact, I would even go so far as to wager that any impoverished, romantic young gentleman would have little choice but to offer elopement if his liaison is discovered. It's either that or die of a broken heart – don't you think, Phoebe?*'

Phoebe was quick to concede that any church-organist-turned-disgraced-eloper was very deserving of her sister's empathy, but also that Sophie's assertion gave like gentlemen such a poor reputation that she was duty-bound to disprove it – which was how she'd set upon Monsieur Dupres, their unfortunate pianoforte tutor.

In her defence, she absolutely did not set out to *encourage* him to fall in love with her – she'd just wanted to prove to Sophie that, *even if* a gentleman was impoverished and hopelessly romantic, he didn't always propose elopement.

And if she'd underestimated Monsieur Dupres on this occasion, she was wholly convinced he was the exception, rather than the rule.

Thomas chose not to understand the matter at all, of course, calling her an ignorant, foolhardy girl he'd gladly pack off to a convent were it not for his unwavering belief she'd get herself expelled, before the sennight was up. Instead, he'd talked of Papa's will and bringing forward the dreaded wedding, which had only hastened her own plan, safe in the knowledge that once everything was taken into consideration, Thomas would have to concede he was wholly and utterly to blame.

It was while she was enjoying the comfort of this certain victory, and her brother's well-deserved guilt, that Phoebe spied her new travelling companions gathering in the frosty grass beside the public road, and felt a first rise of doubt.

If only Thomas had let her have a season... If only he hadn't found the elopement proposal from Monsieur Dupres... If only she'd been able to bring some Fairfax Theatrical Company costumes with her... She could have put them to excellent use where she was going.

The thought gave her a surge of strength.

Where she was going was a secret of the utmost gravity that she hadn't even shared with Sophie, her most suspicious sister. Not only was Sophie unable to keep any kind of secret, let alone under pressure, she would also feel duty-bound to read her one of her sisterly lectures which were beginning to sound, uncannily, like dear Mama's. And the truth was, Phoebe's destination wasn't in the least bit de rigueur for a young lady of her social standing, at all.

A rueful smile crept across her face, one that mirrored the gleam in her moorland eyes. Of all her schemes over the past eighteen years, this one had to be the most daring, and she could only imagine Thomas's rage if he could see her now: clad in their brother's hand-me-downs, unaccompanied, and about to board the common stage. If it were divulged in polite company, it could ruin her and yet Phoebe knew her brother far too well for that. The moment Sophie reported her absence, Thomas would concoct some plausible tale of an indisposed distant cousin, while using every means possible to find her – and all to protect his Monstrous Marriage Masterplan.

Let him search. She'd been dreaming of this adventure her whole life long, and even if it was only for three precious months, it would be enough to sustain her for a lifetime.

It had to.

Chapter Two

Three months and a quart of devil's brew until the wedding

'Thank you.' Phoebe nodded, as a rosy-faced farmwife and her dimpling daughter shuffled down the worn stagecoach seat.

'You're welcome.' The farmwife beamed. 'It's not as if you'll take up much room, I've had roast dinners bigger than you!'

Then she turned to her daughter, chortling in a way that made her entire upper body shake like jelly, as Phoebe slid into a seat nearest the window. She'd paid an extra shilling for a view, but as she turned her face towards the frosted hills she was leaving behind, she was conscious only of another pang of doubt. Knightswood Manor had been her home for eighteen years and, aside from a family trip to Weymouth when Josephine was recuperating from a particularly bad contagion of the lungs, she'd barely left Devon at all. Now she was headed to London, for three whole months, all by herself.

It's this or marry the earl, without so much as a whiff of adventure your whole life long, she chastised herself, as she stretched out and adopted Fred's slightly unconscious expression.

'Excuse me, might I have a little leg room, please?'

Phoebe started as a severe-looking gentleman in the seat opposite glared at her through a tiny, round eyeglass. Flushing, she muttered a low apology. There was, after all, a stark difference between sprawling like a man, and being a total *foozler* as Fred might say.

Fortunately, the coachman chose the same moment to slam the doors with an incoherent shout, and as the coach lurched into a grinding roll, Phoebe drew a deep breath. They were packed in like Cook's favourite sardines, and it was a far noisier affair than she'd ever anticipated, but nothing could override her silent exaltation. She'd done it, she'd escaped! And now she had three long months in which to pursue every heroic adventure she'd ever dreamed of beyond the border of Knightswood Manor.

'Fancy an onion dearie? I find it really helps with the knocks and bumps,' the rosy-faced farmwife wheezed, proffering one of the small, inauspicious roots as though it were a tasty apple.

Phoebe declined politely, noting both the woman and the dimpling daughter appeared to be chomping their way though their market wares with relish. She squeezed her fingers, a sudden memory of the purple-faced earl making her stomach churn; it was not an omen, and she was not going to overthink it.

The severe-looking gentleman cleared his throat.

'I beg to differ,' he offered, with a deprecatory wobble of his eyeglass. 'I always maintain boiled kidneys are the very best antidote to having one's bones rattled to within an inch of one's own grave.'

Several murmurs of agreement reached over the crunch of the wheels, while the farmwife looked the severe-looking gentleman up and down with an expression of avid dislike.

'Well, I don't s'pose you've a basket of *those* about your person now, 'ave you?' she challenged. 'And my dear old Uncle Billy, God bless his soul, who used to travel from Tav'stock to Ex'ter regular, swore by his onions for health *and* luck against highwaymen! So I reckon I'll just stick wiv *them* for now.'

Upon hearing this persuasive account, the entire coach seemed to undergo a change of mind, with one passenger even going so far as to hold out his hand as though in a pledge of undying loyalty to dear old Uncle Billy. The farmwife beamed her delight as she rewarded his support with an extra-large root, before sitting back in smug satisfaction.

The matter settled, Phoebe turned her attention back to the shadowy peaks of Dartmoor, just visible though the smeared window. It was almost three hours until they stopped to change horses, and she was starting to feel the effect of having risen before dawn. Exhaling slowly, she rested her head back against the worn leather seat and let her thoughts drift to London.

There was no way her meagre savings would last three months, which had narrowed her few choices into two even slimmer options: masquerading as a governess for some respectable, yet highly reclusive, family – or joining a theatre company. And since the former was much more likely to result in exposure, she was convinced a short theatrical career was just the thing, with the added bonus of bringing her closer to every fictional heroine she'd ever loved.

Her eyes misted as the many stories she and her sisters had performed to entertain Josephine flitted through her mind. They always made her laugh – and cough – before Mama banned them, but they'd sneak back, anyway, and begin all over again. Back then, she believed she could *do* anything and *be* anyone. She still did – it was only the world who disagreed on account of one tiny fact of birth that decided everything in her life.

Of course, she had no real desire to *be* one of her brothers, she just wanted the same freedom. She wanted to travel, climb trees, swim wherever she liked, and wear trousers with *miracle pockets* whenever she chose – which explained her current choice of country attire. She knew the world would take a lot less notice of a young, bourgeois gentleman of no particular fame or fortune, than a young gentlewoman. Thomas was much less likely to discover her this way, and she could cover her tracks by signing Fred's name with a very credible flourish, which was actually much more pleasing to the eye than his own hasty scrawl, when needed. And while she knew it wouldn't be as simple as walking into the Covent Garden Theatre and demanding an audition for Kemble's new King John, it was still preferable to presenting as a hopeful actress, which would likely bring all sorts of undesirable problems of its own.

Phoebe exhaled as the relentless jolts and bumps began to soothe her heavy eyelids closed, recalling her plan for a character reference, should one be required. Their highly unfortunate and much misunderstood pianoforte tutor, Monsieur Dupres, now resided in London and would undoubtedly furnish her with something suitable if she reminded him of the debt he owed. She was, after all, the one who'd persuaded Thomas to let him go without a hint of scandal, and with full recommendation to future employers. And, if he was at all reluctant she could simply share that she still had his elopement proposal in her possession – as well as the postal address of the *Society Matters Circular*.

She allowed herself a small, wry smile.

As an actor, she could earn her own money and perhaps even tour a little, see a few sights she'd only ever heard or read stories about. Her head filled with the multitude of exotic-sounding places Fred had visited on his Grand Tour last year. He'd had such a splendid time visiting all the European cities with his Oxford friends that they'd taken on somewhat of a fictional gleam for her: Paris, Venice, Rome, *fair Verona*... Perhaps she'd be lucky enough to be cast in a dramatic stage duel to the death; she'd always been better than her brothers at fencing. Or a witty comedy, where she was a female disguised as a male, playing a male actor playing a female... She stared out at the receding silhouette of Dartmoor as her woolly brain tried to compute the layers of dress should such a role ever be offered, and before she knew it, they were cantering through the moorland woods with a carpet of bluebells underfoot, and a chorus of wood warblers for company...

'Taunton! All passengers descend at The Swan. We depart again at one o'clock sharp!'

The coachman's bark stirred Phoebe from a wistful dream

about stretching out on the Fairfax-family chaise's fully sprung seats, while her old governess recounted the many times the stagecoach made her bones rattle like an old ghost. She and her sisters used to dissolve into laughter when she said such things, but today Phoebe had new sympathy. Travel by the common stage was not turning out to be quite the experience she'd hoped.

Stiff and aching, she climbed down the worn step and onto a cobbled courtyard, where she was greeted by a hive of midday activity. Two young ostlers ran to hold the panting horses' heads, while passengers continued to disembark from every corner of the coach. Phoebe couldn't help but stare. She'd boarded so swiftly, she hadn't realised there were just as many people travelling on top of the coach as there were inside, and they looked twice as relieved as she, if that was even possible.

'Welcome to The Swan, ladies and gentlemen,' a pompous voice boomed over the hustle and bustle. 'An establishment of quality, serving persons of quality, the very best in quality food!'

'I wonder what he saves for everyone else then?' the farmwife muttered beside Phoebe.

'This way to our comfortable tap room where we will be pleased to serve you from our fine selection of wines and brews! I'm sure you've worked up a thirst, and you'll be hard put to find a finer local brew south of Bristol! And if it's a bite to eat you're after, I can personally recommend the roast beef!'

The landlord's throaty sales pitch nearly deafened Phoebe as she absorbed her new surroundings. She cast his portly figure a covert glance as he stood on the freshly scrubbed step of The Swan Public Inn, rubbing his hands together and beaming his welcome amid the chaos in the courtyard. He looked every inch the sort her brother would call a *right rum'un*. And yet there was no denying the grumble of her stomach, either.

Indeed, it was just as she was pondering whether sampling the local brew might actually be something Fred would do, and therefore entirely in keeping with her new character, that a new commotion rippled through the courtyard.

'Lawks, Ma! I swear, it's the devil hisself!' the farmwife's daughter gasped, as a high-perch phaeton and two spirited greys thundered into the courtyard at such speed, that Phoebe felt sure they must run straight into the crowd.

A second gasp rippled through the courtyard as the carriage flew past, yet the tall driver appeared quite unconcerned, and merely executed the tightest of turns, before drawing to a sharp halt behind the stagecoach.

Phoebe caught her breath.

Could Thomas have discovered her already? Or was it Fred come to warn her that Thomas was on the warpath?

She had to concede that the latter was a little unlikely since she hadn't even written to Fred yet, but she wasn't taking any chances. She pulled down the brim of her hat and took a swift step backwards, straight into the farmwife's dimpling daughter.

'Oi! Watch me toes!'

'Oh! I'm … so sorry,' Phoebe mumbled, as the driver jumped down and strode around the rear of his equipage, the high gleam of his boots heralding his importance.

'Lawks, I'll live!' The daughter grinned. 'You're so light-footed a gentl'man, I barely felt it at all!'

Phoebe smiled distractedly, trying to side-eye the newcomer's boots and decide if he had Thomas's impatient stride, or something more like Fred's country snail pace. She sucked in a breath as the crowd parted, and then exhaled in relief.

He had neither.

She squeezed the girl's hand in a momentary lapse.

'Thank you, I'm such a clumsy oaf at times!' she breathed, as the girl dimpled beneath a monstrous straw bonnet tied with a garish pink ribbon.

Phoebe shrank back, suddenly aware that certain mannerisms acceptable from Miss Phoebe Fairfax, could be construed as something else entirely from Mr Alfred Fairfax.

'That I'm sure you ain't, is he, Ma? But you can buy me a cider to make up for it … if y'like?'

She stared, uncertain what to make of this dimpling girl, twisting a bonnet ribbon around her finger in a way that clearly meant *something*. Before she realised. The farmwife's daughter was giving her 'the eye' as Fred would call it – she was flirting with her!

Phoebe felt a very undignified bubble of laughter threaten to surface, just as the landlord's pompous voice filled the courtyard again.

'Ah, Viscount Damerel! How lovely to see you, sir! If I'd known you were coming, I'd have reserved the best parlour. As it happens, I've only the smaller of the two left…' He tailed off hopefully as the imperious-looking driver of the phaeton approached.

'Water for my horses, Briggs!' the gentleman returned bluntly.

'Of course, sir! Right away, sir! You, boy, wake up!' he relayed sharply. 'Take the viscount's horses to the stables and no dawdling!'

A young ostler sprang into action as the crowd jostled for a better look at the viscount, who'd managed to change the pompous landlord's whole demeanour with one withering look.

Phoebe's eyes narrowed.

Viscount Damerel looked exactly the sort of gentleman over whom Sophie would swoon, given half the chance. He was tall and well groomed, with hair swept into some fashionable style Phoebe vaguely remembered Fred attempting to copy – he called it a Wyndham Fall or some such thing, or perhaps that was the tie of his cravat, she could never quite recall. He was also impeccably dressed: his coat fitted like a glove, his pantaloons were spotless, and his Hessian boots gleamed more than any pair she'd ever known. Yet despite all this, his nose was a shade too aquiline, his chin excessively proud and there was something in the tight press of his lips that did little to recommend him at all.

In truth, he looked the sort of gentleman who never climbed a tree, despite all the freedom afforded him.

She bristled involuntarily.

Her brothers would undoubtedly call him a 'Corinthian of the first water', but his puffed-up self-importance said only one thing to her: *dandy*. And whatever he thought about having the smaller of the two parlours was lost entirely as he strode inside, leaving the open-mouthed landlord in his three-caped wake.

'No mention of a parlour for the rest of us, eh, Effie?' the rosy-cheeked farmwife quipped, raising one of her thick auburn eyebrows. 'We'll just have to make do with the tap room and a jug of cider instead!'

'I'd much rather the tap room and a cider, than share a parlour with *that* fancy one!' Effie scoffed, pushing her cloak back to reveal a simple country dress cut far too tightly across her shapely chest.

Briefly, Phoebe gazed in abject admiration; she'd never seen such an ample bosom, even on Sophie who was by the far the most comely of them all.

'Won't you join us inside?' the rosy farmwife cajoled. 'You can keep young Effie here company, while I unlace me boots.'

She sighed and leaned forward conspiratorially.

'Bunions,' she whispered loudly, before shooting a look around the courtyard to ensure all those within earshot had heard her correctly.

All Phoebe saw was the basket of offending roots at Effie's feet.

'Young gentl'man don't wanna hear nothin' about yer feet, Ma!' Effie exclaimed, taking Phoebe's arm as though she'd known her all her life.

'What he needs is a drink, like us! Come on.' She dimpled, shaking back her auburn curls and drawing the rapt admiration of most gentlemen nearby.

Moments later, Phoebe found herself being propelled towards The Swan Inn with more strength than she would have ever thought possible of a young girl. And not for the first time since leaving Knightswood, she found a use for Fred's ridiculously high shirt points. She sank her chin inside them as far as she could, comforting herself with the thought that a bustling farmwife and her dimpling daughter were likely to be the very last people in the world Thomas would suspect of harbouring his runaway sister.

The busy tap room was located down a long corridor and towards the back of The Swan Inn. It was entirely unlike any of the tearooms Phoebe had frequented with her family, yet the faint wafts of roast beef and spiced cider were so enticing, it wasn't long before she began wondering if falling in with Effie and her mother might not actually be the luckiest occurrence of her journey so far. A young gentleman travelling alone was unremarkable, but a young gentleman travelling with far more comely companions couldn't be more invisible; and by the time Effie's mother had secured a window table with little more than a wink, Phoebe was convinced she was managing her new-found freedom very astutely indeed.

'Ain't you gonna take off that hat?' Effie asked, pulling at her bonnet and shaking out a tumble of auburn locks. 'Bet your head feels 'ot. I know mine feels like a boiled puddin!'

Phoebe swallowed as Effie and her mother busied themselves with the apparently jovial task of stripping off their hats and winter cloaks. Yet all Phoebe's thoughts were for the fact that she'd completely overlooked the need to remove her own hat occasionally.

Thankfully, Fred came to the rescue once again.

'I confess,' she ventured, recalling her brother's rather alarming experiment resulting in treacle-like locks, 'that thanks to a small *miscalculation* with Macassar oil, I'm rather reluctant.'

She smiled, feigning distinct embarrassment.

'I was *attempting* Mr Brummell's latest creation, with a rather unimpressive outcome, so I do hope you will excuse my manners – or should I say lack of them – Mrs…?'

'Oh, just call me Flora, like the rest of Dunsford!' The farmwife chortled good-naturedly. 'And of course we'll excuse you! Beau Brummell, eh? Well, well, you youngsters do like to chase the fashion!'

She leant forward conspiratorially.

'And while we're getting things straight, you mustn't mind Effie's straight talking, either. It's how my late husband and I raised her. Say what yer think, Effie, we always told her, especially when it comes to the young gentl'men; no girl got anywhere by holding back!'

Her eyes misted over while Phoebe choked on a sip of water, wondering how many fits of vapours her own mama would've had on hearing such advice.

'Glass of ratafia and a plate of chicken please,' she whispered to the serving girl who'd arrived to take their luncheon order.

Flora frowned.

'I meant … a jug of cider, and plate of your landlord's roast beef…' Phoebe substituted in a gruffer tone.

Effie's eyes lit up as her mother sat back, satisfied.

'Lunch for a lord,' they chimed happily.

Precisely one hour later, Phoebe was a little unsure why everything seemed quite so entertaining, but quite certain she hadn't laughed as much since Sophie fell into a muddy horse trough in her new pelisse.

'Well, what I says is, a girl can handle a pitchfork *just* as well as any man!' Effie concluded, stabbing her fork in the air, as though to accentuate the point.

Phoebe nodded in vigorous agreement, before becoming aware that Fred's hat had slid to a new and dangerous angle. She adjusted it, only to find the tap room walls behaving similarly. She stared intently, trying to work out what was wrong with them.

'Ladies, pray do excuse me … I must powder … stretch my legs for a moment!' she declared with a small, energetic hiccup.

'Right you are!' Flora laughed heartily. '*Run-dez-vouz* back on the coach, as they say – though whoever *they* are, I'm sure I've no idea!' she added, draining the last of her cider in one impressive draught.

Beaming magnanimously, Phoebe stood up. Or at least, it appeared she'd stood up because she was definitely vertical, but her legs were behaving in a most irregular manner. Indeed, if she didn't know any better she'd say that rather than standing, she was *actually floating*. Phoebe checked her person suspiciously, but everything appeared to be connected in much the same way as before, and her head was starting to feel very warm indeed, so she paused only to beam again before making for the corridor.

Fortunately, the fresh air was an immediate tonic – even if the corridor did seem steeper than before – and it was just as she was beginning to wonder if she didn't make a more convincing Fred than Fred himself, that she heard the voices.

'I don't care what bookings you've taken, I need your

freshest pair, and I'll pay double whatever anyone else is paying!'

Phoebe paused outside a private parlour, as a raised exchange filtered out into the hallway.

'I understand, sir, of course, sir… It's just the local fight you see, sir, it means a lot of The Swan's horses have been promised already.'

'I don't think you heard me,' a glacial voice returned. 'I have no interest in bookings or the local fight. All I care about is leaving this inn with your fastest horses within the next few minutes – do I make myself clear? I mean to be in Bridgewater by nightfall!'

'But … but … that's impossible, sir! It's already past luncheon and you'll lose the light by—'

'Do we understand one another?' the haughty tone cut in again, leaving Phoebe in little doubt as to its owner.

'Knew he was an arrogant dandy,' she muttered, just as an imperious march sounded across the floor.

In her head, Phoebe made an elegant escape down the corridor, far away from the disagreeable viscount and his perfect eyebrows, but in reality her floating legs dissolved beneath her, leaving her sprawled across the parlour entrance, face to face with his immaculate Hessian boots.

And worse still, Fred's old hat took off like an AWOL pudding bowl.

'Really, Briggs!' the viscount hissed. 'I thought The Swan commanded a rather better quality of clientele than drunkards and scoundrels! I may need to rethink my patronage altogether if this proves not to be the case, and *especially* if fresh horses prove too much of a challenge!'

For a moment there was only a tense silence, then a stream of incoherent apologies filled the air, as the viscount turned and strode away.

Mortified, Phoebe clutched at her exposed head, knowing she needed to retrieve her hat as quickly as possible if she were to avoid detection. She scuttled across the floor in what she hoped was a swift and subtle movement, though she suspected it was neither.

'Kindly remove your *dubious person* from my *quality establishment* this second!' Briggs boomed as she reached the offending item, nearly making her drop it again.

Flushing, Phoebe pressed her hat to her head before turning to face the livid man.

'I won't have drunkards blackening The Swan's good name, and losing me my hard-earned custom, do you hear me? Be off with you now before I send word to the authorities that I've a right *scallywag* here, and no mistake!'

For a second, Phoebe could only blink at the blustering landlord in disbelief. She'd never been spoken to in such a manner, even when she fell through the stable roof, with the groom still abed. Then a loop of her hair slipped out beneath Fred's hat, and landed in a coil on her shoulder. They both stared at the traitorous lock before Briggs lifted his eyes, incredulity all over his face as he started towards her.

So Phoebe did the only thing left for a girl wearing her brother's short drawers *to* do – she picked herself up and fled.

Chapter Three

Three months and one unimpressive highwayman until the wedding

It seemed onions really did possess some beneficial powers.
Not only because their pungent scent helped to soothe
Phoebe's queasy stomach somehow, but because they negated
the need to explain her retreat inside Fred's hat for the next leg
of the journey.

The spinning rooms, the viscount's condemnation, the
landlord's expulsion – it was all too much – especially since
her head pounded like a storm over Haytor. So after claiming
fatigue with her loud and cheerful companions, she lay back
and pulled Fred's hat low over her eyes. And this time she
didn't mind the jolt of the wheels, at all. The only thing she
could think was how her mouth tasted like the skin of a
wizened apple, and her stomach was threatening to empty
itself at any given moment.

Phoebe stifled a groan, grateful for every draught in the
overstuffed coach, as her head bulged with all the stories her

brothers had told about the devilish effect of too much liquor. At the time she'd thought them exaggerating or trying to impress her, but now she knew they were being entirely honest, and silently she berated herself for not being more cautious. The only drink she'd ever been allowed to sip at home was ratafia, and even that had given her the bellyache. It was while she was mulling over *all* the things she'd like to say to her brothers about their very poor life choices, that she at last slid into a lucid sleep – featuring oxen and bunions – and where she might have remained quite contentedly, had a rough lurch not shaken her awake a while later.

Reluctantly, Phoebe peeled her eyes open, though both felt weighed down by a stone apiece. The afternoon light was beginning to fade, and most of her fellow passengers were looking as dishevelled as she felt. She blinked, aware of a dull throbbing at the back of her head. Somehow, and against all the odds, she'd slept for the entire afternoon.

'Have we reached Bristol yet?' she murmured, noticing the severe-looking gentleman was now stretched out like a basking lizard, and using a worn Bible as a night mask.

'Bristol? I wished we 'ad!'

Flora's moan was loud enough to stir the rest of the dozing passengers, while Phoebe watched the severe-looking gentleman snort the Bible off his face, and catch it in his lap.

'What do you mean?' she asked, trying to ignore a painful rise of laughter.

'Listen!' Effie hushed, her eyes as large as side plates.

It was only at this point that Phoebe became glaringly aware that the coach was entirely stationary, in the middle of an empty road, with the winter light fading fast around them.

Briefly, she recalled the lurch, and wondered if they hadn't landed in a ditch, or been forced to stop and fix a wheel.

Which was when she heard voices.

'I said open the door, and no one gets hurt!'

'I will not! The safety of passengers is my responsibility, and I must warn you that at this very moment, my rear coachman has a blunderbuss aimed—'

'Then accept my commiserations!'

There was a poignant moment when a single shot rang out, and then another, before a heavy silence descended. Effie clamped her hand to her mouth, muffling a bat-like shriek, while the rest of the passengers seemed undecided as to whether to cling to one another, or run for their lives.

And all the while, Phoebe's thoughts ran wild.

A highwayman! An actual, real highwayman was holding up their coach!

Suddenly, all the stories she'd ever read about courageous heroines who refused to give up their jewels, before stealing away on the highwayman's horse, chased through her head – framed by the scent of real musket fire. She imagined Sophie's wide-eyed drama, the twins' grins of excitement, Matilda's envy, Josephine's cursory glance, Fred's mild concern, and Thomas – well, Thomas being Thomas, really – all while her own feelings remained somewhat unidentifiable.

It crossed her mind that she might still be under the influence of Briggs's deceptively intoxicating brew, but she didn't allow the thought to linger.

Now was not the moment for her courage to buckle!

This was *exactly* the type of adventure for which she'd yearned, while curled up with her favourite tales of historical heroines. It was a moment to face with fortitude and wit – a story of heroism with which to regale Josephine and Matilda when she returned to Knightswood.

She drew a deep breath.

'Has anyone got a weapon?' she whispered into the gloom.

It seemed as though all the occupants turned simultaneously, but Phoebe wasn't entirely sure it wasn't some remnant of her double vision.

'A Bible?'

'My basket?'

'How about a sword, dear?'

At this, everyone turned again towards a slight lady in a corner of the coach, who hadn't spoken a word for the entire journey. She looked around sixty years of age, wore a flocked dress with a grey shawl and felt bonnet, and was tapping an unremarkable umbrella on the floor in front of her. Phoebe felt her flicker of hope gutter instantly. She looked the very last person in the world to own a sword.

'Come again?' Flora asked doubtfully.

'Well, technically speaking, it's a dress sword,' the lady enunciated carefully, as though they were all hard of hearing. Swiftly, she twisted the handle of her unremarkable umbrella to reveal a glinting épée concealed at its centre. 'Miss Sarah Siddons, daughter of Roger Kemble and Sarah Ward, at your service,' she added, with a wink.

Immediately there was a low gasp, followed by a hushed mutter, as the travellers realised they had theatrical royalty in their midst.

'Did you say you're the daughter of *the esteemed actors* Roger Kemble and Sarah Ward?' the severe looking gentleman repeated, while Effie's eyes widened so much she put Phoebe in mind of one of the twins' toads.

Edward and Henry were thirteen, and keen zoologists. Thankfully, they were much more like Fred than Thomas, if rather too keen on bringing their studies into the library.

'Yes, dear, one and the same! Now, do you want the épée or not?' she added, offering the handle to Phoebe.

'Oh, what a brave young gentl'man you is!' Effie wailed, clutching her hands together in the style of a renaissance maiden. 'See, Ma! Didn't I say he wasn't three sheets to the wind?! He's as noble a young gentl'man as I ever knew – and now he could perish protecting us... Oh, please don't perish protecting us, it would break me 'art!'

Phoebe stared in horror as Effie began to sob. Great big shoulder-shaking sobs that rocked the whole coach as its occupants waited expectantly.

'I assure you, Effie,' she began awkwardly, 'I very much intend not to perish at all—'

But whatever else she was about to say was lost, as she was yanked, unceremoniously, from her seat, and into the wintry eve. Phoebe spun instinctively, theatrical épée outstretched – offering silent thanks that she'd always bested Fred at swordplay – to find herself, for the very first time in her very tedious life, face to face with a *real* highwayman.

And he was quite the disappointment.

Not only was he not at all tall, rugged, or even the remotest bit enigmatic, he also had the audacity to be smirking! She ran her gaze over his fair hair and grubby clothing, before spying his equally unimpressive second, standing a short distance away with a horse.

'Where are the coachmen?' she demanded, conscious her fellow travellers were jostling for the best view out of the coach window.

'Watching the inside of their eyelids!' her adversary grinned.

Phoebe glanced in the direction of his nod, and spied two trussed figures lying in the grass behind his friend.

'Temporarily,' he added with a shrug.

A surge of annoyance coursed through her as she took a step closer, angling the épée, confident she had shaken the worst of her haze.

'Untie them!' she demanded.

She wasn't sure why she was quite so angry, except that this rogue was tarnishing the reputation of all highwaymen, and didn't deserve to be holding up coaches. He wasn't even wearing a proper mask! His was made from old sackcloth, and dirty around the edges. Highwayman indeed, she'd met fiercer chickens!

He laughed and stepped closer.

'Make me?' he smirked, pulling a hand from behind his back to reveal a smoking musket.

'With pleasure!' Phoebe threw, lunging and flicking his musket into the long grass with one swift manoeuvre.

She allowed herself a small smile of satisfaction; it was as much a surprise to her as her grubby-masked opponent that one of Fred's disarming moves had worked so well.

'Hey!' The highwayman scowled, starting after it, but Phoebe followed up too quickly, pressing him back.

'Why doesn't he take off his hat?' someone muttered.

'Macassar oil!' Effie and her mother chimed, just as her

adversary stumbled backwards and found himself prostrate, with the tip of Phoebe's dress sword pressed firmly against his open neck.

'You were saying?' she asked, scowling.

There was such a gasp of admiration from Effie, that Phoebe felt a brief moment of triumph. She couldn't wait to relate the whole affair to her sisters. It was the finest moment of her life, and they would all live off the drama for months.

'I said … make me!' he growled, reaching out to snatch up another sword thrown by his second.

Instantly, Effie filled the wintry air with one of her loudest shrieks.

'Oh, no! He's going to run the young gentl'man through! My heart will be broke in two, like in one of them fancy plays!' she moaned, clutching her chest.

This was followed by a loud chorus of sympathy, from which Phoebe could only conclude that everyone shared exactly the same degree of faith in her skill.

Briefly, she considered declaring her inferior weapon as a point of honour, but then the highwayman was upon her, thrusting his sword so vehemently that her own theatrical counterpart shuddered under the strain.

She gritted her teeth and parried with all her strength, determined not to lose to a blackguard who set such a terrible example for all highwaymen, when she heard the distant echo of galloping horses.

'Go at dusk, they said … it'll be quiet, they said…' the highwayman grumbled as the soft thunder grew louder beneath the pale and wintry sky.

'It's like Taunt'n High Street on bleedin' Market Day!'

He started forward again, his thrusts and swipes wilder and more urgent than before.

'Come on, Will!' his second called nervously, already astride his mare.

'This one ain't worth it!'

'Yes! Come on, Will, be off wiv you!' Effie's mother reprimanded bravely. 'Otherwise, it'll be the gallows for you an' no mistake!'

There was a clamour of agreement which left no one in any doubt that the rest of the passengers were feeling just as emboldened, and only fuelled Phoebe's determination further. Will had proven himself to be an entirely unworthy, sorry excuse for a highwayman, and deserved to be *pinked by a girl*, as Fred would say.

And then there was the no small consideration that he seemed just as intent on winning as she was.

She steadied her arm and met each of his strikes squarely, but it was clear he had the advantage. Strike by strike, he drove her back into the shadow of a large oak, his copper eyes glinting above the grubby edges of his mask, until finally, one wild swipe removed the entire length of her blade from its hilt altogether. There was a brief awed silence as everyone turned to watch its silvery flight across the grass, and then the whole of her right side was consumed by fire.

Bemused, Phoebe fell back into the long grass and inhaled sharply. The tip of Will's sword was buried in the shoulder seam of Fred's shirt, while a scarlet stain was spreading around it. Hazily, she thought of the scolding Martha would give her for ruining one of the good shirts, as Effie shrieked loudly enough for them all. Then everyone turned as a newcomer drew up, and the air filled with the distinctive stride of an incoming hero – sword in hand, dark face scowling.

'A hero that looks more like the highwayman than the highwayman!' she muttered, just as Will retrieved his sword, making the flames leap higher still.

'You … cur!' she yelled, deriving no small amount of satisfaction from the way the word rolled off her tongue.

Little wonder Fred used it so often.

Instantly, there was a loud clamour of support from the coach party, along with a pitiful plea from Effie to *leave the poor gentl'man be*, while Will took off across the grass towards his horse.

Phoebe watched his departure with an odd mix of relief and disappointment. She'd been bested by the worst highwayman in Taunton, in front of a home crowd, while her hair had seen fit to become irretrievably embroiled with a tree root.

Cursing, she tugged hard and finally felt her pins give way, leaving her wild tresses to tumble down at exactly the same moment the incoming hero stepped into blurry view.

'Looking for this?' he asked, offering Fred's hat in an oddly familiar way.

She nodded, her senses swimming as his face came closer. Too close for her not to realise that she actually *did* know him, somehow.

'It's … you!' she accused, as a sudden pressure set her shoulder throbbing with a fresh fire.

'Indeed,' he returned, his perfect eyebrows arching

quizzically. 'I believe we had the pleasure back at The Swan, Mr…?'

Phoebe stared, trying to fight the most alarming realisation. She couldn't really believe it – life couldn't be so unfair – and yet he possessed the very same icy glint.

'Alfred,' she squeaked in a strangled tone, conscious the entire coach party were approaching, and she looked the most unlike Fred she'd looked since leaving Knightswood that morning.

The viscount frowned as he leaned closer and sniffed sharply, making Phoebe cringe despite the pain engulfing her shoulder.

'Well, then, *Mr Alfred*, you appear to have sustained an injury to your shoulder, which is bleeding quite profusely, and undoubtedly worsened by your recent over-indulgence in Briggs's *devil's brew*.'

He paused to raise his thick, supercilious eyebrows.

'Fortunately, my home is but a short distance from here and once the physician has attended, we can send word to your family.'

Phoebe stared defiantly, despite the scorching pain and mist of faces around the viscount's head. He might have been issuing curt instructions for a lame horse, and yet she had sense enough to know she had little choice too.

She exhaled in frustration. So much for finding her inner heroine, she'd barely found her way out of Devon. Yet there was something else, too, a strange mix of feelings she barely recognised at all. It was only her first day, and she'd been drunk, thrown out of an inn, fought a real-life highwayman, and *now*, rescued by the most dislikable gentleman of her new acquaintance. It couldn't be further from the heroic tale of adventure she'd imagined – and yet she'd never felt more alive.

'Thank you,' she murmured in her most Fred-like tone, before she mustered what was left of her dignity, and passed out.

Chapter Four

Three months and one foiled plan until the wedding

The viscount was as good as his word, and while Phoebe's shoulder burned as though a barrel of underwhelming highwaymen had used her for pitchfork practice, she *was* in a very comfortable bed.

She was also staring at one of the largest murals she'd ever seen. At least, she assumed it was a mural, because not one of the smiling cherubs had actually moved, and if she had passed over to the other side she would have expected far less chintz – *unless she'd gone to that other place.*

There was a knock at the door.

'I've brought a supper tray?' a young female voice ventured, before the door creaked open.

Phoebe sighed in relief. She was pretty sure they didn't do room service in that other place, either. She struggled up on her good arm as a mob-capped maid walked towards her, bearing a laden tray.

'Well, it's good to see you awake!' She smiled, setting the tray beside Phoebe. 'Though you mustn't put any weight on that arm just yet!' she said. 'We weren't sure if you was gonna make it when you first arrived, what with you having the fever an' all. But then Mrs Jennings said you'd be as right as rain once the fever broke, and Doctor Chappell agreed you had the *constitution of an ox*. An ox, he said!' the maid repeated, clearly keen that Phoebe share her awe.

Phoebe blinked, suppressing a mix of feelings.

'Which is just as well, as you was nearly run through good and proper!' the maid continued. 'I could scarce believe my ears when m'lord said you fought a dangerous highwayman! How brave you are miss … sir… Oh!'

She turned, but not before Phoebe witnessed her flushed confusion.

'Mrs Jennings said I was to draw your curtains while I was here!'

The maid hurried towards the window while Phoebe willed her fogged brain to clear, not least because she appeared to be wearing a suspiciously frilly night-dress, while bits of 'Fred' were hanging on the nearest armoire.

'How long have I been here?' she croaked.

'How long?' the maid repeated over-brightly, yanking the curtains violently in a bid to cover her embarrassment.

'Well, let's see … m'lord brought you back here just before supper time yesterday, and sent for Doctor Chappell right away. He said the ride from the Bridgwater Road most likely inflamed the wound, hence your delirium, and a good rest would sort you out. He also said that if you was a bigger … person … the wound mightn't have cut too deeply, but what with you being a … when they found out you was a… As you're quite *small*,' she recovered triumphantly, 'that highwayman got you good and proper! Anyway,' she beamed, 'it's really good to see you have some colour today, miss, and if you start eating right, there's no telling where you'll be in a few days!'

She smiled in relief then, while Phoebe stared back with growing horror.

A few more days … when they found out… Thomas!

She sat bolt upright and regretted it instantly.

'I have to get dressed,' she forced out, her head spinning faster than Matilda's nursery top, 'there are people who will be missing me!'

'Now then,' the maid clucked maternally, 'you're no use to no one as you are! Far better you follow Dr Chappell's orders, and stay put for a few days. Besides, His Lordship broke his journey to Bridgwater to bring you here, which he don't do easy for anyone! He set off at dawn again this morning, course, but I don't think he'd take too kindly to the news you'd finished yourself off after all the trouble he's taken. He's such a kindly gentl'man, m'lord…'

She tailed off mistily while Phoebe pictured the viscount with his perfect arched eyebrows and immaculate Hessian boots, demanding the landlord's best horses. She couldn't imagine him doing, or saying, anything that was in anyone's best interests but his own, and the idea that he'd divert his own journey to rescue an injured nobody seemed entirely implausible – unless it benefitted him in some way.

She flushed. And now there was also the indisputable fact that the maid, the doctor, the viscount – and indeed his entire household – knew he'd rescued a girl dressed like a boy, who'd been pinked by the most unimpressive highwayman south of Bristol. Her flush deepened as she recalled the moment she'd fallen in front of his gleaming boots, and how the glitter of his eyes had said everything. Now, he'd think her every bit the scoundrel he'd assumed her to be at The Swan Inn, or perhaps worse. Perhaps, the extent of her disguise would intrigue him enough to make enquiries that would completely undo her, and bring Thomas to her bedside!

Phoebe's eyes widened as the weakness of her plan presented itself in monstrous, chandelier-lit letters. She hadn't considered such a dramatic diversion, and if injury meant her plan to escape to London was thwarted, *what next?*

Luckily, two soft-boiled eggs and some crusty bread provided a happy distraction from this question for a short while, but by the time the maid had left, Phoebe had begun to consider that she might actually be the very worst kind of heroine that time or tale had ever known. She had no contingency plan, no means to send word to dear Fred that she was safe, and worst of all, his shirt and breeches seemed to have entirely disappeared.

It was as she was pondering her sad misfortune to be born this pitiful creature, destined to live without one truly noble, heroic adventure – that didn't include an unimpressive highwayman, dubious dandy viscount or husband old enough to be her grandfather – that she finally fell into a hot and fidgety sleep.

Phoebe shifted uncomfortably. The burn in her shoulder had quietened into a throb she couldn't ignore, while the pale light spilling across the thick Turkish rug confirmed it was after midnight. It was the sort of light that used to make her think of smuggler rings and forest fae, but tonight she could only see the extra hours she'd allowed to slip through her fingers. She must have fallen asleep the moment the maid left the room, and now she'd spent the best part of two nights in the dubious viscount's home *unaccompanied!*

A cold shiver began to web across her skin. Taking the coach to London and sending word to Fred was one thing, spending the night in the country residence of an arrogant bachelor viscount, quite another – one had the hallmark of adventure, the other only scandal. Phoebe conjured his intricately tied cravat, perfectly cut coat and mocking eyes. She had no evidence he was a rake, but something made her believe he was precisely the sort of gentleman her mother would have warned her against.

Everyone would assume *something* had happened.

Of course, she had no idea what that *something* was, only that her mother and friends always lowered their voices when they spoke of it, and that it was important when it came to marriage. This was a fact that had always perplexed her – after all, how could a *lack* of knowledge be an asset in any way?

Cursing in a way that would make her brothers proud, she forced herself to sit up and swing her legs to the floor. Thankfully, someone had had the foresight to place a pair of woollen booties and dressing gown beside her nightstand, which she pulled on a little awkwardly. She couldn't quite manage to tie the whole frilly ensemble together with only one good arm, but reasoned most of the household would be asleep, anyway. Then, pausing only to wonder what Effie and Flora would say if they could see her now, she pushed herself onto her feet.

For a moment everything swayed, like the corridor at The Swan Inn. Then slowly the room steadied again, and she managed a few tentative steps towards the window. Grimacing to suppress a wave of pain, Phoebe pulled at the heavy brocade curtain, before pausing to stare.

The viscount's garden was a moon-drenched, landscaped fairytale!

There were wide, rolling lawns in perfect descending terraces; climbing trees and secret, winding paths as far as the eye could see; and right in the centre, where no one could miss it, a huge marble fountain was supported by an army of celestial cherubs.

It was the sort of midnight garden that belonged to the dreams of children, not a dubious, dandified viscount.

'Sometimes, this world really wants for sense,' she muttered, steeling herself for the walk to the door.

A few minutes later she was leaning against her bedchamber doorframe, fighting another wave of pain, but feeling a lot steadier on her feet. Carefully, she twisted the handle, and squinted into the murky, panelled corridor. It smelled of boot polish and lavender, while a pale stream of moonlight danced along a scarlet carpet. A week ago, she might have been deterred by the thought of the viscount's ghostly ancestors, but right now her thirst was past ignoring.

She stepped outside, the carpet muffling the pad of her booties as she crept along the corridor, which turned into a small staircase, which turned into a longer corridor. Yet she could tell she was approaching the main part of the house because the viscount's gilt-edged relations were getting younger.

Finally, she paused at the top of a grand staircase, lit only by a pair of flickering chandeliers, and peered down into the viscount's hallway. She rolled her eyes. Everything from the dark, moody paintings, to the display of majestic antlers, to the polished mahogany floor was just like him: cold, arrogant, gleaming.

'I expect he levitates over the floor with the help of the fountain cherubs,' she muttered as she gripped the banister.

Slowly, she began easing her way down the wide marble stairs, until she reached the ground floor, where a suit of armour loomed out of the shadows to greet her. Phoebe gasped, and instantly felt ridiculous. She could hardly claim to seek adventure, and then faint at the slightest thing.

'Mary Shelley wouldn't look twice!' she muttered to herself.

She'd borrowed *Frankenstein* from Fred during one of his long summer holidays, and it had made such a welcome change from her usual library novels that she was minded to keep it. Sadly, Fred had other ideas.

Quickening her pace, she crept along the corridor and past numerous closed doors, until at last she reached a large, moonlit kitchen. Then, mumbling pithy comments about the number of preserving pantries any viscount might reasonably need, she downed two glasses of water before holding a cold, damp compress to her wound. The relief was immediate, calming her fractious mood and soothing her nerves until, armed with a full jug and fresh compress, she felt like starting back.

Carefully, and with one eye on her jug, she made her way back along the corridor. It was only as she reached the foot of the stairs that she heard the creak – not the creak of an old house fast asleep, but rather the creak of a body very awake. Phoebe froze, feeling every hair on the back of her neck and arms start to rise, and while she knew it to be utterly impossible, she couldn't help but turn her wide-eyed stare towards the suit of armour, watching from the shadows.

'Would you like some help?' it asked softly.

She inhaled sharply, mesmerised by its glinting, jointed arms, reaching out towards her in the gloom. If she'd been the shrieking type she would have put any self-respecting ghoul to shame, but instead she simply dropped the jug, which fell with a resounding crash, emptying its contents all over the floor.

'Hellfire and damnation!' it swore.

'Excuse me?' Phoebe frowned, uncertain which rules of etiquette applied, yet recalling her mother's distinct instruction about manners being important at all times.

'I was thirsty,' she added swiftly, for the avoidance of any doubt.

There was a soft laugh, which only made her frown harder; it would be just her luck to run into a sardonic ghost.

'Not for a quart of devil's brew, I trust?' it returned, looming forward out of the murky darkness.

For one swift moment, Phoebe wondered if she might still be under the brain-fogging influence of Briggs's cider. Then the puddle of ice water began reaching through her woollen booties, and she was forced to concede that not only was she extremely sober, but that any sardonic ghost was much more likely to be the one living person she least wished to see in the world.

'Obviously not!' she retorted, wondering what on earth he thought of her now he knew she wasn't *Fred*.

She clenched her fingers, wondering why she hadn't just stolen a horse, and put as many miles between them as possible while she still could.

'Your feet are wet,' he observed calmly, shrugging off his fine brocade dressing-gown, and throwing it over the puddle. 'Come into the library, where you can dry off. The fire is still alight.'

Then he turned without waiting for a response, revealing a faintly-lit doorway just behind.

Phoebe stared, thinking furiously. She was obliged to accept her host's invitation, of course – though in this case it was arguably an order – and he was quite correct that her booties seemed to have decided to become the *actual* puddle. But, in removing his dressing gown the viscount had also revealed himself to be entirely shirtless, and distractingly golden.

She flushed. She was no prude, she'd grown up with four brothers who'd spent every summer trying to drown one another in Knightswood's lake, but she also knew that that was vastly different from spending time alone, in a suspiciously frilly nightgown, with a half-naked viscount.

Phoebe swallowed so hard her throat burned, but she could hardly stand in the corridor all night, especially since some might say she owed him a debt of thanks – no matter how regrettable. So ignoring the faint squelch of her wet booties, she followed him through the doorway.

Moments later, she was looking around at a surprisingly warm and cosy library.

She inhaled deeply, savouring the familiar scents of old paper and sealing wax, as her gaze settled on the viscount, stoking the embers of the fire. A small burst of flames responded, and briefly she wondered if everything in his life always did as he bid it.

'Come and sit. I'll help you take those off.'

He nodded at her feet, as though it were the most natural thing in the world for her to be standing in his library at midnight, in a borrowed nightgown and soggy booties.

'Is your shoulder paining you?'

'It aches,' she admitted ruefully.

She reached up to touch the padding of her wound, and was suddenly, starkly, aware that the half knot she'd tied had slipped undone, exposing the full waterfall frill of her ridiculous nightgown. Phoebe flushed furiously. It wasn't exactly indecent, it was the sort of nightgown her mother would wear with lace enough for an army of bedspreads, but it was still the sort of situation that most polite society would consider ruinous.

'I beg your pardon, my lord!' she apologised, fumbling with her good arm. 'I thought everyone would be abed at this hour.'

He was before her in a second, and looking at her in a way that she was sure Fred would call *roguish*.

'But of course, and everything is twice as challenging with an injury. Why don't you let me help you?' He murmured with a new, disarming smile.

Phoebe had never in her life been quite so close to a half-dressed gentleman, let alone one quite so golden, and felt every protest dissolve at the back of her throat as he reached towards her. She could feel his warm breath on her exposed skin, glimpse flecks of gold in his jade eyes, and sense the intent behind his smile. She sucked in a tight breath, her head clouding with a thousand different thoughts and feelings. None of this could be real. She should be halfway to London with Effie and Flora by now, not protecting her virtue from some dubious rake.

'Although it seems such a shame to hide this pretty nightgown,' he added, his eyes darkening suggestively.

All at once everything seemed to slow, and Phoebe was aware only of the beat of her heart overriding every logical, self-preserving thought. She opened her mouth and willed something clever to come out, but all she could see were his eyelids lowering, and a look on his face that quickened her own breath.

As though in a dream, she watched his lips part and fingers drop to brush the cotton bodice of her nightgown. She gasped at his touch, which set a million tiny candles alight across her fickle body, and knew then that the question in his eyes somehow matched the delicious rise of something from the pit of her stomach, that this was fast turning into what Fred would call *a situation*.

Which had to be exactly what the viscount intended.

It was the only thought she needed for a second rise within her – much like the one that had seen her banished to her bedchamber for a week for landing Tom Bilch, the butcher's boy, a right leveller. She still thought it wildly unfair when he'd been the one to call her a *hornswoggler*, but that was beside the point. The viscount was a cad!

Instinctively, Phoebe brought up her good fist in a cross-body punch that would have impressed any one of the Bilch boys, and let it crash into the side of his jaw, watching in delight as his wolfish smile was replaced with shock, pain and finally, fury, as he stumbled backwards. She grinned in momentary jubilation, and then an eruption of fiery pain engulfed her right side.

'Ohh!' she gasped, holding her shoulder and running towards him.

She had no desire to stay in the same room, let alone get any closer, but she'd spotted his glass of iced brandy beside the armchair, and right now it was all she could think about.

In a breath, she'd snatched up the glass and pressed it directly against her fiery wound. The relief was instant, and she exhaled heavily.

'Do you need it?' she asked stiffly, noting the viscount's reddening chin with satisfaction.

She'd dealt him a ringer, but he deserved it.

'Yes,' he growled, grabbing the glass and tossing back the contents in one gulp.

She stared, watching the muscles tense in his neck, and sensing she'd hurt his pride far more than his face.

'Who the devil are you?!' he added, massaging his jaw as he flicked the stopper from the brandy decanter.

'And *I've* the drinking problem?' Phoebe muttered, eyeing his movements warily.

'As least I don't prey on respectable customers, in respectable premises, with a ring of scoundrels and scallywags!' he retorted, refilling the glass. 'And don't even bother trying to defend yourself! You were wearing the worst disguise I've ever seen! Did no one ever tell you that no self-respecting gentleman would ever touch a brown leather hat, no matter how bourgeois?!'

Phoebe stared, her brief moment of sympathy replaced with a rise of simmering heat that resembled one of the twins' ambitious experiments.

'Prey upon customers?' she repeated. 'Worst disguise you've ever seen? Ring of scoundrels and scallywags?!'

The viscount looked her up and down, scowling.

'I speak as I find,' he returned artically. 'Why else would a young, unaccompanied female be gallivanting around the countryside in the company of rogues – and dressed like a tallyman to boot!'

His eyes narrowed to slits.

'In my experience, a chit like you has only one ware to sell!'

Phoebe felt a flare of anger reach through to the roots of her unbrushed hair. She was starkly aware of how wild and dishevelled she looked, and how her shoulder felt as though it was newly afire, but it didn't give him the right to insult her so abominably.

'Is that why you brought me here?' she demanded, 'because you thought … you thought I was a … *a bit of muslin*?'

The words sounded so implausible, even to her own ears, that she had the sudden and uncontrollable urge to laugh. She'd weathered all sorts of insults from her siblings in her time, but no one had ever levelled such an accusation. Thomas and Fred occasionally made veiled comments about women who kept gentlemen company, particularly actresses, but that he could assume such a thing of a girl, dressed as a boy, travelling in the company of farmers, said far more about the viscount than it did her.

'You aren't?' he asked, a genuine frown settling above his perfect eyebrows.

Phoebe sucked in a long breath through gritted teeth.

'Even assuming, for one fraction of a second, that I was such a *person*, do you think rescuing me from a ridiculous highwayman and bringing me here – to your home – entitles you to … *anything*?'

She seethed as he eyed her uncertainly.

'I didn't bring you here thinking that…' he began. 'I was actually trying to assist you! The Bridgwater Road has been plagued by robberies in the last few months, and I didn't realise you were the same boy I caught eavesdropping at The Swan. The moment I realised you were actually a *girl* dressed as a boy, and in the company of rogues… Look, you talk prettily, I'll give you that,' he amended swiftly, 'but why else were you listening outside my parlour door? And three sheets to the wind no less?! Confess, if it hadn't been for Briggs's infamous cider, your intention was to appropriate…'

'I was on my way to get some air,' Phoebe glared, 'and your door opened when I least expected it! I wasn't trying to appropriate anything, I couldn't even walk in a straight line! I've never drunk anything so vile as Briggs's cider in my whole life, and I certainly had no idea it was capable of producing such ill-effects. And Flora and Effie are *not* rogues!' she finished with a growl.

At this the viscount gave a small shout of satirical laughter.

'Spare me,' he muttered, tossing back another glass of brandy, 'I've seen more honest faces at the dock!'

Phoebe sucked in a dangerous breath.

'Well, rogues or not, they never treated me thus! And now that you have insulted me in every way imaginable, I would remind you that I was doing quite well enough before you arrived!'

'Oh, yes, it certainly looked like it – on the receiving end of a farmer's sword! I was there, remember?!' he added, rolling his eyes derisively.

'He wasn't a farmer, he was a highwayman!' Phoebe hissed.

The viscount snorted with derision.

'*And* if I'd had a real sword, I can assure you I would not be standing here today!' she added.

'What do you mean?' he snapped.

'I was using a theatrical épée,' she threw furiously, 'property of Miss Sarah Siddons, daughter of *the* Roger Kemble and Sarah Ward!'

The viscount stared in silent shock, though the muscle in his cheek appeared to be working excessively hard.

'You can't be serious,' he challenged after a beat.

Phoebe lifted her chin.

'I don't lie,' she growled, 'any more than I *appropriate*, keep company with *rogues*, or sell my *wares*!'

The viscount had the good grace to colour a little this time.

'Well, you're a young fool to partake in any kind of duel with a dress weapon, whoever this daughter of Roger Kemble is!' he scathed.

'I had little choice!' she fired back. 'The coach was full, and someone had to stand up to that ridiculous highwayman!'

The viscount stared as if he couldn't decide if she was stupidly courageous or downright mad.

'You talk prettily, your hands have never seen a day's work, you've no idea how to tell a farmer from a scoundrel and you've been taught how to fence...' he mused darkly. 'I've been toying with sending a man to find out where you boarded the stage, or you could just save me the trouble and tell me now – who the devil are you?'

Phoebe paled. It was exactly what she feared. A few discreet enquiries would swiftly elicit the information that only one local young lady was madcap enough to disguise herself as a gentleman, board the common stage and take on a highwayman. She inhaled deeply, and knew she was cornered.

'Miss Phoebe Fairfax,' she returned in her haughtiest tone, fixing her gaze on a candle on the other side of the room, 'of Knightswood Manor.'

There was a heavy pause.

'Miss Phoebe Fairfax, sister to Tom ... I mean, Lord Thomas Fairfax of Knightswood Manor in Devon?' the viscount rattled, paling beneath his scowl.

'I think I know my own family circumstances, thank you, sir!' She glared.

'But ... your clothing?' he accused.

'Belongs to Fred ... Alfred Fairfax ... another brother,' Phoebe replied defensively.

A heavy silence descended in which the viscount's eyes bulged more than Phoebe thought was probably good for anyone.

'If you really are Tom's sister, then why on earth are you

standing in my library, in a frilly nightgown, looking like that!' He groaned, sinking into his armchair, his face in his hands.

For a second, Phoebe wondered if he wasn't a bit touched in the head, then she recalled his arrogant manner from the moment their paths crossed, and realised he was more likely being obnoxiously rude.

'I'm here because *you* brought me here,' she bristled. 'And I apologise if my appearance offends you, but surprisingly enough, a quart of Briggs's cider and a small incident with a sword haven't exactly enhanced my complexion! I've also had a few other pressing matters on my mind, and I really rather think it's none of your business who I am related to, or what I look like. I was doing perfectly well before you showed up like some fictional three-caped hero and brought me here!'

At this, the viscount stood up, looking as though he might actually like to shake her. He stepped forward, his jaw twitching madly as though working to suppress a million uncharitable thoughts, and for the first time, Phoebe drew back. She'd never seen anyone glower quite so intently.

'I had no choice, you silly little fool!' he growled. 'You were bleeding out faster than I or anyone else could stop! And you'd better start thinking very quickly if we're to sort this mess out. For a young lady of quality to travel on the common stage, dress as a tallyman, get drunk, and fight off scoundrels with a *theatrical épée* ... it's ... ruinous! What were you thinking?! And where on earth does Tom think you are?'

'Thomas doesn't know where I am,' Phoebe hissed, eyeing the viscount with vehement dislike. 'No one does, and far better it stays that way! As I've already said, I was *being* Fred and acting as he might ... well, actually, he wouldn't have got out of the coach … but I was simply trying to act a little *heroically*, not get stabbed and have my whole plan ruined by some dubious, interfering viscount!' She scowled darkly. 'Quite frankly, if I hadn't drunk Briggs's horrid cider *and* had to suffer the limitations of a theatrical épée, which had the misfortune to snap at quite the wrong moment – though it *was* very kind of Roger Kemble's daughter to lend it to me—'

'Wait a minute – act a *little heroically*?' the viscount interrupted, his eyes now bulging so much Phoebe thought it best to take another step back. 'So this whole charade is because you wish to have an adventure like one of the heroines in your schoolroom novels? That's it, isn't it? You've run away! Of course you have. You are the original head-in-the-clouds schoolroom chit who has run away and found out the real world is nothing like the inside of a novel! Of all the foolish, hare-brained simpletons…'

His voice shook with such derision, Phoebe actively contemplated landing him another leveller, but decided it was one thing punching a man when she was some roadside nobody, and quite another punching him when he knew her brother.

Instead, she pulled herself up to her full, frilly, wet-bootied height.

'I am a Fairfax, and we don't run away from anything!' she pronounced haughtily. 'I had a very real reason for leaving Knightswood, and the cider, the onions, the duel … they were all just *distractions*! I fully expected to be in London by now, not the back of Bridgwater or wherever we are. And I most certainly did not expect to find myself being rudely interrupted by an arrogant dandy!'

'Onions ... back of Bridgwater ... arrogant dandy?' the viscount repeated faintly, before tipping his head back in another shout of laughter.

At this point, Phoebe reconsidered her suspicion that he was indeed touched in the head, and that she should have made a bolt for the door.

'My brother says any gentleman who spends longer on his cravat than his books, is a dandy!' she glared defensively.

'This the same brother who considers a brown tallyman's hat to be acceptable in polite company?' the viscount retorted, sinking back into his armchair.

Phoebe gritted her teeth, she wasn't about to defend Fred's fashion sense to anyone, but the viscount had no right to judge.

'Either way, we're in a right mess! You know that don't you?' he added, running his fingers through his tousled hair again.

Phoebe was annoyed to find herself thinking it looked better dishevelled, and intensified her glare.

'I've known Tom since Oxford, and he isn't known for restraint when it comes to horses or family! He's going to be livid, I mean *pistols at dawn* livid! This is a matter of honour now. You do see that, don't you? You've been away a whole night, two in fact, and he will assume you've been...'

The viscount glanced down at Phoebe's suspiciously frilly nightgown and to her surprise, reached out to deftly re-tie her dressing gown.

Phoebe scowled harder.

'You're going to respect me now that you know who I am?' she challenged, despite the shiver snaking across her skin.

He stood up, staring intently, and for a moment she

thought he might discard his new-found chivalry. Then he turned and stalked towards a fresh shirt hanging on a stand beside the library entrance.

'I'm going to respect you *more* now I know who your brother is!' he muttered, pulling it over his head, and as he did so Phoebe was conscious of the oddest pang.

Then he reached towards a pull cord.

'Wait, please,' Phoebe interjected, with a sudden rise of fear. 'I can't go back to Knightswood … not yet. There's a very good reason I left, and if you make me go back now it will all be for nothing … I'll lose the only freedom I ever had!'

The viscount paused to look at her with the same cold glint that she recognised from the roadside.

'It seems to me, Miss Phoebe Fairfax,' he drawled, 'that if gallivanting around the countryside dressed as a bourgeois tallyman is your idea of freedom, then you're in need of your brother's protection more than you realise. Young ladies of quality don't get to be heroines!'

Then he pulled the bell with fervour.

Chapter Five

Eleven weeks and one concocted fairytale until the wedding

The journey back to Knightswood was conducted in silences and scowls.

Mrs Higgins, the viscount's kindly housekeeper, who Phoebe latterly discovered was the owner of the suspiciously frilly nightgown, had also produced a distinctly unfrilly niece. Tilly was small, unsmiling, and had a head full of enviable corkscrew curls; but she was also the right age to be a plausible lady's maid, and had agreed to accompany them back to Knightswood, on the promise of three sugared mice and a new ribbon.

Unfortunately, Tilly had none of her aunt's bustling kindliness, and had looked askance at Phoebe more than once since leaving Ebcott Place, the viscount's home, giving her the distinct impression that she thought her every bit as objectionable as her employer.

'You were travelling to Taunton with your lady's maid

when your chaise and four were set upon by the Somerset Highwaymen, who forced you to hand over your belongings at sword-point,' the viscount repeated, as though Phoebe were a child who'd failed to learn her basic letters. 'That was when the accident occurred, resulting in your current injury. It was not long afterwards that I came upon the pair of you and, upon perceiving your injury, escorted you back to Ebcott Place, where my staff tended to you. Then, once you were fit to move, I delivered you back to your brother's care,' he finished, returning his stare to the rolling Devon countryside.

'Did they also steal my clothes?' Phoebe asked.

'I beg your pardon?'

'I was simply curious as to whether you'd wish me to say the highwaymen stole my clothes, because that would also answer the question of my lack of female apparel,' she explained. 'We'll have every potential angle covered,' she added, over-brightly.

He glowered then in a way that took her back to the moment in the library when she thought he was going to strangle her.

'I don't think that *angle* is necessary at all,' he growled, returning his attention to the window.

'Then I believe I am fully conversant with your fictional account of my situation, thank you, my lord,' Phoebe returned, conscious Tilly was scrutinising them both.

She lay back her head and closed her eyes, contemplating the last few days. Her wound had made a speedy recovery under Mrs Higgins's excellent care, and once letters had been exchanged with Thomas outlining a very generous version of the actual truth, Phoebe had little to do except wait and think about all the choice words her brother would lay at her door the moment she arrived back at Knightswood. It was inevitable in the end, of course, but she'd rather hoped she might have a heroic tale or two to tell by then.

Instead, she had only a debacle of a duel with the most disappointing highwayman in all England, involving an épée with a distinct mind of its own. In fact, she had the sneaking suspicion that her abysmal performance would barely even warrant a *mention* in any of the windswept, heroic novels she and Josephine loved so much.

If only she hadn't drunk the cider, if only she hadn't tried to best the highwayman, if only she hadn't been injured … what then?

She inhaled deeply, trying not to wonder what may have transpired had the viscount not come into her life, before she recalled the ringer she landed to his jaw. Her thoughts darkened with satisfaction. She may have lost her only chance of freedom and adventure, but at least he wasn't in any doubt as to how she felt about it.

'I don't pretend to know the details of your private life, Miss Fairfax, but you might do better to embrace the fortunate position into which you were born, rather than regret one that exists only between the covers of a novel,' he offered suddenly. 'There are plenty of young ladies who would happily trade their own position with yours, as I'm sure you're aware.'

Phoebe could feel Tilly measuring her reaction with interest, while she wrestled every pithy retort about the viscount keeping his perfect aquiline nose out of her business, from the tip of her tongue. It didn't help that he had a point. She was fortunate in many ways, of course, but none of it compensated for an entire lifetime lost to a gout-ridden, onion-scented earl without one truly noble adventure to show for it. And this sorry escapade most certainly did not count.

Briefly, her thoughts flitted back to the night she was alone in the viscount's library, to the way his fingers had brushed over the thin cotton of her nightie. It was so fleeting, and yet had somehow burned itself into her memory. She drew a shallow breath. She'd never been touched in such a way, and the memory caused as many conflicted feelings as the event itself.

Were these the moments that passed between a man and a wife when they were wed? One of the moments married women whispered about?

The thought of such a moment ever passing between herself and the earl was suddenly more repugnant than she could put into words. She suppressed a rise of nausea as she pictured his clammy, purple fingers reaching for her, his beady eyes undressing her, and yet still she was uncertain whether she was more afraid of being left alone with the earl, or never experiencing such a moment in her life again.

'I am sure there are many who would agree, my lord,' she returned coolly, 'though, as you say yourself, the details of my private life are exactly that.'

Then she watched Tilly's jaw drop with satisfaction, before swinging her gaze back to the window, certain her victory would be woefully short-lived.

'You must understand the gravity of this situation, Phoebe?' Thomas ranted from behind Papa's gold inlaid walnut desk. 'If Damerel here hadn't been prepared to intercede, and help concoct a … *fairytale*, your escapade would have very likely ruined us all!'

He'd ushered them into the library for the meeting, which was warning enough in itself as Thomas rarely used the room, except to share news of deaths or betrothals.

'We would kiss goodbye to any favourable matches, let alone with the Earl of Cumberland, which would, in turn, endanger the chances of all your sisters! Really, Phoebe, this folly of yours is beyond any kind of comprehension! Do you understand the disquiet you've caused? I have burned the midnight oil trying to fathom how to tell the earl that his betrothed has seen fit to run away on the common stage, dressed in her brother's clothes!'

Phoebe felt the viscount's eyes flicker towards her at the last, though she kept her eyes trained forward. Thomas had at least spared her the indignity of a chastisement in front of Tilly – let the viscount think what he liked.

'Did you fathom it – in the end?' she asked, hardly daring to hope for such a lucky twist of fate.

Thomas eyeballed her furiously.

'No, I did not!' he bellowed. 'And you have Sophie to thank for that foresight! If she hadn't persuaded me that Fred would know exactly where you were, I'd have been forced to ask if the earl wouldn't take your sister, instead, though the Lord knows if he'd have been minded! He could have his pick of any of the debutantes this season. Do you understand that? He's an earl!'

A million uncharitable thoughts about double-crossing sisters hurtled through Phoebe's head, while Thomas nodded abruptly at the viscount.

'Apologies, Damerel, this is one of those damned domestic affairs that needn't trouble you,' Thomas snapped. Do stay the night, though. You can put me in a better temper while I consider how best to correct ignorant, ungrateful wards who haven't the least clue about the world, or their good fortune in it!'

There was a moment's silence as Phoebe dropped her gaze, certain the viscount had to be enjoying her dressing down immensely.

'Alas, I thank you for the invitation, Fairfax, but I have more pressing engagements this evening,' he returned in an oddly curt tone.

'I'll send the carriage for Tilly in a few days, just to lend the story a little more credence and stem servants' gossip,' the viscount continued. 'You could say her aunt missed her, or some such thing?'

Thomas stood up and rounded the desk to shake the viscount's hand.

'Thank you for your assistance with this trouble, Damerel. I am damned indebted to you … damned indebted, indeed. I've a suitable retribution to consider now, but I shan't forget it, you have my word on that.'

Phoebe looked up as the viscount nodded, and wondered briefly at a world that elevated a rake's fictional story above her own dismal truth.

She watched as he made his way to the library door, before turning back.

'I think, if I were in your situation, Fairfax, I might consider a *not inconsiderable* injury retribution enough,' he offered quietly. 'It is also worth mentioning that, while the whole escapade was reprehensible, to say the least, Miss Fairfax's courage, when faced with the Somerset Highwaymen, was something to behold indeed. Some may even have called it … *heroic*. Good day to you. Miss Fairfax.'

There was a strange silence as the door closed, and for a moment, neither Phoebe nor her brother moved. The last thing she expected was an appeal for clemency on her behalf, let alone the most curious compliment she'd ever received. An odd charge suffused her veins as she lowered her gaze. He was an insufferable snob, a dangerous rake, and a backhanded compliment at the eleventh hour changed nothing – yet she was perversely sorry to see him go.

'You're damned lucky you ran into such a decent fellow, Phoebe, or this could have ended very differently indeed!'

Thomas's tone was caustic, yet she could tell even he was slightly mystified by the viscount's parting comment.

'Kindly remove yourself to your bedchamber and remain there until I send word that you may do otherwise. If you're in need of a diversion, I suggest you distract yourself with your embroidery or the Bible!'

And for once in her life, Phoebe was most happy to oblige.

Chapter Six

Ten weeks and four shrinking walls until the wedding

'Lord, Phoebs, you just never think things through!' Sophie chuckled, rummaging through a drawer of stockings.

'It's one thing to try for London, but why you had to go drawing attention to yourself in such rambunctious style, I'll never know. Ah, here it is!'

She pulled out her favourite pearl inlaid slide, and slid it neatly into her tumbling curls, before shaking them out à la mode.

Phoebe lay sprawled across her bed, watching her sister's adept fingers, and knowing she too should try to be more content. But then Sophie didn't have to live her whole life within ten, painfully short weeks.

'Well, I think Phoebe was *exceptionally* brave when faced with *excessive* danger,' Matilda pronounced, lunging forward

with an old parasol, 'and anyone would consider that
exceedingly—'

'Embarrassing?' Josephine cut in from the corner of the
room, her nose buried in a newly purchased novel entitled,
Pride and Prejudice.

Matilda laughed, while Phoebe pulled a face.

'What *were* you going to do once the director of the Covent
Garden Theatre realised you were actually a girl, though?'
Sophie added, her pretty eyebrows darting northwards. 'I
mean, I think I would rather marry the crusty old earl, than
live in a single room above a shop, counting my ha'pennies!'

'Well, yes but that's only because you don't actually *have* to
marry the crusty old earl,' Phoebe returned crossly. 'It's
different for you,' she added, rolling over to eyeball the ceiling.
'You've got time and choice on your side.'

Sophie started to frown.

'More choice than me, at least,' Phoebe amended. 'And
anyway, don't you ever get fed up with it all? With the
smallness of everything? Don't you ever want to know why
we're supposed to be content with corsets, embroidery, and
four shrinking walls, when our brothers get to do, and see, so
much more? Take Thomas and Fred, they got to go to
university, drink as much devil's brew as they wanted *and*
chase halfway across Europe, all on the pretext of studying
ancient civilisations. Fred had never even heard of
Herculaneum before last summer! And before that they got to
race horses, climb trees, and rip whatever clothing they like, all
because they were born with a—'

'Phoebe!' Sophie gasped, shooting a look at Josephine and

Matilda, both of whom suddenly wore an expression of avid interest.

'Well, it's fact!' Phoebe grinned with a shrug. 'So, why shouldn't we talk about it? Or our right to education *beyond* the cross-stitch and Fordyce's sermons?!'

'You forgot dancing – with two left feet!' Matilda injected. 'And what's devil's brew, anyway?'

'Nothing you need worry about,' Sophie closed hastily. 'And you know that's just the way things have *always* been, Phoebs,' she added in her next breath. 'Why should we expect things to be different for us?'

There was a brief pause while Phoebe rolled over to eyeball her sister.

'Why *shouldn't* we expect things to be different for us?' she countered. 'Who decided we had to live by a set of rules? Who invented *reserve* and *meekness* and *virtue* and said we had to observe them all?'

'Phoebe…' Sophie warned.

'And why shouldn't we have as many adventures as our brothers? I warrant we'd put the opportunities to far better use and emerge far greater heroines, if put to the test.'

'Pray God we won't be,' Sophie muttered, closing her eyes.

'Was that what you were trying to do?' Josephine quizzed. 'Be a heroine? Because it seems to me you don't need to wear trousers, or fight a highwayman, to do that!'

There was a poignant silence while everyone turned to look at the greatest bookworm among them, still safely ensconced between the pages of *Pride and Prejudice*.

She shrugged.

'Surely, if we feel we need to live up to some *male* idea of heroism, or even that depicted between the covers of a novel, then we're probably missing the point altogether? The heroine in this book turns down a marriage proposal on the basis of the gentleman's treatment of her sister,' Josephine continued, tapping her page thoughtfully, 'though to be honest, they have a few other issues, too… I just think heroism itself shouldn't be defined by an act, or a type of behaviour, but rather the way we respond to things, as well as each other, of course.'

There was another protracted silence while everyone stared at Josephine in admiration.

Matilda was the first to find her voice.

'Personally, I still think heroism is all about *exceedingly extraordinary* feats that no other girl will try without fainting – or crying – or some such namby-pamby thing!'

'Matilda Fairfax!' Sophie scolded indulgently.

'You may be onto something, Jo,' Phoebe conceded, gazing at the ceiling. 'But I'm definitely not referring to *romantic heroism*, I haven't the least interest in it. I'm talking about *real, intrepid, battling the seven seas* heroism!'

'But that's exactly my point!' Josephine sniffed. 'Isn't it all one and the same? We can all be heroic in big and small ways, loud and quiet, if we so wish?'

'We can…' Phoebe frowned. 'But right now I want the type of adventures our brothers have. The sort of adventure I can look back on and tell my grandchildren about, to prove I had spirit and wasn't afraid to ride alone or travel to foreign shores…'

'…or fight unimpressive highwaymen and nearly end up killing yourself,' Sophie laughed, rolling her eyes. 'But are you sure you aren't in the least bit interested in romantic heroism,

Phoebs?' she quizzed, pulling a curl forward so it draped becomingly down her peachy neck. 'I thought Viscount Damerel seemed quite the romantic – if slightly austere – hero … rescuing you, bringing you home, supplying a cover story… Plus, "Viscountess" has a nice ring to it, doesn't it?'

She paused to survey her handiwork, while Matilda feigned being sick.

'Viscount Damerel is nothing more than a conceited, interfering dandy!' Phoebe returned flatly, forcing the image of the viscount's half-naked silhouette from her head. 'I pity anyone who finds themselves married to a gentleman who thinks nothing of taking other people's horses for his own purpose!'

She could feel Sophie's scrutiny.

'Let alone his complete disregard for anything but his own lofty self-importance!'

A memory of the viscount shrugging himself into a fresh shirt, skittered through her mind. She closed her eyes and drew a breath.

'And if it's a fancy title you're after,' she finished, 'you could have embraced the opportunity to become a countess in my absence!'

At this Sophie became suddenly, and intensely, embroiled with an uncooperative curl.

'*Balestra!*' Matilda interjected, lunging forward with one of Sophie's favourite parasols.

'Keep your guard close until you lunge, then bend and stretch,' Phoebe corrected as her youngest sister paused to re-tie the stocking around her forehead.

'Don't encourage her!' Sophie scolded, retrieving both her

stocking and parasol in one deft move. 'It's bad enough you think you're Boudicca, without filling Matty's head too!'

There was a brief pause while the elder sisters contemplated each other frankly.

'Lord, Phoebs, I agree we *deserve* to have as many adventures as our brothers,' Sophie exhaled, finally pinning down the errant curl, 'but there are some things within our ability to change, and some that aren't. Whatever his reasons, Papa left an instruction in his will for his *eldest* daughter to wed the earl when of marriageable age and – while I don't envy you – that *is* you! I'm not even out for another year, and we both know Mama wouldn't have approved of my taking your place, for any reason. Besides, isn't a last wish kind of ... binding?'

Phoebe gazed around at the bedchamber she'd shared with Sophie when they were children. She was absolutely right, of course, Mama had always been such a stickler for manners and etiquette, and would have taken to her bed for nothing less than a week over Phoebe's latest escapade. Quite how she'd have handled the notion of her prettiest daughter having to take Phoebe's place didn't even bear thinking about.

'At least Mama would have let me have a season,' Phoebe muttered, tracing the shadow of the afternoon sun across Sophie's embroidered coverlet.

She couldn't recall a time when they hadn't gathered in this room to play, fight or dream up their latest theatrical adventure and she wondered despondently, how many of these cosy afternoons she had left with her sisters.

Tilly, the decoy maid, had been duly dispatched after a week, and apart from a stiff enquiry after the health of her wound, Thomas had avoided Phoebe's company. She wasn't entirely surprised – it was his way – but his absence of conversation about the earl and the wedding was making her nervous. It would be just like him to spring it on her when she was least expecting it.

'I don't see why you don't just tell Thomas you're too injured to marry soon,' Matilda frowned, hoisting herself up onto the window seat. 'That's what I'd do… And then I'd light a beacon on Exmouth cliff, and wait for a pirate ship to come and find me!'

Everyone paused to look at Matilda, who was busy reaching out of the latticed window to grasp a large ivory magnolia petal.

'Well … the first part has merit,' Sophie considered. 'Don't lean out that far, dearest!' she added sharply, 'not unless you want to land in one of the groundsman's barrows!'

Matilda laughed, and hooked a foot under the ledge.

'It's not such an untruth, anyway, is it?' she grinned, 'I heard you tell one of the grooms your shoulder was aching like the d—'

'Yes, yes, dearest, it does ache a little,' Phoebe interrupted, side-eyeing Sophie who was glaring intently.

'I suppose it's worth a shot though, isn't it?' Sophie mused after a beat. 'I mean, even the earl couldn't object to a period of convalescence after such a *terrible* fall from a horse.' She rolled her eyes at the additional story Thomas had invented for the earl and remainder of their small Devon social circle. 'Perhaps we could even badger Thomas for a trip away, somewhere?'

'Mama would insist on Bath,' Josephine muttered, still

buried in her book, 'and that Phoebe took the waters – like an old maid.'

They all started to laugh.

'Well, it's not exactly duelling with highwaymen or sailing the seven seas,' Sophie managed, when she'd recovered, 'but you wouldn't be counting down the days at Knightswood, either.'

She reached to tuck a lock of tumbling hair from her sister's face.

'And you never know, Bath might actually prove to be unexpectedly adventurous? Just with less swords … and onions…'

Phoebe caught Sophie's hand.

'You know, I wouldn't have expected you to take my place with the earl, not for all the tea in China,' she muttered protectively.

'It's my duty, and…'

'Maybe,' Sophie returned, her eyes dancing with mischief, 'but not *quite* yet! Why don't we ask dear old Harriet to recommend a convalescence stay with Aunt and Uncle Higglestone, in Bath? Thomas could hardly refuse if it comes from Mama's lady's maid. She *is* the final arbiter on all things polite and proper, after all!'

Phoebe stared at Sophie, a glimmer of hope in her indigo eyes. Miss Harriet Godminster had retired after Mama's death, and now lived in the local village, but she still held the kind of power afforded to all domestic staff who'd watched their charges grow out of breeches and petticoats.

Even Thomas was afraid of her.

'I do believe dear Harriet would be happy to vouch for us,'

Phoebe returned with a slow smile, 'especially since she considers I should be bed-bound with a lavender compress, anyway.'

'Then it's a plan!' Sophie grinned. 'And I shall persuade her we all need to accompany you – just to ensure you don't over-excite yourself!'

'In Bath? In March?!' Phoebe remonstrated, yet even she had to admit to the new pulse of excitement seeping through her veins.

It wasn't London or the Grand Tour, but it wasn't Devon either, and who knew what could happen in ten whole weeks?! It was more than enough time for an adventure or two – perhaps even enough time to do something a little heroic…

'What's the plan? What's devil's brew?' Matilda scowled, interrupting Phoebe's daydream. 'And why won't anyone tell me what gentlemen are born with?!'

Chapter Seven

Nine weeks and one Bath escape until the wedding

'Harriet was the fiercest I've ever known her!' Sophie confided mischievously. 'She just hissed at Thomas, and flapped on about you looking pale and needing convalescence and *gentle diversion* until he looked as though he might just agree to anything! Honestly, Phoebs, she was about as protective as any mama goose could be, without actually popping you under her wing!'

They all started to laugh.

Phoebe gazed around the Fairfax family chaise, which was making light work of the miles to the City of Bath, on this bright spring day. Thankfully the twins, Edward and Henry, had already returned to school, which meant they didn't have to put up with their amphibious entourage; and while Thomas had read them all the longest lecture about family reputation, and how they were all to be paragons of virtue while staying with their relatives, nothing could dampen Phoebe's spirits.

Her shoulder, while not fully healed, was feeling a lot more comfortable, there had been only the sparsest of references to her impending nuptials, and she had nine whole weeks to call her own.

Things could most definitely be a lot worse.

'I wonder if we can persuade Aunt Higglestone to take us to the Assembly Rooms?' Sophie mused. 'I remember Mama saying she and Aunt attended no end of Assembly Room gatherings during their season, and that it was the very best place to see – and be seen.'

Aunt Higglestone was a beloved relative who, much against family wishes, had made a scandalous love match with ambitious banker, Horace Higglestone. Yet what Uncle Higglestone lacked in social connections, he more than made up for in dividends, thanks to a long career at one of the most profitable banks in London. Happily, their aunt was not shy in sharing the fruits of his success and this generosity not only helped to redeem herself with the family, but also benefitted her elder sister's large progeny enormously.

Coincidentally, her aunt's story also confirmed Phoebe's growing suspicion that the universe favoured younger siblings as a rule, and she made a silent vow never to elevate the expectations of any child above another, should she ever have the misfortune to find herself a mother.

'We none of us are out yet, remember?' Josephine sniffed, her nose buried in a smuggled library edition of *Sense and Sensibility*.

'And I expect Aunt Higglestone will have had strict instructions from Thomas to march us directly to the Tap

Rooms and back again, without so much as a nod at any ancient Roman ruins!'

Her tone was so indignant they all laughed, but Phoebe had the feeling that Josephine wasn't far wrong. Thomas considered Aunt Higglestone a safe relative, not only because she was childless – meaning she was ready to lavish all her attention on her marvellous nieces and nephews – but also because she was bourgeois enough not to attract the attention of any of the rakish inset, who could distract or lead them astray.

'Pooh! You can keep your Assembly Rooms and ancient Roman ruins, I just want to see if there are any *extremely* naked statues!' Matilda pronounced, pushing her nose into the air.

'Matilda Fairfax!' Sophie remonstrated in a scandalised tone.

'Well, if you won't tell me what men are born with…'

'Even if there are any *extremely* naked statues,' Phoebe intervened, feeling the heat of Sophie's glare, 'who's to say if they're any reliable guide? Most Roman statues are depictions of gods, and there's nothing godly about any living man I know!'

'Goodness, Phoebs, you sound just like dear Harriet,' Sophie laughed.

'Well, I think we should prevail upon our aunt to take us on as many outings as possible,' Josephine declared, oblivious to the conversation around her. 'After all, there's absolutely no point in going to Bath and not seeing the sights! I, for one, have been reading up on The Old Temple, and where the ancient Romans used to worship the goddess *Sulis Minerva*, who believe it or not…'

'I believe it! And there's absolutely no point, whatsoever,' Phoebe agreed swiftly, lest her beloved bookworm sister describe every historical sight she'd already bookmarked for their trip.

'We'll persuade Aunt to take us to all the important historical sights while we're there – any *extremely naked statues* a bonus!'

Matilda giggled as Josephine settled back to her book, leaving only Sophie's purposeful stare.

'You wish to see extremely naked statues as well?' Phoebe quizzed.

'I was just wondering the same of you?' Sophie retorted, resting her head back.

'Happily, I think Josephine has enough historical sights planned to entertain us all,' she added, a mischievous sparkle creeping into her eyes, 'I was thinking rather of a certain *rakish member of the ton* sights.'

Phoebe rolled her eyes to cover the surge of feelings she always felt whenever her sister brought up the viscount. She'd expressed her avid dislike several times since her return, and been vague enough about her stay at Ebcott Place to close the subject forever, but she could tell Sophie wasn't convinced.

To be fair, neither of them had stayed away from Knightswood without the other before, and there was no denying the viscount had a certain wild attractiveness – when he wasn't glowering. But there was something more, too, something that had garnered Sophie's suspicion. It wasn't the first time her sister had been suspicious, of course – she was born that way – but it was the first time Phoebe couldn't convince her otherwise. Unlike Thomas, who hadn't asked *any* questions about her time away, whatsoever.

Phoebe's throat tightened as she stared out at the disappearing countryside, thinking of that brief moment in the viscount's library. It had been such an intimate act for a man who barely knew her, one who most definitely didn't respect her. And yet it had burned itself into her head, as though she'd never truly been alive before.

How had he made her feel such violent emotion, when she disliked him so intensely? It didn't make any sense.

And then there was the way he seemed almost to vouch for her, before he left.

'Miss Fairfax's courage, when faced with the Somerset Highwaymen, was something to behold indeed. Some may even have called it … heroic…'

'…and are you even listening?!' Sophie scowled, dragging her back to the clattering wheels and pale March sunshine.

Phoebe forced a smile.

'Sorry, I was thinking of Misty.'

It was Sophie's turn to roll her eyes.

'There's no point sighing over a horse you can't ride, home or away,' she chastised. 'And besides, who needs a pony when there may be thoroughbreds in Bath?!'

Phoebe couldn't help but chuckle.

'And even if Thomas has written with the strictest chaperone instructions that *glue* our amiable aunt to us day and night, do you think we might cross paths with more fashionable members of the ton at the Pump Room?' Sophie added, with a twinkle.

'Who knows?!' Phoebe exhaled. 'From what Harriet said, it

will be filled with scheming mamas, their precious unmarried daughters, and ageing bachelors with gout – my speciality!'

'Actually, there's an ageing bachelor in my book, Colonel Brandon?' Josephine sniffed, without looking up. 'He doesn't have gout and seems rather lovely.'

'There are always exceptions,' Phoebe conceded darkly, 'but to my mind anyone above forty is counting the days until they're scented of onions!'

'In truth, I suspect the fashionable set won't be looking to spend time with chits from the schoolroom,' she murmured to Sophie, while the others laughed, 'and even if one or two do notice us, they won't number Viscount Damerel! He's an abominable dandy and far too superior to seek out the company of a few country misses!'

'He did help you out of a fix, though, Phoebs,' Sophie cajoled, her eyes narrowing. 'And it sounds as though your first meeting could have been misconstrued…'

'Why else were you listening outside my parlour door? And three sheets to the wind, no less! Confess, if it hadn't been for Briggs's infamous cider, your intention was to appropriate…'

The viscount's words echoed through Phoebe's head, and she felt her hackles flare instantly.

'He did what any decent human would do, who found an injured person on the roadside, and wasn't completely devoid of scruples or moral inclination!' she snapped. 'I don't afford him a hero's cape because of that!'

'Colonel Brandon found Marianne in the pouring rain,' Josephine sniffed, 'and carried her all the way home. The Dashwoods thought *he* was pretty heroic.'

'Well, Viscount Damerel is nothing like Colonel Brandon!'

Phoebe retorted. '*And* I warrant he only stopped in the first place because there was a roadside audience!'

She coloured faintly, recalling the way the viscount's swift action had both driven the highwayman away and prevented further injury. Yet he'd also been ready to take advantage of her vulnerability before discovering her identity… Far better her sisters thought him the dubious, dislikable dandy he'd already proven himself to be.

There was a brief silence before Josephine coughed, and then all thoughts of the viscount and the fashionable set were forgotten.

'Are you warm enough, dearest?' Sophie frowned anxiously. 'Do you need another blanket? I do believe Matilda has enough for two shrimps!'

Phoebe watched as Sophie plied their younger sister with gloves, handkerchief, and herbal poultice to inhale, all of which the long-suffering Josephine accepted without complaint. They'd shared care of their sister since Mama passed, and she hadn't had a lung spasm or infection in two years, which their doctor hailed as a near miracle. The last thing they needed was for Josephine to fall ill while they were in Bath.

'You know, I do believe the waters will do you the power of good,' Sophie cooed, tucking the blanket around Josephine with practised ease, while Phoebe quietly assessed her.

Sophie was the undisputed queen of fuss, but she alone had the knack of calming the worst of Josephine's attacks, which had made her both fortunate and indispensable. Happily, their sister looked a good, healthy colour today.

'And while you and Phoebe are recuperating, Matilda and I

can keep watch for any caped Colonel Brandons – unscented, of course!'

The coach filled with more laughter, as Phoebe settled back to watch the sunlit, springtide hedgerows speed by. Sometimes she wished her sisters a thousand miles away, and sometimes she wasn't sure she could breathe without them.

Chapter Eight

Eight weeks and one pair of parasol pirates until the wedding

Aunt and Uncle Higglestone lived in a bourgeois villa, in a bourgeois street, in the most bourgeois part of Bath, and Phoebe couldn't love them more for it if she tried.

Every part of Wood Lodge with its small, gated gardens, breakfast terrace and musty, well-stocked library warmed her soul, and she could have spent a very pleasant few weeks traversing between the Abbey, the Baths and all the classical colonnades and neat squares, were it not for the fact that her impending nuptials were drawing closer every minute of every day. And while it was no secret that there was to be a wedding in the family, her aunt seemed far more preoccupied with the itinerary of their stay than taxing Phoebe with questions she couldn't answer.

'I thought we might try a different walk after our visit to the Pump Room today,' their aunt chattered brightly, over a generous portion of kippers and eggs.

Phoebe speed-buttered her toast, trying not to meet Sophie's gaze. They'd started every day of their visit so far with a dutiful trip to the Pump Room, and while she wasn't about to challenge anyone who believed the waters to be healing, their sour taste suggested quite the opposite.

'Do we need to go to the Pump Room today, Aunt?' she appealed. 'They were quite busy yesterday, and I do wonder if a crowded room is altogether good for Josephine?'

Josephine flashed her an indignant look, while Matilda snorted into her hot chocolate.

'Nonsense, child! The benefits of the waters far exceed a little crowding, and I do believe they're putting some colour in *your* cheeks, as well as Josephine's...' Her aunt frowned anxiously. 'Both of you were as pale as ghosts when you arrived! I said to your uncle: I can't wait to see what the waters do for those girls... Didn't I say that, Uncle Higglestone?'

She prodded her studious husband with her elbow, who grunted his support from behind a leatherbound copy of John Galpine's *British Botany*.

Phoebe ignored a kick beneath the table, and bit into her toast. She had yet to hold a full conversation with her uncle, beyond *good morning* or *would you please pass the butter*, and was quite tempted to see if cutting a pair of eyeholes in his morning newspaper, or the latest periodical on British plant life, would help. Sophie was aghast when she suggested it and made her promise to do no such thing.

'Phoebe says the water tastes like mud!' Matilda offered mischievously.

Phoebe glared at her younger sister, and made a mental

note to withdraw the offer of a trip to North Parade to buy sherbert lemons.

'It does,' Uncle Higglestone concurred unhelpfully, from behind his periodical.

'Indeed? Well, how *young ladies of quality* would know such a thing is a great mystery to me!' their aunt remonstrated with a twinkle in her eye. 'All the same, it is Thomas's dearest wish that *both* of you benefit daily from the waters, and exert yourself as little as possible.'

She smiled mistily.

'He does so care about you all, and we mustn't misplace the trust he has shown in me since your dearest mother…' She tailed off to fumble for a lace kerchief she always kept for moments such as this.

'Mother would be so happy we are here with you!' Phoebe rushed, alarmed her aunt was about to weep all over the breakfast table. 'And I believe the waters have worked wonders already, I feel much fitter and quite well!'

She smiled brightly. It wasn't a complete lie, her shoulder had knitted very well, and she was certain fresh air and time would do the rest.

'In fact, I was wondering whether, in celebration of my swift recovery thanks to your care, Aunt, my sisters and I might enjoy a short ride one day next week?'

At this, her aunt forgot all about their dearest mother, and inhaled sharply.

'A ride? On a horse, dear? So soon after your accident?! Oh… Now *that* I am sure Thomas would not allow!'

She paused to fan herself rapidly.

'However…' She smiled conspiratorially at the cover of

Uncle Higglestone's periodical. 'Your uncle and I are not against *small* pleasurable diversions, and may know of something that will delight you young ladies very much indeed, don't we, dearest?'

There was another grunt, which could have meant any number of things, but clearly satisfied their aunt.

'An evening picnic at the Sydney Gardens, next weekend!'

She paused to glance around with a look of real triumph.

'There will be fireworks and lanterns and music and more fireworks! We attended one last year and were quite taken by the whole event, weren't we, Uncle Higglestone? We're positive it will be just the thing to entertain you young ladies!'

She ploughed on without waiting for an answer.

'Now, there is the spring weather to consider but so long as we take warm pelisses, we really can't complain about the temperature. There is also the Sydney Hotel itself, of course, should we require shelter for one of you more delicate souls.

'But, on the whole, we believe you will all enjoy it, and it's low enough on the seasonal agenda for your brother to be content, too. Actually, I was rather wondering if we might pop into the modiste on the way back from the Pump Room this morning, as I suspect you might not have anything *quite* suitable for a spring picnic, have you?'

Aunt Higglestone finally paused to beam round the table.

Sophie was the first to find her voice.

'A spring picnic? And a *real* modiste?' she whispered in a hallowed voice, as though all her Christmases had come at once. 'I think we'd all be thrilled, Aunt!'

'There's a picnic in the book I'm reading...'

'Will there be meringues and candy floss...?'

'Who will be there, *exactly*?' Phoebe's voice rose above the clamour of the others, as she skewered her last piece of buttered toast.

'Why, most of our acquaintances, dear! The Sydney Gardens social picnics are public and very popular, but so long as you avoid any *undesirables*, they are entirely suited to respectable families.'

She lowered her voice conspiratorially. 'Bath is a little more relaxed than London you see, so you don't need to fret *too* much about not being officially out yet.'

Phoebe suppressed another smile, certain she couldn't fret anywhere as much as her aunt, who fretted enough for the entire world.

'Anyway, I've already taken the liberty of writing to your dear brother, and asking if your uncle and I could take you to a few *respectable* social gatherings for some gentle diversion. He was reluctant, such is his care for you all, but after I explained we'd be chaperoning you closely and the picnic hardly ranked on the Bath social calendar, he really was quite content.' She beamed.

Phoebe could well imagine Thomas had only made it through the first couple of sentences of Aunt Higglestone's very proper letter, before consigning it to the fire – but could have hugged her all the same. She'd begun to think their daily trip to the Pump Room, followed by a *bracing* walk along the canal tow path, was going to represent the peak excitement of their stay, and even she was struggling to see how she could turn one of those excursions into a remotely heroic adventure.

'Isn't the modiste next to a bookshop?' Josephine enquired.

'I don't need a new dress, I need a bandana and pantaloons!' Matilda announced, stabbing her poached egg.

'I've always dreamed of attending a society picnic with a Prussian-blue parasol—' Sophie began dreamily.

'I do hope you won't be put to any terrible great expense on our behalf, Aunt!' Phoebe overrode, glaring at all her sisters. 'We have brought our best dresses with us, and you and Uncle Higglestone are already looking after us, after all.'

'Oh, hush now, dear! It will be our pleasure, and exactly what your dear mama would wish, too! Now, as I understand it, Thomas has the special *attire* for your forthcoming announcement well in hand…'

Phoebe glanced up sharply. It was the first she'd heard of the betrothal plans for a while, and her aunt's reference suddenly felt too real. A small, hard lump formed in her throat.

'… but I can't imagine you've had the chance for too many frivolous shopping trips these past few months,' Aunt Higglestone continued brightly, 'and this will give me the opportunity to spoil my lovely nieces.'

'None! We've had none!' Sophie rushed, glaring at Phoebe. 'I mean, dearest Harriet has no match when it comes to hems and frills, but Thomas considers hand-me-downs suitable for every occasion and, well, none of us have had the stomach to ask for anything new since…'

There was a poignant silence.

'Since Papa had the poisoned toe,' Josephine filled.

Uncle Higglestone grunted behind his periodical, as their aunt stretched a conciliatory hand over her favourite harebell butter dish.

'Well, then, that settles it! We'll each have a new muslin

before the week is out, and I'll wager we can even find something in Prussian blue at Madame Paragon's! Oh this is going to be such fun!'

'This is not fun!' Matilda scowled, slumping in the back room of *Madame Paragon's boutique dressmakers for gentility.*

'Shh!' Phoebe frowned, peeping through a jade velvet curtain separating them from the dressing space.

Sophie was parading in her fourth shade of blue muslin, while the rest of the Fairfax clan awaited their turn with significantly less enthusiasm.

'Aunt Higglestone will hear you.'

'But they all look so *extremely* the same!' Matilda moaned. 'Why can't Sophie just pick one? I had a choice of two, so chose the one I could cut up for a bandana and pantaloons when I tire of it!'

'You must do no such thing!' Phoebe chided, though her lips were twitching. 'Sophie, for one, will never forgive you, but you must also consider that Aunt Higglestone is paying a small fortune for these dresses.'

'But you always do exactly as you please! You didn't take a single dress with you when you ran away, I checked your armoire! You wore Fred's clothes and drank *devil's brew* and then you had a duel with some pretend sword and—'

'It was Miss Sarah Siddon's theatrical épée!' Phoebe objected. 'Plus, I never ran away! And what have I said about mentioning devil's brew?!'

Matilda crossed her arms and scowled.

'Anyway, you're not the only one who likes adventures!'

Phoebe considered her headstrong younger sister in exasperation, before snatching up a gentleman's cravat from a colourful pile on the sideboard.

'Did you know, I also fought a *dastardly* pirate once?' she murmured, tying the red cloth, bandana style, around her forehead.

Matilda stifled a shriek of laughter and snatched up another, while Josephine smirked and let her book slide to rest.

'Which one?' Matilda demanded breathlessly.

'Why Captain Blackbeard – or was it Bluebeard? The one with the best beard!' Phoebe pulled a face. 'Now, choose your weapon! Pistols or swords?'

'The sword – every time!' Matilda squeaked, grabbing a parasol from a holder in the corner.

'My favourite, too! Now *en garde*, me heartie!' Phoebe challenged, pulling out another parasol, while her younger sister lunged with something resembling a banshee's shriek.

'Of course, Marchioness Carlisle, and dear Lady Carlisle,' Madama Paragon's voice rang out. 'I was only thinking this morning that the rose silk became Miss Aurelia's graceful figure so beautifully. Do excuse me while…'

Which became the precise moment that the jade curtain was pulled aside, revealing Phoebe and Matilda mid-battle.

'Oh … my!' Madame Paragon gasped, her eyes dancing.

'Really, Phoebe and Matilda! What *on earth* are you doing?' Aunt Higglestone exclaimed, goggle-eyed, while Sophie dissolved into a fit of silent giggles.

Phoebe dragged her eyes from her stricken aunt to two

highly fashionable ladies of the ton, eyeballing her with something between horror and delighted amusement.

'I… Please accept my apologies… We didn't realise there were more customers in the shop,' Phoebe garbled, trying not to look at Sophie.

'Not at all, Miss Fairfax!' Madame Paragon returned valiantly. 'We have been some time with Sophie's fitting, have we not, Mrs Higglestone? It is only natural young ladies would wish to … entertain themselves.'

'Indeed! But one would hope they would do so in a rather less hoydenish way!' the Marchioness of Carlisle pronounced, the feather on her elaborate hat nodding in violent agreement. 'When my daughter is in need of *entertainment* she reaches for her paintbox or harp – you might try them! Our order please, Madame Paragon…'

'Of course, Marchioness Carlisle,' Madame Paragon returned, stepping past Phoebe to retrieve a pale yellow silk gown, trimmed with lace.

It looked expensive, and as Madame Paragon sealed the box, Phoebe stole another look at Madame Paragon's customers. She'd listened to Sophie long enough to know both were dressed in the very latest fashion, with wide-brimmed bonnets trimmed with fluttering ribbons, and day dresses finished in shimmering gauzes and blonde lace. She also recognised the younger lady's hair was dressed *à la chinoise*, thanks to Sophie's regular attempts to achieve the same. She inhaled deeply. They clearly hadn't had so much as one heroic adventure their whole lives long, and she disliked them on principle. Yet they were also the type of well-connected persons her aunt, Thomas, and the Earl of Cumberland would wish to impress – which meant she had no choice but to wish it, too.

She forced a smile at the haughty marchioness, while pulling the cravat from her head.

'I'm not convinced it does cure the headache tied thus around the forehead,' she chattered brightly, 'but I do declare your presence has proven a tonic – I cannot thank you enough, Marchioness … Lady Carlisle.'

Then she sank into a deep and dramatic curtsey which prompted the younger Lady Carlisle to snort into a delicate lace handkerchief, while the marchioness stared suspiciously at Phoebe.

'Indeed! I favour bedrest and lemon tea myself,' she returned through pursed lips.

'A safe choice, though perhaps bandanas are a new fashion among the young ladies this season,' the modiste placated, with a twinkle.

'To be sure!' Aunt Higglestone chimed in nervously. 'And it is such a fortuitous pleasure to see you, Your Ladyship! Mr Higglestone and I were rather hoping the girls would make Lady Aurelia's better acquaintance at the Sydney Gardens picnic this weekend. We hear there are to be fireworks, and a Merlin Swing for the young people…'

Aunt Higglestone beamed encouragingly, while Lady Aurelia glanced at her mama.

'So I understand!' the marchioness returned.

'Yet even if the circus is in town, Mrs…'

'Higglestone,' their aunt supplied obligingly.

'Aurelia is used to rather more sophisticated diversions than the jugglers and swings of Sydney Gardens…'

'Indeed! Though the Sydney Gardens picnic is commonly agreed to be one of the more entertaining events of the Bath season, Marchioness,' a low tone interjected, 'my brother and I certainly look forward to it.'

There was a moment's silence while everyone looked across at the two new visitors standing just inside the open shop door, and Phoebe felt her every thought grind to a halt. It was so unlikely as to be impossible, and yet there was no denying the perfectly-tied cravat, the immaculate Hessian boots, or the same supercilious stare that took her right back to the roadside in a breath. And beside him, there was a younger gentleman in army regimentals, with dancing chestnut eyes and a mischievous smile, which Phoebe would have liked in any other circumstance.

'Oh! Viscount Damerel, Captain Damerel!' the marchioness gushed, the peacock feather dangerously out of control. 'How fortuitous to see you here, for Aurelia has been quite disappointed not to see you both at the Assembly Rooms of late, have you not, Aurelia?'

Aurelia managed to simultaneously simper and look entirely unconcerned, while Phoebe stared, feeling as though she had slipped into some ridiculous parallel universe where all the most awkward people of her small acquaintance had suddenly decided to become the best of friends.

How long had they been standing there? How much had they seen? The door had been open for some time…

Swiftly, she hid the incriminating parasol behind her back and side-stepped behind a nearby mannequin.

'It is kind of Lady Carlisle to notice my absence, when she herself has so many admirers,' the viscount returned smoothly, 'as I'm sure all the ladies here must – including Miss Fairfax?'

Phoebe re-emerged nonchalantly.

'Viscount Damerel, Captain…' she forced, sinking into a curtsey and ignoring her sisters' glances.

'I trust you are fully recovered Miss Fairfax, and finding Bath to your liking?' the viscount asked.

Phoebe raised her eyes as far as the topmost shiniest button of his elegantly cut morning coat of dark olive green. Quite how one human being managed to achieve so much perfection on a daily basis, was beyond her understanding. No doubt he'd read all the books in his perfect library, too.

Without warning, a memory of his silhouette in the library firelight reached through her crowded thoughts. Her eyes flickered to his to find the same curious gleam reaching across the room between them now. She caught her breath and dropped her gaze, though she was aware of a dull flush creeping across her face.

'I am, thank you, my lord … thanks to the generosity of my aunt and uncle,' she mumbled, noticing her aunt turn pink with pleasure, while the marchioness just glowered.

'That is most pleasing to hear,' the viscount returned in a mellow tone. 'I trust you and your sisters will make the most of your stay. I find Bath can be pleasing when it comes to light diversions, if a little lacking in … *heroic* adventures.'

Phoebe glanced up sharply while the captain grinned, yet there was no time to respond.

'Oh, Viscount, you really are so droll!' the marchioness crowed, securing his attention once more. 'We find Bath the perfect antidote to the crush of the Ballrooms in London – not that Aurelia didn't enjoy those, too.'

She paused to trill unpleasantly.

'I'm sure she would be happy to share some of her favourite diversions with you, if you'd care to accompany us? Captain Damerel?'

'It would be a pleasure,' the viscount returned, just as Madame Paragon caught a parcel from the countertop and pressed it into his hands.

'Here is your order, Viscount, thank you for your custom, as always!'

'Excellent timing, thank you, Madame Paragon. Good day to you, Mrs Higglestaff,' the marchioness closed with a triumphant, feathery nod.

'Ladies,' the viscount bowed, before turning to follow.

'Higglestone,' their aunt corrected, faintly, as the door closed with a thud.

Chapter Nine

Eight weeks and one brotherly letter of concern until the wedding

Oxford, 28th March

And so, dear sisters, having learned that you managed to divert our dear eldest brother from his Monstrous Marriage Master Plan – at least temporarily – I feel it incumbent upon myself to pay our kindly relatives a visit, both to congratulate you on your escape, and to persuade you to show me a few of the delights of Bath.

Until then, I would be most grateful if you could desist from any more deadly duels or other pirating activities.

Your doting brother,
Fred

P.S. I am also very much looking forward to assessing whether our dear uncle does, indeed, require surgical separation from the Bath Chronicle and Weekly Gazette, as you suggest.

'Does he say when he's coming?' Josephine sniffed into a new copy of *Persuasion*, which she'd found wedged behind a well-thumbed *Encyclopaedia of Botanical Species* in their uncle's library.

'I'm not sure what delights we're supposed to show him – we haven't exactly seen many ourselves!' Phoebe muttered, looking over her brother's typically short letter for anything she may have missed.

'Oh, hush, Phoebe!' Sophie scolded, too in love with her lace-trimmed Prussian-blue gown to find fault with anything.

'There's the Pump Room, The Royal Crescent, The Circus, Queen Square, Pulteney Street, The Guildhall, not to mention the Upper Assembly Rooms and Sydney Gardens of course...'

'But those are all boring places! And we haven't even been to the last two yet!' Matilda grumbled.

'Seconded,' Phoebe nodded.

'Yes well ... that's about to change this weekend, isn't it?' Sophie placated. 'New dresses *and* a society picnic – even the viscount and his brother said they thought the Sydney Gardens picnic to be one of the more entertaining events of the Bath season!'

Phoebe shot her happy sister a swift glance. She hadn't said much after their debacle of a visit to Madame Paragon's, but she had the feeling the dancing-eyed captain had left almost as much of an impression as his brother – who appeared to have irritated every rational thought she ever possessed.

'We should all be grateful, we could still be stuck in Devon with a new governess and the cross-stitch!' Sophie added.

'Actually, I quite like the cross-stitch,' Matilda frowned, reaching for Sophie's rouge.

Thoughtfully, Phoebe replaced Fred's letter in her writing box, and stood up to smooth down her gown. Despite her entreaties for something plain and simple, her aunt insisted they all had two new dresses apiece. This one was cut from lavender-figured satin, with a festoon flounce caught up with rosettes, and sleeves made of fine net clasped all the way to the wrist. Phoebe surveyed herself critically; there was still no competition with Fred's breeches, but there was something about the cut of the dress against her fair skin and burnished hair that made her feel grown-up. Almost.

'You look different in that,' Matilda added, with two bright pink cheeks, 'like a lady … sort of … well, as much of a lady that you can look, anyway!'

'Thank you – you look the least like a pirate you've ever looked, too!' Phoebe retorted, bunching up a shawl and throwing it at her grinning younger sister.

'Matilda!' Sophie scolded, snatching back the rouge. 'She's right though,' she added as Matilda grumbled. 'I've never seen you look so ladylike, Phoebs! You make a very pretty debutante, the earl will have to watch his step!'

'I don't think the earl can see past his stomach to do that!' Phoebe retorted, pushing out her own stomach, to ape the earl's bulbous stoop. '*Well, well, your brother could do with feeding you up a bit, but you'll do … nothing worse than a skinny countess, I say,*' she mimicked, strutting across the floor and waggling a finger at an enthralled Matilda, who dissolved again. 'And as for Bath and its many delights…' She straightened to pick up a fan and bring it to her face, her eyes rolling. 'Well, it's a step up from quadrilles and French, I'll give you that!'

'Now that I do agree with,' Sophie smiled. 'The Pump Room is a thousand times better than conjugating *Être* and *Avoir* until one feels they couldn't ever eat another croissant…'

'I never feel like that,' Matilda declared.

'And yet, how I wish we could really enjoy everything without thinking of propriety or expectations,' Phoebe added wistfully. 'How gloriously free that sounds!'

'Perhaps you should ask the captain to challenge the earl to a duel, on account of his onion-scented person, and release you from Thomas's Monstrous Marriage Master Plan?' Matilda suggested, scrubbing her cheeks with a cloth.

'He is by far the more amiable of the brothers, it's true!' Sophie giggled. 'Though perhaps the viscount would care to oblige, he did rescue you—'

'The viscount would sooner shoot me!' Phoebe retorted swiftly.

'Phoebe!' Sophie objected.

'Well, it's true!' Phoebe defended. 'From the moment I made his acquaintance he has done nothing but mock and ridicule! He is the proudest and most insufferable kind of gentleman, who has made me realise that there are few things more precious in life than freedom from those who view females as chattels, or inferior beings, in every way!'

She paused to draw breath as Sophie regarded her curiously.

'Well, if it's a little freedom you want, perhaps Miss Phoebe Fairfax of Fairfax Theatrical Company could help?'

'You want me to *imagine* myself enjoying Bath without

propriety or expectation?' Phoebe frowned, feeling her sister might be underestimating her predicament just a little.

'No, you ninnyhammer!' Sophie exclaimed, much to Matilda's delight. 'I'm just saying that while you're in Bath you can be whoever you want to be, whenever you want to be her … as long as you're Phoebe when needed, too.'

'Complicated!' Josephine muttered, not even lifting her eyes from her book.

Phoebe stared at her pretty cornflower-eyed sister, wondering when she got to be so duplicitous, and yet even she had to admit the idea was attractive.

'You mean, invent someone who can have a few adventures?' she quizzed.

'I mean, become someone whom Bath society would accept as entitled to enjoy a few diversions without a chaperone, such as a … mysterious widow of independent means, visiting Bath after her husband's early demise to … the dropsy!'

'Not the dreaded dropsy!' Josephine objected, glancing up. 'It's so depressing! Why not irritation of the nerves? Much more romantic!'

'Pah!' Matilda jumped up, her eyes gleaming. 'Any early demise is excessively dull – unless he was murdered, gruesomely, in a duel! But if a mysterious widow means Phoebe can do more than drink mud water while we're here, then I say she should do it!'

She paused to survey her older sister critically.

'Two minutes!' she exclaimed, running from the room.

'We might regret this,' Sophie muttered.

Seconds later, the twelve-year-old reappeared with a rolled-up blanket, which she then discarded, with the air of a court magician, to reveal several items hidden inside.

'One of Aunt Higglestone's wigs?!' Sophie gaped in horror. 'Just because Phoebe's going to pose as a widow, doesn't mean she needs to look positively medieval!'

'Actually, it's a cap and wig powder!' Matilda defended hotly. 'And spectacles. Phoebe will need a good disguise if she's to pass undetected, she can't just go out as she is!'

There was a brief silence while they all acknowledged the wisdom of the youngest Fairfax, before Phoebe grinned and took the items from Matilda.

'A deceased husband would explain an absent chaperone,' she mused. 'And a level of disguise would be highly useful should any person of our acquaintance be out at the same time.'

She popped Aunt Higglestone's cap on her head and tied it beneath her chin. Instantly, her sisters dissolved into laughter.

'It actually suits you!' Sophie snorted, wiping away her tears.

'But still, how is she to actually go anywhere?' Matilda asked, her forehead creased with concern. 'She can hardly waltz directly in and out of Aunt and Uncle's front door, after all!'

'Are you forgetting our sweet and delicate older sister holds the fastest, tree-scaling record across Dartmoor?' Josephine smirked, nodding towards a maple tree just outside the bedchamber window. 'I'm sure the lack of a door isn't going to prove too much of a problem, even with an injured shoulder.'

Phoebe glanced at the tree with its conveniently thick and

twisted branches, just waiting to assist an intrepid widow to the ground, and felt a flicker of hope. She wouldn't make the same mistake as last time; there would be no devil's brew, no duels, no interfering viscounts – just a little freedom … before everything changed for good.

She drew a breath.

'Which just leaves the question of a name,' she murmured, her mind filling with myriad possibilities before inspiration struck.

She sank into a curtsey.

'May I present to you … Mrs Mary Smith!' She grinned. 'Younger cousin to Miss Sarah Kemble, otherwise known as Miss Sarah Siddons, darling of the theatre, and daughter to *theatrical extraordinaires*, Mr Roger Kemble and Sarah Ward!'

There was a brief pause before the bedchamber erupted in a chorus of groans and laughter.

'Mrs Mary Smith, younger cousin to Miss Sarah Siddons, darling of the theatre,' Sophie nodded, wiping her eyes. 'It's perfect!'

'It sounds *excessively* old,' Matilda grumbled.

'Or a governess's name! Everyone will expect you to talk about manners and coach-springs!' Josephine warned.

'I don't care,' Phoebe returned brightly. 'And Mrs Mary Smith won't care! She's a young widow from theatrical royalty with none of the trappings of an unmarried debutante, which means she can explore Bath's *many delights* without Thomas, dearest Aunt, or anyone else, suffering some kind of terminal apoplexy.

'Unlike Phoebe Fairfax, Mrs Mary Smith is quite free!'

'It's glued,' Phoebe complained.

'No, it's not, it's dressed, dearest – there's a difference!' Sophie frowned, adding another pin before Phoebe could dismantle her tumbling creation, duly powdered with wig powder until her dark copper locks looked almost blonde.

'Now it's perfect, so don't you dare touch it again! I want everyone to meet a *sophisticated* Mrs Mary Smith, not one who falls out of trees!'

'I haven't yet fallen out of the tree,' Phoebe objected. 'I scaled it twice today, just to practise, and didn't so much as snag a stocking!'

'*Anyway*,' Sophie continued, rolling her eyes, 'the Upper Assembly Rooms will be a squash tonight – or so the modiste said when we collected our ribbons – which means it should be relatively easy to mingle without fear of anyone identifying you.'

Phoebe raised her inky eyes to Sophie's cornflower-blues, knowing exactly to whom she was referring.

She still couldn't quite believe the universe had crossed her path with the viscount's again – and in a modiste's in Bath of all places. She closed her eyes and felt the humiliation anew. He already thought her a hare-brained fool, and now she'd confirmed it with her childish pirating antics – in front of one of the most dislikable matrons of the ton. She recalled his supercilious stare, and the way his eyes had gleamed when she'd met his gaze.

'*It seems to me, Miss Phoebe Fairfax, that if gallivanting around the countryside dressed as a bourgeois tallyman is your idea of freedom, you're in need of your brother's protection more than you realise. Young ladies of quality don't get to be heroines.'*

And why were her traitorous thoughts determined to keep reminding her what he thought?

She squeezed her fingers as she drew a deep breath. Let him think what he liked, she was a Fairfax first and would never apologise for it.

'In truth, I'm just looking forward to actually seeing a little of Bath, without anyone having a fit of the vapours,' Phoebe shrugged, picking up the spectacles and trying them.

'Really?' Sophie quizzed. 'And here I was thinking you might have more pressing matters on your mind.'

Phoebe glanced at her wily sister. It was true she was feeling the ticking clock on her nuptials more than ever, but it seemed a little ambitious to hope an alias might attract a new suitor who was not only willing to overlook a peculiar dress sense, but was also desperate to marry within seven short weeks.

'Well, I can't wait to hear all about it,' Sophie continued, leaning forward to rub rouge on her sister's scowling face. 'Bath is much more relaxed than London, so it should be easy for Mrs Mary Smith to have a little fun before the dreaded betrothal announcement…'

Her sister chattered on brightly as Phoebe conjured a picture of herself standing at an altar, next to the earl. She suppressed a deep shudder. She might laugh with the rest of her sisters, but in truth, the thought of calling herself the Countess of Cumberland in less than two months was terrifying. And it wasn't so much the wedding day – she could grit her teeth and get through that – it was the thought of what came afterwards that haunted her.

She closed her eyes and swallowed the ready rise of nausea. There was time yet, and she was determined to use it.

'Do you think old purple-face will be there tonight?' Matilda asked, retying her cream sash as a trusty sword belt.

'No one could be that unlucky!' Phoebe returned with feeling.

Chapter Ten

Eight weeks and one game of Questions and
Commands until the wedding

The Earl of Cumberland wasn't at the Upper Assembly Rooms.

It did seem, however, as though most of Bath were, and from the moment she'd shinnied down the old maple with her petticoats tucked into her stays and ball slippers between her teeth, Phoebe had begun to feel quite hopeful, indeed. The private Hackney carriage hire had proven a lot easier to navigate than the packed stagecoach, no one had stared suspiciously at her powdered hair, and the cap had elicited only respectful glances – including one sympathetic nod from a society matriarch.

The Assembly Room was also just as Sophie predicted: full of starry-eyed debutantes, a handful of eligible gentlemen – and a concerning supply of ineligible ones, too.

All in all, apart from one small misunderstanding with a

nosy footman – who actually turned out to be the Assembly Room announcer – Phoebe was convinced things had started as well as they could for any girl in search of adventure.

She sipped her ratafia and allowed herself a small smile. She'd made it – she'd escaped, and so far, no one had given her so much as a second glance.

'Mrs Smith?' a lady in lime chiffon, with a matching ostrich plume enquired. 'Do excuse me, but I believe the announcer mentioned your family name was Kemble? Are you, by chance, any relation to the wonderful Sarah Kemble? I believe her stage name is Sarah Siddons?'

Phoebe swallowed, feeling as though the first chink may have just appeared in her otherwise very shiny plan.

'Oh, why, yes!' She smiled, praying the lady's knowledge of the actress was limited. 'I'm a *much* younger cousin, recently bereaved.'

'Oh, I was hoping you'd say so!' the lady exclaimed, clasping her hands dramatically. 'I mean in regard to the cousinly connection,' she added hastily. 'I just adored her Lady Macbeth!'

She lowered her voice and fluttered her fan.

'My artistic soul pines for the stage, and though this is far from common knowledge, I'm certain that were my circumstances different...'

'Really, Cordelia, I don't think your Cheltenham Tragedies are any sort of secret in Bath!' a sharp tone interjected. 'Clearly, Mrs Smith is here to enjoy Bath society, and does not wish to be bothered with your theatrical nonsense, am I not right Mrs Smith?'

To her great consternation, Phoebe found herself looking

directly into Lady Aurelia's perfectly peachy countenance. She was wearing the extravagant yellow silk gown that Phoebe had glimpsed in Madame Paragon's, and even she had to admit it became Aurelia's golden hair and forget-me-knot eyes very well. Tonight, she'd finished her ensemble with a cloak of midnight blue, set back off her fair shoulders, and a pair of delicate, white kid gloves that Phoebe would never dare wear herself, for fear of them being a completely different colour within the hour. She thought briefly of her scramble down the maple earlier that evening, and bit her lip. Aurelia was undoubtedly a young lady of quality, and the sort of girl who really should marry the earl, and produce a whole troop of purple-faced, onion-scented offspring for his pleasure.

'Delighted to make your acquaintance, Miss …?' she murmured, keeping her eyes low as she dipped a curtsey.

'… Lady Aurelia Carlisle,' Aurelia supplied airily. 'Do walk with me a while, Mrs Smith?'

Phoebe exhaled silently. She was certain Aurelia would not be the type to withhold should she have seen through her disguise. She nodded politely, and together they began to perambulate around the busy room.

'Though you may call me Aurelia,' she added after a few moments, 'for I've a feeling we're going to be the best of friends, don't you think?'

Phoebe smiled, the ratafia creating a safe and fuzzy comfort in her stomach. This was proving easier than she thought.

'Are you enjoying Bath, Mrs Smith?' Aurelia continued. 'I must say, I am finding it rather *ennuyeux* after London.'

She paused to flutter her eyelashes at two young men in

gleaming army regimentals, who bowed low as they passed by.

'These soldiers are such incorrigible flirts, don't you think?' Aurelia added, accepting a sherry from a passing footman. 'One can't believe a word they say.' She smiled and held up a kid-gloved hand at a portly gentleman, who was ogling the room.

'That's Lord Avery, one of Mama's *dearest* friends… He makes my skin crawl – do you know that feeling?'

Phoebe pictured the earl's moist, purple lips and nodded. She knew the feeling exactly.

'Is he your intended?' she asked tentatively, wondering if she and Aurelia had more in common than she first realised.

'Good gracious me, no!' she exclaimed with wide-eyed horror. 'I'd rather marry a codfish! I mean, he's offered, and he's tried to…' she paused to screw up her nose. '… *kiss* me on more occasions than I care to recall. But I've been promised to someone far younger and wealthier since the cradle.'

'Oh well, that's a relief,' Phoebe mumbled, wishing she'd taken a glass of sherry when she could.

'Yes, but I would welcome your advice with *a little spot of bother* all the same?' Aurelia continued in a hushed tone.

She glanced around, before turning back with a demure smile.

'Given you are a married woman of the world, and I merely a debutante?'

'Married and bereaved,' Phoebe amended swiftly.

'And excessively content with it, too, I warrant!' Aurelia tittered.

'Oh no,' Phoebe started awkwardly, 'it's just I—'

'Don't worry, I completely understand,' she reassured, guiding Phoebe into the corridor, before lowering her voice to a whisper. 'In truth, I know all about the duties of a married woman too.'

She smirked knowingly while Phoebe stared, starkly aware they were now leaving the protective bustle of the Assembly Room, for a quiet corridor with much more lighting.

'And that it doesn't always have to be *a duty* at all?' Aurelia continued, bestowing a dazzling smile on a passing gentleman who gazed as though enraptured.

Phoebe stared at Aurelia's cherry-bow lips, hardly knowing what to think. As Mrs Smith, she'd really only just met the marchioness's pretty daughter, and yet she seemed determined to share some deep, dark secret that Phoebe had absolutely no desire to hear.

'Lady Aurelia, much as I'm enjoying this delightful tête à tête, I really should—'

'I think I may be with child.'

Phoebe blanched, while Aurelia continued to smile as though she'd just confessed a slight headache.

'I beg your pardon?' Phoebe whispered.

Aurelia leant closer. 'I said, *I think I may be with child*,' she repeated, as though Phoebe might be hard of hearing.

Phoebe inhaled silently, feeling every polite response forsake her. Her thoughts whirled, while every hushed whisper and innuendo she'd ever overheard at Knightswood – courtesy of the butcher's boy, the domestic staff, and the gamekeeper – spun to the forefront of her mind.

She's fast… He's always been frisky… Needs the herd to sow his oats… Her flank is thickening.

She dropped her gaze to Aurelia's tiny waist, and frowned.

'You don't look...' she began.

'It's early yet,' Aurelia whispered. 'But I am a little *late*... And as you are a widowed woman of the world, I wondered if you know *how* to know ... for sure?'

Phoebe swallowed, feeling wholly inadequate to the moment, before it struck her. Aurelia had done the thing married people do – the thing she'd possibly wanted to do with the viscount! She closed her eyes and forced his golden silhouette from her mind. Now was not the time.

'From my experience of such things,' she whispered, in what she hoped was a convincing, maternal tone. 'Being *late* for anything, has no bearing on ... one's flank thickening.'

Then she added a smile for reassurance, and waited for Aurelia's relief.

To her great surprise, Aurelia only stared with narrowing eyes, before tipping her head back and laughing as though she might never stop.

'Oh, that's good! Very good! I needed that.' She sighed, wiping her eyes.

Briefly, Phoebe wondered if she wasn't a little touched in the head, and considered her with new sympathy.

'I trust your betrothed has been understanding?' she tried again. 'Perhaps family could be informed? Arrangements brought forward?'

At this Aurelia stared.

'My betrothed?' she repeated, before collecting herself. 'Oh yes, my betrothed... He is, *most blissfully*, unaware, and as we are not contracted to marry until I reach my twenty-first birthday, long may it continue! After all, there's little point in not enjoying some freedom while we can, is there?'

A million conflicted thoughts flew through Phoebe's head. She was all for freedom, but if Aurelia and her betrothed had done the thing she'd possibly wanted to do with the viscount, there seemed few good reasons to exclude him now.

'I just thought that someone as *worldly* as yourself,' she continued, 'might be able to assist me with— oh Captain Elliot! How delightful to see you!'

Phoebe stared at Aurelia's adept change in tone, as three young officers in regimentals approached.

'I do declare this Assembly is a positive squeeze, and yet no gathering is of any interest without you, of course.'

The officers approached them with varying levels of interest as Aurelia morphed into the very epitome of a society debutante. Phoebe shifted uncomfortably – she wasn't used to being the object of curiosity, disguise or not.

'You are ever the gracious flatterer, Lady Aurelia.' Captain Elliot smiled, bending low over her hand before turning to Phoebe.

Phoebe stiffened, taking in the captain's perfectly coiffured hair, strong jaw and fine chestnut eyes, which were brimming with mirth. He was immaculately dressed in crisp white pantaloons and spotless boots, while his regimental coat was decorated with a clutch of gleaming medals that belied his ready charm. Yet all of this paled next to Phoebe's growing certainty that, somehow, they had already met… Before she realised.

Captain *Elliot* was none other than Captain Damerel, the viscount's amiable brother!

'Mrs Mary Smith,' she murmured as she curtsied, feeling the least like Mrs Mary Smith she'd felt all evening.

'Enchanted to meet you, Mrs Smith!' he returned, his eyes dancing. 'Any friend of Lady Aurelia is a friend of mine!'

Phoebe blinked.

These soldiers are such incorrigible flirts, don't you think? One can't believe a word they say.'

Could Aurelia have been suggesting her *little spot of bother* wasn't down to her betrothed?

Phoebe began to feel a little warm beneath her wig, as her head filled with myriad new possibilities.

'Why don't you join us for a game of whist, Captain?' Aurelia cajoled. 'It is so hot in the Assembly Room.'

'I wish I could, but I'm promised for the quadrille,' the captain returned with one of his dazzling smiles. 'My friends would be honoured to make up a four, though, if that would be agreeable? Lady Aurelia, Mrs Smith, it has been a pleasure.'

Phoebe sunk into another curtsey as the charming soldier made his parting bow, exhaling beneath her breath.

'Well then, who's for a round of faro?' Aurelia exclaimed, all her previous cares seemingly forgotten.

'But, don't you also wish to return to the dancing?' Phoebe attempted, the bustling Assembly Room holding considerable new appeal.

She was suddenly and glaringly aware that if the captain was at the Ball, then the viscount could be, too, and she would be far better off in the busy Assembly Room than a quiet corridor.

'Heavens alive, no! That's the last place I wish to go!' Aurelia rolled her eyes as she led the way to one of the private card rooms. 'There're far too many boring people when my *new* favourites are right here! Now do let's go, before someone else takes the table…'

The soldiers, introducing themselves as Smithfield and Brent, didn't need a second invitation and reluctantly, Phoebe accompanied them.

'What about stakes?' Smithfield asked, with hair that reminded Phoebe forcibly of a mop.

'I don't play too deep with the ladies, don't like to steal their pin money!' he added before turning to guffaw with his friend for far longer than was necessary.

Aurelia closed the door with a smile.

'Oh, don't you worry about that,' she returned, a glint in her eye. 'I never play for money!'

'Then, what do we play for?' Phoebe frowned, worrying how long her disguise would last at these close quarters.

'I can think of *a few* options,' Aurelia smiled coquettishly. 'But for today, how about a Question or Command?'

The soldiers started to grin, while Phoebe stared doubtfully into Aurelia's narrowed eyes. Firstly, she'd closed the door, which didn't seem awfully proper at an Assembly Ball; secondly, she'd downed two drinks quite swiftly, and Phoebe could still recall the ill effects of Briggs's devil's brew with alarming clarity; and thirdly, while she rather enjoyed Questions and Commands at home, it could prove rather challenging for *Mrs-Mary-Smith-younger-cousin-to theatrical-darling-Sarah-Siddons.*

Yet, Aurelia had offered the hand of friendship, and wasn't the purpose of the evening to enjoy some freedom? To experience a little of Bath life before everything changed?

She shook back her sleeve frills with determination – unlike Thomas, she rarely lost at faro.

Phoebe began losing straight away. It wasn't so much bad luck, as the fact that the soldier with the mop-head kept shuffling his seat towards her, which ruined her concentration.

'I'll take a question,' she conceded when the first game was lost, certain it had to be better than a command.

Mop-head smiled.

'Certainly… Have you been widowed long, Mrs Smith?' he asked in a foppish tone.

'Pooh! Mary doesn't wish to answer boring questions about her dead husband!' Aurelia pouted. 'Her cousin is a famous actress! And everyone knows actresses live the most exciting lives!' Her eyes lit up as she leant forward and lowered her voice. 'They go to all the best soirees, wear the latest French fashion and have as many secret *liaisons* as they wish!'

She paused to titter into her sherry.

'So I think Mary must have many daring stories to tell,' she continued, her eyes gleaming. 'And better questions might be… Did you ever join your cousin on the stage? Fight a valiant duel? Kiss a prince perhaps?!'

She emptied her glass, as Phoebe forced all persistent and vexing thoughts of the highwayman and the viscount from her head.

'Yes, do tell us about your theatrical exploits, Mary,' the mop-head soldier leered suddenly, closing his hand over hers. 'Especially those involving *soirees* and *secret liaisons*…'

He paused to guffaw as Phoebe recoiled, and retrieved her hand.

'That's three questions!' She objected, decidedly grateful she'd not opted for a command.

'My game, my rules!' Aurelia flashed, refilling her glass once again.

'Well, I might have performed in a *few* productions,' Phoebe conceded slowly, grateful none of them had actually witnessed Fairfax Theatrical Company's production of *Hamlet*, when Sophie's raft ran aground and Ophelia's deathbed became a decidedly muddy affair, '… and fought a duel…' The moment Sarah Siddons's blade chose to take flight, flew through her head. '*And* worn miracle trousers – which, I assure you, are far more exciting than all the French fashion in the world! You don't know how lucky you are,' she added, side-eyeing mop-head.

'I knew it as soon as I saw you!' Aurelia exclaimed, reaching for another drink. 'You have the look of an adventurer! But what of kissing princes? Or kissing anyone? I'm in favour of kissing generally, you see.'

She giggled at Brent, who shifted his chair closer.

Phoebe frowned, conscious they now appeared to be squashed along two sides of the table, when there were four very good ones available.

'Yes, do tell us about the kissing!' the mop-head soldier echoed, picking up her hand and doing something wet and slimy to the back of it.

The earl's moist lips came to mind, and she felt a swell of nausea.

'Are stage kisses as real as they look, or did you save those for your admirers after the duels?' Mop-head smirked.

Much against her will, the night in the viscount's library

reached out of the fog of her brain again. She was certain he'd wanted to kiss her. Had he admired her? Or was she merely a distraction?

'I'll respect you more now I know who your brother is.'

She gritted her teeth and yanked her hand away, aware that Aurelia was not going to give up. 'Command – I choose command!' she substituted swiftly, hoping her change of mind would turn all thoughts from kissing.

'What fun!' Aurelia giggled. 'As you lost the game and haven't answered the question, it now becomes a matter of honour. And there are really only two commands that settle a matter of honour in my book – a race, or…'

Phoebe swallowed, picturing Aunt Higglestone's face if she were to ask to borrow a horse to settle a card debt, when she wasn't even permitted to ride.

'Or?' Phoebe frowned, crossing her fingers beneath the table.

'Or a kiss!'

At this, everyone around the table began to laugh in a way that Phoebe found highly unnecessary, as it really wasn't funny at all.

'But because we are all friends, I'm quite prepared to share your debt with you!' Aurelia added archly.

Then she lurched towards the younger soldier, and pressed her lips to his in a way Phoebe had only read about in a novel Harriet had once banned.

Phoebe stared in shock, before realising Smithfield had also slid his roving hand around her waist, and was starting to loom towards her. Horror-struck, she recoiled from his pursed lips, but the more she leaned away the more her chair leg locked, and he seemed only too happy to interpret squirming as encouragement.

Which left her no choice at all.

Muttering one of Fred's favourite curses, she made a grab for Aurelia's half-drunk sherry, and emptied it over the soldier's leering mop-head.

Which was also precisely the moment that the door opened. For a second, no one moved and then slowly, Phoebe turned her gaze towards the doorway to find a curious footman, a dancing-eyed captain, and a belligerent marchioness looking back – and behind them all, a haughty stare that made her want to retreat inside her widow's cap for good.

Phoebe inhaled raggedly as she glanced back at Aurelia, only to find that she'd somehow managed to slide away from Brent, leaving herself and mop-head looking very cosy indeed. She flushed to the very roots of her powdered hair.

'What is the meaning of all this, Aurelia?' the marchioness demanded, making all the candles in the candelabra flicker uncertainly.

'When the captain said you were enjoying a round of cards with an unknown Mrs Smith and two gentlemen of the regiment, I must admit to not being best pleased, but to find you *in a private room*, with an *actress*, and *two foot soldiers*? Do you not realise what the world might think? Thank goodness the viscount knows us well enough to trust your behaviour stems from childish innocence, and nothing more!'

Phoebe's chest thumped as she lifted her eyes to the viscount's, but they were so heavily lidded they revealed nothing. She glanced back to Aurelia.

Why would it matter what the viscount thought – unless they had an understanding?

Briefly, she stared, feeling as though a bucket of icy water had been emptied over her head.

Could the disagreeable viscount actually be Aurelia's betrothed?

'If I may be per ... permitted to def—' mop-head began to stammer through a shower of sherry drops.

'You may not!' the marchioness snapped so fiercely he blanched.

'Might I recommend a more discreet tone, Marchioness?'

The viscount's tone was dispassionate and his eyes cold, taking Phoebe back to the Swan Inn in a heartbeat. He closed the door, before directing one of his piercing stares at all those gathered. Phoebe felt herself wither instantly, certain he would see straight through her disguise, yet, when his gaze swept the room, it seemed to pass over hers without a flicker of recognition. She exhaled silently, relief coursing her veins plus something else, too – a shadow of disappointment – despite it making no sense whatsoever.

'While the reputation of actresses and officers are of lesser concern, Lady Aurelia is still enjoying her first season, and you would not wish her name to be blemished by inadvertently stirring up the same interest you are seeking to avoid.'

It was the marchioness's turn to blanch.

'You are quite right of course, Viscount,' she conceded, as the captain avoided eye contact with everyone, his lips twitching.

'Aurelia has only been out a short while, and there mustn't be the slightest hint of scandal...'

'Oh, Mama!' Aurelia cooed suddenly. 'What a fuss to be making when I have behaved just as I ought.'

She got up and slid her arms around her stiff mother.

'I must admit to being a *trifle* surprised when Mrs Smith offered a brief enactment of *a romantic tragedy* but I've never been in the company of an actress, or her cousin, before, and certainly didn't wish to appear rude. I do see *now*, of course, that it was entirely unsuitable behaviour for an Assembly Ball, no matter how innocently instigated.'

Then she fluttered her china-doll eyes so hard they actually began to water – while Phoebe stared, unsure whether to feel aghast or impressed.

'There, there, child, I did not consider your behaviour would be anything but what it should be,' the marchioness consoled, throwing Phoebe and the mop-head soldier a caustic look. 'Whereas the pair of you should be ashamed of yourselves! Trying to lead my child astray with your … *ignoble* behaviour!'

Phoebe flinched.

'Count yourselves fortunate I've no wish to make this evening's events public, otherwise I'd ensure no one in Bath ever opened their doors to you again!' the marchioness proclaimed.

'Aurelia?'

Then she swept from the room, taking Aurelia with her, while the captain finally gave in to his mirth.

Chapter Eleven

Eight weeks and suspecting the captain until the wedding

'And it wasn't even in the least bit heroic!' Phoebe groaned as their smaller carriage pulled up at the Sydney Hotel, behind their aunt and uncle's comfortable chaise.

She'd recounted the full agony of the Assembly Ball, while Josephine and Matilda were safely ensconced with their kindly relatives, and Sophie was suitably horrified.

'Which bit? The Ball? The questions? The kiss?' she asked faintly. 'At least it was an adventure I suppose...'

'I never kissed the mop-head!' Phoebe protested. 'Though he did get a little too close for comfort.'

She closed her eyes and shuddered.

'I've no idea why the universe keeps sending all the codfish my way, but it's the kind of adventure I can be doing without!'

Sophie's lips twitched as she eyed her sister with concern.

'And the viscount was there … but he didn't recognise you?'

'He was too busy being disagreeable to the disagreeable marchioness!' Phoebe retorted, taking care not to look her sister in the eye.

The whole evening had been a disaster, but it was the viscount's appearance that had occupied her thoughts since waking. While his attendance at the same Assembly Ball in Bath was regrettable, his appearance in a highly embarrassing situation not of her making felt misfortunate indeed. Her only consolation was that he seemed too preoccupied with protecting his betrothed from scandal, to notice that *Mrs Smith* was the same *hare-brained simpleton* he'd found on the roadside a few weeks before.

A dull flush reached across her cheeks as she conjured his overbearing displeasure. He seemed to have a unique ability to agitate the most peculiar mix of emotions, and currently she was unsure if she felt more chagrin, disappointment or relief.

'So, now what?' Sophie asked, pursing her lips.

'Well, Mrs Mary Smith has clearly taken the polite world by storm, so the possibilities are endless…' Phoebe rolled her eyes.

'That was never the intention!' Sophie laughed. 'Besides, this arrived for you this morning.'

Phoebe stared as her sister handed over a thick, cream-coloured envelope with beautiful ornate lettering. She didn't recognise the hand, but for some reason she knew the sender right away.

'It came just before we left. I took it directly from the hall table and I don't think Aunt or Uncle noticed.'

'Mrs Mary Smith,' Phoebe frowned, just as the carriage door was yanked open.

'Hurry up, you two! Or we'll miss the picnic!' Matilda danced, whirling around in front of the gated entrance to The Grand Georgian Hotel.

'Hush now, dear,' their aunt fussed. 'There's plenty of time! And do tie your pelisse, though it is so unseasonably warm I do believe we may be able to promenade without... What do you think, dearest?' she asked Uncle Higglestone, who was still immersed in a smuggled copy of the *Bath Chronicle and Weekly Gazette*.

'Oh, yes, quite, quite,' he mumbled absent-mindedly. 'Though perhaps we'd best not throw all caution to the wind, lest the girls wish to see the fireworks, or Merlin Swing?'

'Ooh, yes! I wish to see all of it!' Matilda grinned, her eyes wide with excitement.

'Maybe a walk to the lantern boats after supper, too?' Phoebe smiled, glancing at the busy entrance to the dusky garden.

Josephine had read the Bath's Royal Pleasure Gardens pamphlet aloud numerous times over the past few days, so Phoebe could readily understand Matilda's excitement. The gardens were unlike anywhere any of them had ever been before, with entertainers, a bandstand, a Grecian Temple, an assortment of classical ruins, and numerous lantern-lit nooks and pathways.

'A walk to the lantern boats after supper sounds very agreeable.' Her aunt nodded approvingly. 'Now, then, girls,' she said, regrouping their small party inside the entrance. 'While the picnic is by invitation only, the gardens themselves remain *public*, and there is always the chance of crossing paths with an *undesirable*.'

She enunciated the last word very carefully while shaking out her new ivory parasol and giving the busy gardens one of her suspicious looks.

'Don't worry, Aunt,' Matilda placated, 'Phoebe is an old hand when it comes to undesirables, did you know she once fought—'

'Where is the picnic, exactly?' Phoebe interjected, taking hold of her sister's arm and propelling her swiftly towards a miniature ruin with water cascading over its cracked walls.

'Have you seen this?'

'But I was just—'

'Matilda!' Phoebe remonstrated as soon as they were out of earshot. 'How many times do I have to remind you? There must be no mention of highwaymen, duels, trousers, card games, wig powder, or anything else vaguely incriminating!'

'That list is too long!' Matilda returned, scowling.

'Oh, it's *so* pretty,' Sophie chimed in loudly, peering closely at the ruin. '... Or devil's brew, or questions about what men are born with,' she added under her breath, making Matilda scowl even harder.

'I don't see why…,' she objected.

'Well, if it isn't the intrepid pirates!' a new jovial voice exclaimed. 'Although, there appears to be no swordplay among you this evening, only a host of delightful young ladies ready to enjoy the Sydney Gardens spring picnic. What a happy coincidence! Captain Elliot Damerel at your service, Miss Fairfax and Miss…'

'Fairfax – they're all Fairfaxes!' Aunt Higglestone beamed, bustling forward.

'Good evening, Captain, and Viscount Damerel, too! What a pleasure! I do recall your mentioning you might be here this eve, and it is delightful to make your further acquaintances. May I present Miss Phoebe Fairfax, Miss Sophie Fairfax, Miss Josephine Fairfax, and Miss Matilda Fairfax, my wonderful nieces!'

Phoebe straightened instantly, relieved to find herself behind a wall of excitable sisters, amid the clamour of greetings. She inhaled deeply. To cross paths with the viscount at the modiste's and Assembly Ball was unlucky enough, but to run into him again at a garden picnic felt an injustice of the highest order.

She raised her eyes reluctantly, taking in the brothers' gleaming Hessian boots, spotless pantaloons and fitted coats of superfine cloth before reaching their faces – one filled with mirth, the other seemingly devoid of anything at all. The viscount regarded her directly, and she felt a brief rise of agitation, wondering what part of a spring family picnic a disdainful viscount could possibly find of interest.

'And of course, you remember Mr Higglestone? From the races?'

Clearly, neither had any such recollection of the owlish Uncle Higglestone, who'd found himself on the receiving end of one of Aunt Higglestone's sharpest prods, but were too polite to say so.

'But of course! It is a pleasure to meet you again, Mr Higglestone, and *all* the very fair Miss Fairfaxes too,' the captain responded.

Phoebe watched the pleasantries being exchanged, feeling as though her stomach was already aboard the Merlin Swing. Even if the viscount hadn't seen through her disguise at the Assembly Ball, it was clear he still thought her a hoydenish miss – while the captain was a prime suspect for Aurelia's *spot of bother*.

'We have a party bent on pleasure this evening, Viscount,' her aunt continued delightedly. 'Why don't you accompany us for a short while?'

Furiously, Phoebe trod on Sophie's boot, but her sister appeared to be entirely transfixed by the captain.

'That is kind, but—' the viscount began.

'We should be delighted!' his brother returned, overriding the objection.

Phoebe inhaled silently. She could hardly blame her sisters' excitement. The captain's smile was clearly disarming, and his dancing eyes full of mischief, too, but the viscount was the last person with whom she wished to spend time. An echo of his ridicule in the modiste's reached through her thoughts, and she bristled instantly.

What gave him the right to make his opinion so evident? He held no authority over her or any of them, nor was likely to anytime soon.

She glanced at Sophie, who was dimpling far more than necessary, as they joined the busy main path.

'Do the Misses Fairfax like to ride?' the captain enquired, proffering an arm to Sophie, who happily fell into step beside him. 'If so, I can certainly recommend Prior Park, especially before breakfast.'

'Oh, do call us by our first names, Captain Elliot,' Sophie

insisted. 'The Misses Fairfax makes us sound like old governesses!'

She trilled off into a frivolous laugh while Phoebe glared at the back of her animated head, thinking all sorts of uncharitable thoughts.

'Is riding of interest to yourself, Miss Fairfax?' came a much quieter enquiry. 'Or perhaps I should ask if your shoulder has recovered sufficiently yet?'

Startled, Phoebe glanced up to discover that the viscount had fallen in beside her, leaving Josephine and Matilda to bring up the rear of the party with their beaming aunt and uncle. She drew a deep breath, starkly aware that the proximity between them might yet prompt him to realise that she was the fast widow who'd led his betrothed astray.

'I love to ride, and my shoulder is much recovered, thank you, sir,' she returned stiffly. 'I also like to climb trees, swim, and do all the things my brothers do, given half the chance!' she added, lest he think her any less the girl he'd met on the roadside.

'And I warrant are much better at such pursuits than they are, too,' the viscount murmured.

Phoebe glanced up, but his expression was schooled.

'I must own to being somewhat surprised that the picnic is one of your seasonal highlights,' she frowned, after a beat. 'It seems rather tame entertainment for a gentleman...'

'Yes?' he prompted.

Phoebe swallowed, his proximity was beginning to unnerve her.

'For a gentleman of your *sophistication*?' she finished,

recalling the way he'd threatened to withdraw his patronage at The Swan Inn.

A curious smile played around his lips.

'Actually, I think you would find my tastes quite *variable,*' he returned, a gleam creeping into his eyes. 'And, unlike balls, these gardens feature horses – which always have my distinct approval.'

'Is that what brings you to Bath?' she quizzed.

He paused to chuckle and, quite inexplicably, Phoebe caught her breath

'Unfortunately, not,' he returned. 'I'm in Bath on family matters and will return to Ebcott Place when they are concluded.'

There was a moment of quiet while Phoebe fixed her gaze ahead, conscious of the oddest rush of feelings. Undoubtedly, he was speaking of his betrothal, and she was certain he and Aurelia would suit exceedingly well – which didn't explain her agitation at all. Except that, perhaps, it made her think of her own wretched, forthcoming announcement.

'You are fortunate that you have some control over your future,' she commented, after a beat. 'It is a privilege most ladies must forego.'

'I am. Though in my experience, not all ladies wish for *adventure,* as you do.' He frowned faintly, dark eyebrows arching.

'Perhaps most gentlemen don't wish for a young lady then,' Phoebe retorted. 'Perhaps they actually wish for a songbird they can admire and remove from its cage occasionally, so it can perform!'

'Rather a songbird than a wife who doesn't know how to behave!' the viscount countered.

'Marriage shouldn't be a behaviour test!' she flared. 'And if a lady lacks imagination or adventure, it's because she hasn't been allowed to dream further than a respectable marriage. In my view, the frailer sex are rarely frail at all! We are just as curious, and just as capable, as any man, though some of the polite world would term us dangerous radicals for such thoughts.'

'Indeed!' he returned, his eyes glittering. 'As evidenced by the success of your recent endeavours, I suppose.'

She felt a sudden scorch of heat reach across her cheeks.

'And why shouldn't I wear trousers and drink devil's brew and duel if I so wish?' she demanded. 'Surely, I am just as capable of managing myself as any gentleman?'

'Phoebe!' Aunt Higglestone called in a strangled, yet polite tone.

She bit her lip, conscious she was drawing attention to herself, even if they couldn't hear what she was saying.

'I'm sure there are many who would agree,' he acquiesced coldly, 'and yet such behaviour in young ladies of quality would be reprehensible to many gentlemen with a name and reputation to protect.'

There was a poignant pause, during which all Phoebe could hear was Sophie's tinkling laughter, and she wrestled with an overwhelming urge to land the viscount yet another leveller.

Thankfully, Matilda came to the rescue.

'The Merlin Swing!' she shrieked, her ribbons catching the breeze as she bolted ahead. 'Last one there is a *gundigut!*'

'Matilda Fairfax!' their aunt wailed after her, shaking her parasol in dismay.

Chapter Twelve

Eight weeks and suspecting Aurelia until the wedding

'Well, what does it say?' Sophie whispered as Phoebe unfurled the letter beneath the crisp white tablecloth.

They'd finally arrived at their supper spot, after a long, meandering walk that had almost settled Phoebe's ruffled nerves. She cast a look around. The sun had melted into a late pumpkin dusk, and the gardeners had begun lighting miniature lanterns in the copse of trees surrounding them. It really was the most picturesque spot.

'Do you think there are any severed ghosts' heads around?' Matilda asked loudly, much to the disapproval of several nearby mamas. 'Josephine said the Romans buried the heads of their favourite horses here.'

'Not beneath the picnic tables, dearest,' Aunt Higglestone placated hastily.

'Here, read it yourself,' Phoebe muttered, passing her sister the letter.

Dear Mrs Mary Smith,

Please excuse my behaviour at the Assembly Ball, I had few options remaining.

Look for me at the Sydney Gardens picnic, when I hope we will be able to promenade together, and resume our friendship.

Yours affectionately,
Lady Aurelia Carlisle

'Well, she doesn't exactly waste words,' Sophie concluded, turning it over.

'But she addressed it to Mrs Mary Smith, at Aunt and Uncle's address!' Phoebe frowned.

'And she tried to make me kiss a mop-head!'

'True, but she also says she wishes to resume your friendship, and signs it *affectionately*,' Sophie countered. 'And she's friends with the delightful captain, too … isn't she?'

'Mmm, she's making sure I know she knows,' Phoebe mused. 'And don't forget the *delightful* captain may have something to do with Aurelia's *situation*, too!'

'Yes,' Sophie returned, looking crestfallen for a moment. 'What did you and the viscount speak of anyway?' she added after a pause. 'You appeared quite … animated.'

Phoebe shrugged. 'The viscount continues to prove himself to be no more enlightened than any gentleman of our acquaintance, and so judgemental of my own view as to be a veritable dinosaur. Truly, I pity any lady he is to call his wife!'

Sophie regarded her sister thoughtfully, just as Matilda's voice rose above the general chatter.

'But how can you call it a *picnic* when everyone sits at a table and eats with knives and forks?' she protested.

Thankfully, the arrival of supper beneath the stars prevented too much discourse on this point, and by the time they'd all polished off pigeon pie, cold lamb, salmagundi, various breads, and numerous puddings, the evening was considerably advanced. Alongside the steady stream of dishes, there was an even steadier stream of young ladies and their mothers, asking why Phoebe and Sophie hadn't yet been seen at the Assembly Rooms.

'I vow if one more doting mama asks me if she can expect to see the two of you at Bath's *most illustrious* balls, concerts, and theatrical events, I shall give them your brother's address myself!' Aunt Higglestone warned with a hiccup. 'And it wasn't for the want of asking, I'll have you both know,' she added, waggling a finger. 'At your ages I'd been out for a season already, and received offers from a number of— Marchioness Carlisle!' she exclaimed, as a grand family made to sweep past their table.

Phoebe held her breath, suddenly reliving the dressing down she received at the Assembly Ball. Mrs Mary Smith may have escaped detection so far, but hawk-eyed Marchioness Carlisle was a different matter altogether.

'*So* many cheekbones!' Sophie whispered, while Josephine snorted into a glass of negus that her aunt promptly confiscated without so much as a sideways glance.

'A pleasure to see you again, Mrs ... Higglestaff,' Marchioness Carlisle pronounced.

Aunt Higglestone inhaled.

'And your *lively* nieces, too… We weren't going to come at all, but then the viscount persuaded Aurelia she would find the fireworks quite diverting! I trust you're enjoying the evening's entertainment?'

'We are enjoying the gardens very much!' Aunt Higglestone gushed generously. 'And we're delighted to see you and the delightful Lady Aurelia again so soon, too!'

Phoebe cast a covert look at Aurelia, standing demurely beside her mother. There was no trace of the girl who'd got drunk, played Questions and Commands, or kissed a soldier before blaming the whole thing on unsuspecting Mrs Mary Smith at all.

'All the delightful Misses Fairfaxes,' Lady Aurelia trilled with a pretty laugh. 'How lovely it is to see you all again, and looking so well, too! Is not this picnic spot divine? I do so admire it and wonder if Mama and Aunt Higglestone might permit Phoebe and I a short promenade, so we may appreciate it fully?'

Phoebe felt her aunt beam her approval, before she even opened her mouth.

'I should be thrilled,' she replied. 'Besides parlour games, promenading is one of my favourite things!'

'How did you know?' Phoebe asked as soon as they stepped onto the pretty wooded path circling the picnic area.

'Know what?' Aurelia teased through her fluttering broderie fan.

'Know it was me!' Phoebe returned. 'And do spare me any airs and graces, I know you aren't who you profess to be.'

'Is anyone quite who they profess to be in polite society?' Aurelia pouted, as Phoebe eyeballed her with abject dislike. 'You don't really do small talk, do you?' she added.

'Not with people who feign friendship, no.'

'Feign?' Aurelia frowned faintly.

'You blamed everything on me! The side room, the card game – even that mop-head's...' Phoebe paused to shudder. 'I'd be the gossip of the ton if your mother hadn't hushed everything up!'

'Well, your terrible powdered hair and cap certainly would be!' Aurelia snorted.

'You don't understand!' Phoebe scowled, her temper flaring. 'Mary Smith was my only chance...'

'Of an *adventure*?' Aurelia quizzed. 'You do know we all dream of those, don't you?' she added with a sigh. 'And we can have them, too, so long as we're prepared to accept a few small...'

Captain Damerel, is that you stealing up behind us?' she diverted loudly. 'I do believe I'd know your tread anywhere! And please don't say you're the search party!' She paused to roll her eyes. 'It's been barely five minutes and I can still *see* the picnic tables!'

Phoebe stared as though Aurelia had taken leave of her senses, just as low voices reached along the path behind them. In disbelief, she glanced back to discover the captain and his infuriating brother were indeed turning the leafy corner behind them, and briefly, she smothered a desire to curse the universe and everyone in it.

'Please be assured your secret assignations are always safe with us, Lady Aurelia!' the captain called gamely, though Phoebe detected a fleeting strain. 'I am also impressed by your powers of detection, you would be an asset to the military!' He nodded at Phoebe. 'Miss Fairfax,' he added with a smile. 'I do hope you'll excuse our interruption, Alex was quite insistent on a walk. Did you enjoy your al fresco picnic? We partook last year, and particularly enjoyed the venison if I recall correctly – quite the finest picnic platter I've ever seen!'

He turned to his brother and chortled good-naturedly.

'It was delicious, thank you, captain,' Phoebe returned, avoiding the viscount's gaze, 'though my sister was rather unimpressed by the lack of jam sandwiches!'

She was still stinging from their last conversation, and had no desire to pretend to exchange civilities now, especially in front of Aurelia.

'Perchance she wishes for a quart of devil's brew, with which to wash them down,' the viscount muttered.

Phoebe stiffened, while Aurelia chuckled with delight.

'Oh, my lord, what droll things you say!' she smirked. 'Pray, what is this *devil's brew* you mention? Perhaps I should try some.'

'I was referring to my youngest sister, sir,' Phoebe returned in her most dignified voice, 'who is still but twelve years old!'

To her satisfaction, the faintest flicker of chagrin passed across the viscount's impassive face.

'Excellent!' he recovered swiftly. 'Then let us hope she remains incurious for as long as possible; there are few things less appealing than a lady who likes her liquor.'

'I assure you, sir, that none of my sisters are so afflicted!'

Phoebe retorted. 'Though I would challenge anyone who called them incurious.'

'Lord, Alex!' the captain chortled. 'You sound like the vicar! I see no reason why a lady need not enjoy herself as much as any gentleman, providing it does not compromise her of course. Personally, I feel the fairer sex would be *twice* as responsible with *half* our freedom, were we just to relax our collar points a little. This is 1820, after all!'

Phoebe flashed the captain a look of intense gratitude.

'And yet we would risk every decent offer of marriage, were we to admit to any of the mischief in which you gentlemen indulge on a daily basis,' Aurelia purred with a gleam.

'Truth!' the viscount nodded abruptly. 'Far better to accept the reality of the world in which we live than dream of one that doesn't, for surely that must lead only to disappointment.'

'Then I am destined to be a disappointed dreamer, sir!' Phoebe ground furiously.

'I too, Miss Fairfax,' said the captain. 'And I often remind my brother there is room for dreamers and pragmatists alike in this world!' He smiled. 'Now, I believe we have detained you ladies for far too long, and you will be much missed from your party. Lady Aurelia, Miss Fairfax…'

Phoebe sank into a curtsey as the gentlemen made their bows, and waited only until they were out of earshot before spinning to address her companion.

'What were you saying before? About an adventure?' she asked, the viscount's insufferable arrogance making her blood boil.

A gleam crept into Aurelia's eyes, as she picked up her skirts.

'This way,' she nodded, stepping off the path.

Phoebe hesitated only briefly, before following her into the trees.

'Of all the people to run into unchaperoned!' Aurelia rolled her eyes. 'And yet here, it is perfectly respectable for us to have a short walk – unlike in town where one has to be presented, and chaperoned, and presented again until one feels quite exhausted! What do you think? Isn't the season a bore?' She yawned prettily, pushing her way through two thick rhododendron bushes.

'I wouldn't know, I've only attended one Assembly,' Phoebe muttered, staring down at a crumpled pamphlet entitled *Mary Wollstonecraft and Women's Equality*.

It seemed particularly poignant, with the viscount's words still ringing in her ears.

'Our education being solely for the purpose of marrying has rarely made sense to me,' she added. 'My brothers are encouraged to learn and travel, while we are treated as little more than fragile butterflies, to be collected and pinned. As though we don't have minds and voices of our own at all!'

Aurelia paused to look back at Phoebe, a look of curious satisfaction on her face.

'I knew you were a bluestocking!' she replied. 'And in answer to your question about how I *knew*: you gave yourself away! When I asked if I looked with child, you pulled exactly the same expression you pulled in the modiste's, when we discovered you fencing with a parasol. Oh, how funny that was! I knew right away it was you, but what I couldn't understand was why you'd gone to such garish lengths to attend a boring Assembly Ball of *all* things!'

She smirked before stepping through to a pretty, lantern-lit glade, where she withdrew a small ivory snuff box from her reticule, flipped it open, and raised a pinch.

'And I certainly don't intend to be collected and pinned!' she observed, inhaling swiftly. 'When I marry, I shall run a fashionable townhouse, host parties of the ton, own more ball dresses than I can ever hope to wear and be a dutiful wife in every way, but … I shall also have as many adventures as I wish, because for people like us marriage is a business contract. So you see, there's no need to be quite so concerned about our education, when *fragile butterflies* can be masters of their own disguise! Snuff?'

Phoebe shook her head, suppressing a rise of feelings as she recalled the viscount's view.

'Such behaviour in young ladies of quality would be reprehensible to many gentlemen with a name and reputation to protect…'

Somehow, she doubted Aurelia's intentions accorded with his own expectations of his marital union – and yet she was sure they couldn't be more suited, either.

'It's my own special recipe,' Aurelia smiled, taking another pinch. 'Finely ground tobacco, scented rose petals and something extra with a little *rush* at the end!'

Phoebe watched as Aurelia inhaled again, her delicate eyelashes fluttering, before stepping back to steady herself.

'Do try it. Consider it a … first step to equality!' She giggled.

'I'm not really sure snuff is up there with education and worker's rights,' Phoebe muttered.

'Oh, la, you're so stuffy! And I thought you were looking for adventure? Such a shame – I really didn't want to tell your aunt and uncle about your little Assembly Room escapade, but it seems you leave me no choice!'

She spun abruptly and started walking back across the glade.

'Tell my relatives anything, and I will have no choice but to divulge your *situation*,' Phoebe threw, beginning to regret her willingness to accompany Aurelia anywhere.

Aurelia turned back.

'Bravo!' she smirked. 'I was beginning to doubt you had it in you! But you see, we really aren't that different, after all.'

'I beg to differ,' Phoebe snapped. 'I would happily give up marriage and all it entails, for one true adventure – whereas you will use marriage and all it entails to have a thousand!'

'Well, the moral high ground does have its price,' she sighed, 'but if you're prepared to help me – if *Mrs Mary Smith* is prepared to help me – then I can promise an adventure in return…'

Phoebe glared silently, the viscount's mockery still infuriating her. She didn't want to help Aurelia at all, but his snobbish arrogance felt like everything she despised most. What right did he have to judge her family in any way? They'd come to Bath with one purpose in mind, and social disaster or not, she had no intention of becoming *incurious*. Now, or ever.

She reached out and took a small pinch of snuff, eyeing Aurelia warily.

'No private rooms or parlour games!' She scowled.

And then she inhaled before she could change her mind.

Instantly, the glade whirled like a carousel, while a

delicious rise of feeling coursed through her veins. It was like nothing she'd ever experienced before, except perhaps at the Midsummer Fair, when she and Sophie had consumed so much candy they challenged the Bilch brothers to a three-legged race, and even so, this was different. This made her feel *so deliriously* happy!

Slowly, she spread her arms and turned on the spot, watching the way shafts of light from the hanging lanterns glistened with magic, or fairies, or possibly both. Briefly, she wished her sisters were there to see them.

'Come on!' Aurelia called from the far side of the clearing.

She laughed then, but to Phoebe's surprise it no longer sounded irritating, just highly infectious, and within seconds she too was laughing so hard, she felt sure she might actually pop her corset.

'It's just a little further, so long as you're not afraid of the dark?' Aurelia called, disappearing down another narrow path.

Phoebe couldn't recall ever being afraid of the dark – and was far too mesmerised by the fairies to concern herself now.

She hurried after Aurelia into the next glade, wondering if she might have misjudged her, after all.

'In truth, it's because of my *situation*,' Aurelia began as Phoebe joined her beneath a maple tree 'and my marriage to the viscount on my twenty-first birthday, that I find I'm in need of a little assistance.'

'Yes … well … as we've already ascertained, I know nothing on the matter that will assist you,' Phoebe returned doubtfully, willing the glade to stop spinning. 'But perhaps if you tell the viscount, he will—'

'Tell the viscount?' Aurelia scorned. 'He must know nothing, you little goose! Why else do you think I'm asking for *your* help?'

'Well, bring the date forward, then,' Phoebe tried again. 'And no one need know anything at all.'

Aurelia threw her eyes skywards.

'And why would I want to tie myself down even *sooner* than my parents planned?'

Phoebe frowned. It was one thing disliking the viscount, vehemently, quite another being complicit in deceiving him.

'The truth is, there is someone who can help me, but she's an actress, and not company I can easily keep. However, the widowed cousin of a famed actress?' A slow smile spread across Aurelia's face. 'She can go wherever she pleases. All you need to do – all *Mrs Mary Smith* needs to do – is slip backstage at the theatre and collect a package for me. What could be easier than that?'

'That's all?' Phoebe asked, willing the fairies to disappear now.

Aurelia nodded.

'And I thought a girl seeking adventure – such as yourself – might enjoy it. Have you ever been backstage at a *real* theatre?'

Phoebe shook her head, and then regretted it; she'd always wanted so much to experience a real theatre.

'Fine,' she conceded reluctantly. 'But then Mrs Mary Smith leaves Bath for good.'

'As you wish!' Aurelia nodded, her eyes gleaming. 'Now, we really do need to go back. This way, come on.'

Inhaling deeply, Phoebe followed Aurelia through two large hydrangea bushes to find herself on a main, lantern-lit path. She felt cheered immediately, and had just turned in the direction of faint music and a small crowd, when a loud whinny distracted her.

Startled, she glanced up to spy a small shelter and a series of watchful eyes, staring back in the murky dusk.

'Misty!' she exclaimed joyously, before making her way across the path.

It wasn't Misty, but a chestnut mare bearing a remarkable likeness to her Dartmoor pony, and, without hesitation, Phoebe buried her face in her homely scent, letting all thoughts of infuriating viscounts, garden fairies, and mysterious actresses slide from her mind.

'There doesn't seem to be *anyone* waiting,' she frowned, looking around the immediate vicinity.

'No one, at all.' Aurelia smiled, looming up out of the dusk. 'Plus, we'd get back twice as fast. Of course, the viscount said you might still be feeling too delicate for riding, but…'

Phoebe was astride the mare in a heartbeat; the thought of the viscount passing any such comment on her person all the encouragement she needed. She pushed her aunt's warning from her mind, as Aurelia pulled the reins from their tether.

'Excellent!' Aurelia laughed in her tinkling way that always put Phoebe in mind of a ballroom chandelier. 'I'll follow on Diamond, who looks a little forlorn.'

Phoebe nodded, barely listening, as she turned the mare with ease. It felt so good to be back in the saddle, with stars peeping through the sky above and the soft sound of hooves beneath.

'Really, I've no idea why Aunt was so against a ride,' she muttered to herself as she reached forward to scratch the mare between the ears. 'Riding should play a part in every convalescence.'

Which was precisely when the sound of a resounding slap filled the air.

For a briefest of moments, everything stilled, and then the mare sprang forward as though several impressive carnivores were in direct pursuit. Phoebe didn't immediately connect the sound with the mare's rump, or indeed, Aurelia herself, but after spending several seconds clinging to the neck of a bolting horse, she had little choice but to accept the two were highly likely to be related.

'Get back! Move!' she yelled to the looming crowd, with as much dignity as she could muster.

The crowd, however, seemed singularly disinterested in their impending doom. With a valiant effort, Phoebe leaned forward and shortened her reins. She was a seasoned horsewoman, but she also knew that the very worst thing she could do was force the mare into a violent halt. So instead, she drew a deep breath and reverted to one of Fred's favourites.

'I said … mind your lazy rumps!' she yelled.

Happily, this time the crowd heard every word, and with a series of audible gasps, parted to let her blaze through, giving Phoebe the chance to observe two highly important things: the first was that the crowd actually appeared to be a long queue of people waiting on one side of the path; and the second was that the last of them looked disturbingly familiar.

Phoebe shrank in disbelief. Even though she was beginning to suspect the *little extra* ingredient in Aurelia's snuff to be something quite different from ground tobacco and rose petals, she'd know those perfect eyebrows anywhere.

Numbly, she clung on as the horse bolted down the main path, only becoming aware of a second rider in pursuit as they approached a bridge over the canal. But the terrified mare showed no signs of slowing, even when a trio of revellers spilled out of the bushes before them. Then, just when Phoebe thought she must ride right out of the garden itself, she glimpsed a familiar party beside the lantern boats, on the canal-side below them.

'A walk to the lantern boats after supper sounds very agreeable.'

The echo reached through the fog in Phoebe's head as she stared, transfixed by the silhouette of a child, dancing along the pontoon as though it were a park bench. And all at once, nothing else was important.

Without hesitating, Phoebe swerved and forced the mare into a dangerous leap, barely skimming a hedge and the outstretched branches of an old apple blossom, before landing and stumbling to a halt. Then she slipped from her back, and plunged down the bank, all thoughts of fairies and riding replaced with a stone-cold fear for her errant younger sister.

'Matilda!' Phoebe yelled, as an explosion of fireworks lit up the sky in such myriad colours that everyone was completely mesmerised.

Which just happened to be exactly the moment that Matilda lost her balance, and fell with a barely discernible splash, between two of the largest lantern boats. For a second, everything stilled again, and then the world loomed back in multicolour, together with a delighted cheer from the bank.

'Phoebe!'

Matilda's cry was barely audible as Phoebe flew towards her, a strange asphyxiation threatening her throat. Then she, too, was plunging into the black canal water, without so much as a backward glance.

Unlike Matilda, Phoebe was a strong swimmer, but she also knew the real enemy was the weight of the boats themselves, especially when tethered to the pontoon. She struck out fiercely and reached the first lantern-lit craft within seconds, before drawing a deep breath and ducking down into the long weeds beneath. The water was deep and dark, and the swaying tendrils deceptive, but she kicked and fumbled among the icy weeds until finally, her hands closed around a small arm. Then frantically, she pulled with all her strength, just as someone else loomed up beside her and began pulling too. For one confused moment she thought it was Fred, and then the only thing that mattered was reaching the surface before her chest burst.

'Matty,' she choked on the sweet dusk air, as two gentlemen pulled her sister's still body from the water.

'Matilda!' she heard her aunt shriek. 'What have you done, child, what have you done?!'

Then Phoebe, too, was hauled onto the narrow pontoon where she watched in a numb haze as her rescuer rolled Matilda onto her side. For a moment, there was only a deathly hush, when even the lantern boats seemed to still until, finally, there was a small cough and a splutter.

The crowd exhaled in abject relief.

'Give her your cloaks,' the rescuer muttered. 'She needs comfort and warmth.'

Aunt Higglestone was beside her in a heartbeat, throwing her arms around Matilda's limp form, before wrapping her in a dozen proffered cloaks. Then, as the crowd closed around them, he stood up.

Phoebe drew in a ragged breath. His hair was soaked, his shirt glued to his chest, and there was canal water dripping from his pantaloons. He looked every inch a Michelangelo that had been left out in the rain, yet there was no mistaking his stony expression, either.

'You are the original head-in-the clouds-schoolroom-chit who has run away and found out the world is nothing like the inside of a novel! Such behaviour in young ladies of quality would be reprehensible to many gentlemen with a name and reputation to protect.'

His words resonated between them as she stared, unable to believe that he was the rescuer. And that she was destined to be the object of his disapproval too. Gritting her teeth, she pulled a long piece of pond weed from her hair, acutely aware that she'd defended a right to swim in her petticoats earlier.

She drew a hollow breath.

'Sir... I cannot thank you enough ... that was...' She faltered, unsure what to say to a glacial viscount turned unexpected rescuer, twice in a matter of weeks.

'Anyone would have done the same, Miss Fairfax,' he replied in a chilled tone. 'What is perhaps less understandable, is your *theft* of a horse while—'

To Phoebe's horror, he broke off to lean forward and inhale, with exactly the same expression she first saw at the roadside.

'—under the influence, *again*.'

'Then let us hope she remains as incurious as possible, for there are few things less appealing than a lady who likes her liquor.'

The injustice of his accusation was such that no heated

retort or witty comeback seemed appropriate. Instead, Phoebe could only eye him with bristling resentment, as he retrieved his evening coat and squelched back up the bank.

'Phoebe! Wrap a cloak around yourself, child, or you'll catch your death, too!' Aunt Higglestone fretted, suddenly beside her. 'We've sent for a carriage, and the sooner we get you both home and properly warmed the better! Oh, what a thing to happen!' she added, her voice cracking. 'I know I mustn't be maudlin, dearest, your uncle detests it so, but *thank goodness* you were nearby! And Viscount Damerel, too, what a surprise that was! I can't imagine what we would have done if you hadn't—'

She broke off her pink-eyed lamenting to stare as a riderless chestnut mare trotted past them, whinnying reproachfully.

Phoebe closed her eyes and exhaled, wondering what had happened to their small pleasurable excursion.

Of one thing she was certain – as soon as her aunt knew all the facts, she would ban her from outings for the rest of her woeful little life.

Chapter Thirteen

Seven weeks and suspecting the captain again until the wedding

Phoebe was banned from all outings for the rest of her woeful little life.

Or as least she would have been, had it not been for the arrival of the jovial Captain Damerel with an armful of yellow roses, the following afternoon.

'I came as soon as I thought you might all be recovered enough to receive visitors.' He smiled at his welcoming committee, who were assembled decorously in Aunt Higglestone's best sitting room.

'Well, Sophie is quite well enough,' Matilda grinned, 'but Phoebe and I have red noses, and Josephine has a cough, so she's not allowed to go anywhere.'

'Matilda!' their aunt scolded, before smiling wanly at the captain. 'It is lovely to see you again, Captain Damerel. As you can see, the girls are all nearly recovered, save for one of my nieces, who has a tendency towards bronchospasms and is abed for a few days. She wasn't involved in the *incident*, but I fear the evening air may have exacerbated her condition. I should not have taken her, I fear, but it is hard when one is blessed with such lively nieces!'

Then she sniffed so woefully that Phoebe felt twice as guilty as she already did.

'It wasn't your fault, Aunt,' she reassured, trying to avoid another monologue of self-reproach. 'Josephine catches a cold if we so much as open a window at home, and as for the rest, well, Mama used to say Matilda and I have a talent for drama!'

Phoebe had spared her aunt the unabridged version of her evening's excursion, including the hallucinatory snuff and Aurelia's very deliberate provocation, but there was no avoiding the horse theft or the viscount's pursuit – which had resulted in his being there when Matilda fell into the canal.

Both her relations were suitably aghast when they'd heard the story, a reaction somewhat offset by Josephine's pronouncement that Phoebe had *still* saved Matilda's life, horse theft or not; until it became clear that while half the ton had indeed witnessed her daring rescue, many more had glimpsed her careering through the gardens, clinging to the neck of a feral chestnut mare.

'Which only goes to prove that no one of consequence should ever trust a pony at a public picnic!' her aunt bemoaned into her fourth kerchief of the morning.

Phoebe looked down at the embroidery that had been pushed into her hands the moment the captain was announced. She'd spent half the morning berating herself for ever trusting Aurelia in the first place, and the other half wondering if bad backstitch represented the sum of her life for the foreseeable future.

'Well, I favour a bit of drama over polite conversation any day!' the captain boomed jovially.

She looked across at the sunny-tempered military man and wondered, for the umpteenth time, if he really could have anything to do with Aurelia's spot of bother. It seemed so very unlikely, especially since he was the viscount's brother, and yet he and Aurelia were clearly on familiar terms too.

'Will you be returning to your regiment soon, Captain Elliot?' Sophie asked.

She was seated in the window, a position she'd chosen when the captain was announced, to showcase her green taffeta and sunlit ringlets to their best advantage.

Phoebe suppressed a frown as he turned to engage her sister directly. His interest was no surprise, Mama always regarded Sophie as her finest work, and the daughter most likely to contract an advantageous marriage, yet Sophie was also well aware of her suspicions. Her determination to ignore this, and continue fluttering her eyelashes as though they were the latest Parisian fashion, was most undermining.

'Oh, yes, I think it's a wonderful idea, don't you think, Phoebe?'

Phoebe blinked as they all turned to look at her, conscious she'd been lost in thought for a few moments.

'Why … yes of course … if you think so?' she stalled.

Sophie rolled her eyes, before shaking back her ringlets and rising to her pretty slippered feet.

'The captain has invited us to a small private soirée next

month! Doesn't that sound fun? Is it not kind of him to include us among his select family and friends.'

Phoebe frowned, eyeing her sister intently. She'd seen that stubborn gleam before, and it was one that didn't take kindly to challenges, yet they were both aware of the social restrictions before their presentation.

She'd also been consoling herself with the thought that she'd never have to face the viscount again, but how could she possibly avoid him at his own family dinner?

'Well, it's a very kind invitation, but would we even be permitted?' she murmured, looking at her aunt.

Sophie laughed prettily.

'It could be a chance to quell any rumours – show everyone we really are quite civilised – and not even you could attract drama at a private soirée!'

Her eyes narrowed briefly, leaving Phoebe in no doubt of her intent. She meant to attend, whatever the cost.

'My hesitation is no reflection on your generous invitation of course, dear Captain,' Aunt Higglestone rushed, clearly flustered by the thought of appearing in the least bit impolite, 'but rather of the fact that my eldest nieces aren't officially out in society yet. However, I have to say I see little problem with a *small* soirée with *select* family and friends – this is Bath, after all – and we're certainly very grateful to your dear brother, the viscount, for his assistance at the picnic, too. Are we not, dear?'

This last was directed with some purpose at Uncle Higglestone, who'd managed to sequester himself in the corner of the room with a botanical journal detailing the mating rituals of wood ants. He grunted appropriately.

'Mr Higglestone called on the viscount this morning,

though he wouldn't hear of our covering the cost of his suit when it must have been quite ruined – he was soaked to the skin after all...' Their aunt broke off to fan herself suddenly. 'Indeed, Mr Higglestone and I owe your brother a very large debt, Captain Damerel, for we are quite certain the outcome would have been very different without his assistance. On this basis alone, we would accept your kind invitation, except the final say must come from my eldest nephew, their guardian.' She nodded and smiled, her cheeks the colour of rosy apples. 'I will, however, write to him *without delay* and impress on him the kindness you have shown, and the family nature of the soirée, and of course the fact that this is Bath – not London – and in truth, I already feel hopeful of a positive outcome.'

The captain gazed at Mrs Higglestone in admiration, his eyes dancing.

'That is encouraging, indeed,' he responded warmly.

'In the meantime, please do pass on our warmest wishes to your dear brother, as well as our sincerest gratitude for his assistance with both Misses Fairfax – again.' She nodded rapidly.

Phoebe had long ceased listening to the small talk and was wondering whether she ought to send her own letter to Thomas, in case he suffered any momentary lapse of character and actually considered her aunt's request. She looked up to find Sophie eyeing her carefully, before turning her own pretty smile on the captain.

'Did you say it's a *masked* soirée, Captain Damerel?' Sophie enquired. 'Should we look to Venice for inspiration?'

A sunny beam lit up his fair face, and briefly Phoebe

wondered what goddess had visited his mother in order to reap such a difference in her sons.

'Oh, Lord yes, please do. The more *carnivale* the better! It's a family thing our mother insists on holding in Father's memory. It'll also mark my farewell – for I'm to rejoin my regiment in May – as well as provide an opportunity for a formal family announcement.'

Phoebe narrowed her gaze at the jovial captain, while Sophie looked positively crestfallen.

'Oh, you're leaving so soon?' she exclaimed. 'And … a formal family announcement? How exciting?'

She forced her voice to be light, but Phoebe knew her better.

'Perhaps,' he returned with a wink. 'Though I'm sworn to secrecy – a matter of family honour and all that – proving that even confirmed bachelors can be trustworthy, occasionally!'

'Well, we all know you *are* that,' their aunt laughed indulgently, 'and we won't press you on the matter, either. I'll just see what I can do about the soirée, though I won't make any promises just yet. My eldest nephew can be *quite* protective of his wards.'

'I still don't fully understand why Aurelia would give you fairy snuff and spook your horse, if she needs a favour?' Sophie repeated doubtfully. It was nearly midnight, and they were in bed, discussing events of the past few days. 'I thought she wanted to resume your friendship.'

'She's not interested in friendship,' Phoebe muttered sleepily from where she lay.

'And isn't *Mrs Mary Smith* a slightly dubious companion for Aurelia now? I mean, after the Assembly Ball scandal?' Sophie added in a hushed voice.

'I really don't know,' Phoebe shrugged, 'but apparently not enough for it to matter when Aurelia needs an alibi. I have thought about leaving her in the lurch – but that would make me little better than her, and besides, a part of me really wants to go. When am I ever likely to go backstage at a real theatre again?'

There was a brief pause.

'Well, I suppose as long as you stay away from soldiers and cards and snuff and ponies you should be fine!' Sophie giggled. 'And whatever you do, don't agree to any more games of Questions and Commands.'

Phoebe swatted her with a pillow, unable to help laughing too.

'Definitely no more soldiers,' she groaned, 'especially those resembling kitchen utensils!'

She paused, as a thought struck her.

'It's a little ironic that this whole adventure started with a theatre and a disguise,' she mused. 'Back then I wanted nothing more than to be someone else, somewhere else, but now I'm just grateful to be here with you all, instead.'

Sophie rolled over and hugged her sister fiercely.

'As well as the rest of Bath, of course!' Phoebe added.

They laughed again, while Phoebe eyed her sister thoughtfully.

'You like him, don't you?'

'Who?' Sophie replied, making a big pretence of puffing up a feather pillow.

'You know who,' Phoebe returned.

'Well, I don't dislike *him*,' she replied, playing for time, 'I mean, who could? He's like … human honey!'

'Phoebe knew exactly what she meant. She pictured the captain's immaculate uniform, his beaming smile and the way his eyes seemed to understand before any words were uttered. But all that was for nothing if he thought to compromise a lady, and then return to his regiment without a second thought.

'Sophie…'

'Okay, okay I do like him! I think him the kindest and most good-natured man I've ever met.'

There was a short, poignant silence.

'But … what of Aurelia?' Phoebe murmured after a beat.

'What of Aurelia?' Sophie challenged, before sighing. 'Look, the captain could be entirely innocent for all we know. Plus, it was kind of him to take the time to call and invite us to his family soirée. And if we're discussing the Damerels, what about the viscount?!' she added in the next breath.

The frankness of her question took Phoebe aback.

'What do you mean?' she quizzed. 'What *about* the viscount?'

His derision at the canal flickered through Phoebe's thoughts, stirring the most violent array of feelings. She gritted her teeth, picturing the way his eyes had raked over her soaking wet dress, instantly reducing her to the ignorant girl she'd felt that night in his library, wearing only a nightie and wet booties. He had the innate ability to make her feel every bit as foolish as he clearly thought her, and why the universe seemed determined to cross their paths at all was a mystery of epic proportions.

'He's quite the rudest, most condescending gentleman I've ever had the misfortune to meet,' she muttered, rolling onto her back. 'He and Aurelia are perfectly suited, and I'd rather marry *Earl Crusty-Roll of Onion Manor* than spend any more time in the company of such a man!'

'Phoebe!' Sophie protested, dissolving into infectious giggles again.

Within seconds, they were both stuffing their pillows in their mouths for fear of waking the entire household.

'It's so like you to have been twice rescued by a gentleman you cannot even abide!' Sophie gasped when she could. 'And yet for a while I thought perhaps you did like him, because he's different to everyone else,' she continued. 'Proud yes, but also a little … *heroic,* I think?'

Phoebe rolled her eyes.

'Fetching a doctor for an injured person and helping drag a schoolchild from pondweed does not make him heroic!' she rounded. 'It makes him interfering – in the extreme! And the truth is, no matter what rare and strange stars aligned to make the viscount and captain brothers, we barely know either of them.'

'So, what's the plan, then?' Sophie asked.

Phoebe rolled over to face her sister.

'I'm going to go to the theatre,' she exhaled. 'I'm going to rid our lives of devious debutantes and dubious viscounts, and then we're going to make the most of *every* opportunity remaining to us, before Thomas announces my betrothal to Earl Crusty-Roll!'

'Now *that*,' Sophie grinned, 'is a fine plan!'

Chapter Fourteen

Seven weeks and one theatrical debut until the wedding

It was two bronchospasms and one very abridged production of *Romeo and Juliet* later that Phoebe found herself bowling through Bath in the Carlisle family chaise.

'We'll be just a little late, perfect for avoiding any pre-show conversation,' Lady Aurelia chattered, as though they really were the best of friends, engaged on an enjoyable theatrical excursion.

Phoebe gazed at her pale satin evening gown, affixed with ribbons, lace, and a matching hair piece, together with elbow-length cream gloves. She looked the perfect young debutante, as she returned Phoebe's frank gaze.

By contrast, Phoebe had left Josephine abed with a bronchial cough that had concerned Dr Cox enough to prescribe cook's best chicken broth and drops of laudanum, twice a day. The laudanum had soothed her, but Phoebe was concerned to see her sister without interest for a book and suspected the lethargy had more to do with the medicine, than her weakness. This development had also vexed Matilda, who seemed determined to persuade their aunt she could enjoy herself immensely on any excursion, no matter which sister was on her deathbed.

All of which had made tonight's preparation twice as challenging.

'How lovely it is to see you looking so well, Miss Fairfax,' Aurelia chattered on. 'Or Mrs Mary Smith, as I should call you now!'

She paused to tinkle with laughter as Phoebe arranged her black velvet cloak over the pretty damson silk she'd borrowed from Sophie, persuaded it was far more a widow-like ensemble than anything else she owned.

'After your very unfortunate incident at the picnic, I admit I was quite concerned about your health, but your aunt assured my mother you have the constitution of an ox! In truth, I must own to having had the headache myself the following morning, but really, it paled next to your plight – a bolting horse and a dramatic rescue from the canal? Whatever next? Of course, we were all most relieved to know your sister was well, and I wouldn't hear of anyone saying how *ridiculous* you looked when you emerged, your hair utterly ruined and your dress clinging in that … most unbecoming way.' She patted Phoebe's arm. 'I also made sure to tell everyone that it didn't matter one jot that you abandoned me, as Viscount Damerel ensured I was quite safe with Captain Elliott and his officers, who are always *most* attentive.' She smiled smugly.

'I'd be wary of too many close attentions if I were you,

Aurelia,' Phoebe returned drily. 'They can result in *little spots of bother*.'

The smile was wiped instantly.

'Oh, how droll you are!' Aurelia recovered, after a beat. 'I can see why the viscount finds you so entertaining!'

Phoebe regarded Aurelia impassively while her thoughts whirled. She was quite used to being considered a foolish, hare-brained simpleton as far as the viscount was concerned, a drunk, even. *Entertaining* was something entirely new.

'Anyway, the viscount called on me the following day, which was kind; so gallant and noble to be thinking of me while you were the one careering dangerously through the crowds of people, and creating such chaos! But, of course, the greater show of gallantry has to be his complete abdication of concern for his own safety when he dived into those canal waters, little knowing what they might contain. I'm sure my friends talk of little else.'

'Well, he knew Matilda and I were in there for a start!' Phoebe returned scathingly. 'And he didn't dive, he jumped – anyone would know it would be asking for the headache, diving into that canal. Finally, I'm certain the viscount would find me rather less *entertaining*, if he were to learn the full extent to which *you* entertain yourself!'

She lay her head back against the seat, satisfied to see Aurelia looking more startled than she ever had before. She might not understand the full intricacies of Aurelia's situation, but she understood enough to know it could be a far more scandalous problem than her own.

'He'd never believe you!' Aurelia returned, after a beat.

'He might once your corsets begin to pop!'

'It won't get that far!' Aurelia retorted.

Yet her tone was far from confident.

'Oh, have no fear,' Phoebe exhaled, with a quiet air of triumph. 'I have every interest in drawing this matter to a close tonight, and then I would thank you to leave all the Fairfaxes well alone, for as long as you're in Bath.'

'With pleasure!' Aurelia snapped.

It turned out the Carlisle family box at the Bath Theatre Royal was so close to the stage that, for the first half of the production, Phoebe was unexpectedly spellbound. She'd spent countless happy hours directing Fairfax Theatrical Company, but this was a theatre of dreams, with a lavishly costumed cast, performing one of her favourite Shakespeare comedies, *Much Ado About Nothing*. It was exactly the type of production in which she'd imagined herself, had she made it to London.

She had to give Aurelia some credit for forethought, too. Their late arrival, combined with the darkness of the auditorium, ensured that no one could identify exactly who was accompanying Lady Aurelia Carlisle. And anyone who did look their way could be assured she was suitably chaperoned. Phoebe stole several glances at her wily adversary during the opening scenes, knowing that despite her newly established upper hand, she should not be underestimated.

'I think Beatrice a most dull character, don't you?' Aurelia whispered as the audience applauded. 'Teasing poor Benedict when he's just returned from war. Far better she just secure a husband she doesn't detest and get on with things. All that witty banter is quite exhausting!'

'Exhausting or exhilarating? Perhaps it shows they are well matched?' Phoebe countered.

She knew Aurelia was only describing the strategy she was employing herself, yet there was a wistful note in her voice she hadn't noticed before.

'Always *such* a bluestocking!' she smirked. 'Anyway, it's all just Shakespearean foreplay, neither of them care a jot really!'

Phoebe frowned, certain Aurelia was playing a part herself tonight and wondered if the mood would loosen her tongue.

'How did your *situation* come to be?' she whispered. 'Did something happen with the captain?'

A smile flickered across Aurelia's face.

'Now wouldn't that be something?' she murmured. 'The captain is nearly as handsome as the viscount, don't you think? Such fine shoulders, both of them…'

A faded memory of the golden viscount, silhouetted in front of his library fire, crept into Phoebe's mind. She flushed faintly, as Aurelia leaned forward.

'But as for his involvement,' she glinted. 'In truth, I…'

'In truth, *I* am not sure whether I'm more intrigued by your hushed conversation, or the fact you're attending the theatre in company your mother has decried,' a low tone drawled, making them both draw apart sharply.

Phoebe inhaled, as Aurelia spun with the ease of a seasoned actress.

'Why, Viscount Damerel!' She smiled coquettishly, fluttering her fan. 'What a pleasure to see you! I thought you considered Shakespeare's comedies *trop ennuyeux*!'

'On the contrary,' the viscount returned, stepping into the small theatre box as Phoebe shrank back and prayed for divine intervention.

'I find the war of words between Benedict and Beatrice most edifying. *"Some Cupid kills with arrows, some with traps",'* he murmured with a raised eyebrow.

'Oh, you are so droll!' Aurelia tittered, as Phoebe silently berated herself for ever thinking she could go anywhere with Aurelia, without the viscount making an appearance.

'What say you, Mrs Smith?' He turned suddenly, his gleam closing down the space between them. 'I may not approve of Lady Aurelia's company this evening, but I do approve of her choice of diversion. Is the play to your liking?'

Phoebe stared at the sudden narrowing of his eyes, at the gold flecks glittering within, and felt every scrap of her previous confidence evaporate. And suddenly they weren't in the theatre at all, but back on the banks of the muddy canal, exchanging furious looks that meant nothing and everything all at once. His hair was dishevelled and he was looking at her as though she was dredged up from the depths of the silt, and yet – there was a fire in his eyes that matched the thump in her chest, word for word, breath for breath.

She swallowed, feeling her tongue leaden, and her head pound. She felt sure he saw right through her, that perhaps he always had; but he'd addressed her as Mrs Smith, and she had no choice but to answer in kind. She clenched her fingers and dug deep.

'It is – thank you, Viscount,' she nodded, imitating Harriet's prim manner as best she could. 'Though I have to say that few young ladies I know would ever faint in such circumstances. In my experience, gentlemen are rarely without fault, and ladies are far more robust than they look.'

'Indeed,' he returned, the muscle in his cheek working overtime, 'though I believe there is a fine line between the robustness you describe, and behaviour that is unacceptable in our polite world – behaviour such as that you demonstrated when last we met. In truth, I am somewhat surprised that the marchioness saw fit to let you accompany Lady Aurelia this evening. I had thought her sense of propriety far stricter!'

Phoebe felt her cheeks burn as she seethed inwardly, imagining all the ways she would like to remind the viscount that she didn't care one jot for his opinions or archaic notions of propriety. Instead, she inhaled deeply, and promised herself this would be the very last time he ever had the opportunity to insult her.

'Perhaps,' she replied coldly, 'if gentlemen were able to elevate their marital ambitions beyond behaviour and reputation, they might discover we are just as curious and capable as they are. But until that time, I suspect ladies will continue to fall into two distinct groups – those they marry, and those they misjudge!'

Phoebe waited by the backstage door in a state of bleak contemplation. How an unimpressive highwayman, an épée with a mind of its own, a calamitous picnic and a dubious, interfering viscount, could represent the sum total of her Bath adventures to this point – standing at the stage door of the

Theatre Royal, asking for a seasoned actress by the name of Carlotta – was most dispiriting.

Her only consolation was that if at first the swarthy stage manager had looked ready to slam the door in her face, he'd changed his mind as soon as she mentioned the actress.

'Well, you're late,' he muttered, looking her up and down. 'But I s'pose there's no harm done if you're quick. Follow the corridor along to the girls, and Lotta will be waiting.'

Phoebe dived through, grateful to be free of his scent and lingering stare, even if his commentary seemed a little odd. She was also highly relieved to escape the auditorium. The viscount's appearance had changed everything, and even though he'd taken his leave before the end of the interval, she now wished for nothing more than to collect Aurelia's parcel and return home.

'And no nicking anything, either!' the stage manager called, as she hurried past an impressive array of wigs and swords.

Phoebe bristled on behalf of all widowed, bourgeois actresses everywhere, but felt it wisest not to respond.

It quickly transpired that *following the corridor along* was code for walking through every dressing area that existed backstage, and if the cast were at all shy of their performances, they certainly didn't share the same reservations about their person.

'What is it about officers?!' she muttered exasperatedly as a second, half-dressed lieutenant attempted to thwart her progress.

'You're a pretty one!' he said warmly, standing in her path. 'Far too pretty for this motley regiment, and especially in that damson eye-catcher. Perchance you're in need of some protection m'lady?'

Then he twirled his ridiculous moustache in the most affected way, before reaching forward to pinch her cheek. A ready flare of anger rose within her. This whole evening had been a disaster, and the last thing she needed was another mop-head thinking he could treat her as though she'd just wandered in from the street.

'None at all – sir!' she scowled, lifting the heel of her pretty boot, another loan from Sophie, and bringing it down quite deliberately on his stockinged foot.

To her great satisfaction, his face began to turn a similar shade to her dress, just as they were interrupted by a sullen, dark-eyed female.

'Mary Smith?' she called abruptly, silencing whatever curse he was about to drop. 'Come on, we've only a few minutes 'til curtain's up!'

Phoebe exhaled as the livid actor hopped away, and nodded. She was surprised Aurelia had given the waspish actress her name, but relieved to have found her quarry all the same.

'Hurry now, there's no time to waste, the dressing room's just down here.'

Carlotta swept in front, all high drama and dressed hair – her silken robe not even close to covering her corset and petticoats – while Phoebe followed, feeling doubtful. Things weren't going quite the way she'd expected, and she couldn't begin to fathom how a barely dressed actress might be the answer to Aurelia's situation. In truth, by the time they arrived in a bigger dressing area, filled with females in a similar state of undress, she'd begun to question whether she'd come to the right place at all.

'Excuse me, you are Carlotta, are you not?'

At this, the entire room suddenly hushed, and looked at Phoebe.

''Ere, she's a fancy one!'

'I'll give yer sixpence if you let me borrow yer dress?'

'Yes, of course!' the dark-eyed actress returned sharply. 'Now, here's the poultice,' she added, pulling a slim envelope from a hanging prop basket and passing it across. 'It needs to be made like a tea, and you drink all of it.'

Her eyes narrowed as she glanced at Phoebe's waist.

'And I suggest you cancel any performances for at least a week! Course you probably know all this already, such is the price we actresses pay for entertaining, eh…?'

She paused to laugh raucously as Phoebe felt a dull flush creep up her neck. At least she understood why Aurelia had needed her to collect the poultice now. They all thought her a widowed actress, and she still felt *a bit of muslin* as Fred would say – a society debutante would create a scandal beyond all imagining.

She looked down at the small envelope and suppressed a scowl. Aurelia had been nothing but hostile since they'd met, but she was here now, and she couldn't rid herself of the feeling that she also needed a friend more than anyone else she knew. Her brief, wistful moment in the theatre box flitted through her head, and she bit her tongue.

'Now, as for payment… The costume is here and you need only stand in for the wedding scene. I'll be back before Act Five, as Frank said…'

Phoebe stared blankly as Carlotta yanked a lacy wedding dress from a wooden rail, and dumped it on a chair, before walking briskly to unhook Phoebe's own dress.

'Wait!' Phoebe protested, trying to wriggle out of her surprisingly strong grip. 'I'm only here for *the poultice*! I'm Mary Smith!'

'We know who you are!' Carlotta grinned. 'Cousin to the one and only Sarah Siddons! Theatre royalty no less! We're expecting big things of you, what wiv you having Kemble blood and all.'

She grinned before pulling off Phoebe's cap and wig in one deft move.

'That's better, you ain't an old maid no more! Now, luckily we're about the same size so let's get the costume on, and get you side stage. Rosa? Lucia? Give us a hand to hook her up… Now, there ain't much to say as you've done *Hero* afore, but just make sure you keel over good and proper, you know how our audience loves a fainting!'

'No, I said wait!' Phoebe threw in a panic, twisting and grabbing hold of the hem of Sophie's favourite dress before it disappeared for good. 'There's been a misunderstanding. I can't fill in for you!'

'What? You can't back out now! Your friend told Frank you was an actress, that you trained with your cousin, and was highly proficient with a theatrical épée an' all!'

Carlotta paused, her dark eyes narrowing.

'She said *Hero* was your favourite role!'

Which was precisely the moment that Phoebe realised that Aurelia had said a lot more than she'd admitted. She pictured the viscount's face if she stepped out on stage while he was watching, and the blood drained from her face.

'There must be some other way!' she returned fiercely, yanking on the hem of the dress, while Rosa and Lucia put up a significant fight with each of the puffed sleeves.

'A deal is a deal!' Carlotta countered. 'This is my livelihood, and the boss will have me out on the street if I let him down. Now take the costume, or I'll have to take back—'

'I'm not going out on that stage,' Phoèbe hissed. 'I'm not even the fainting type!'

Which was the precise moment that two very separate, yet distinct, things happened.

The first was that there was a resounding rip as Sophie's favourite bodice parted company with her favourite skirt; and the second was that the room filled with the very last voice she wanted to hear in the world.

'Do excuse my interruption, but I wonder if I might be of assistance, Mrs … Smith?'

Phoebe spun in disbelief, to find herself face to face with the condescending viscount, again – while she was in her petticoats, again.

'Oh, Your Lordship, you should have said you was coming, I would have dressed up for the occasion!' Carlotta purred, sashaying forward in a way that suggested she would have done exactly the opposite.

'Thank you Carlotta, but I wasn't planning on being here,' he replied, halting her progress with a single glance. 'It's actually Mrs Mary Smith I've come to see, who I understand is under contract elsewhere, and therefore unable to take on any additional roles. Please pass on my apologies to all concerned.

And, Mrs Smith, as patron of this theatre, I'm afraid I will have to escort you from the premises.'

'Be my guest!' Carlotta flared, her expression changing instantly. 'She's overrated! And overpaid! Her dress weren't no common muslin, I can tell you!'

Enraged, she spun to collect up the pieces of Sophie's dress and fling them at Phoebe, who scowled furiously, before clutching them close and fleeing the room.

'Mrs Smith...'

The viscount's call echoed down the empty corridor as Phoebe raced towards the backstage door. She had no desire to hear whatever searing judgement he had to impart, but was also starkly aware she was about to exit Bath Theatre Royal in her corset and petticoats, and without a penny to ensure her safe journey home.

Bracing herself, she forced herself to slow and turn to face the viscount, his cloak billowing behind like a sycophantic cloud of self-importance.

'You can't leave like that!' he glowered, reaching to unhook his theatre cloak as he strode to catch up.

In the next breath, it was fixed snugly around her shoulders and she was being bundled out into the cold evening air.

'I don't know what game you think you're playing, Miss Fairfax,' he growled, as soon as the door closed behind them. 'But this isn't some roadside in Somerset, or even a canal-side in Sydney Gardens! If anyone else had recognised you, watched you going backstage, walked in on that fight between you and Carlotta... You'd be ruined! And why aren't you ever fully dressed?!'

He paused to inhale deeply, his expression darkening into

something she couldn't quite read as he glanced down at her stays and scowled.

'Why are *you* always looking over my shoulder?!' Phoebe demanded, shaking with fury and chagrin. 'You are not my guardian or my brother! How and with whom I spend my time is of no concern to you whatsoever!'

She wanted to say so much more, but that would also incriminate Aurelia, and even though she deserved no loyalty, Phoebe couldn't expose her entirely. Instead, she slipped the poultice into her petticoat skirts, and watched the viscount's eyes narrow to glittering jewels.

'I have no desire to be either your guardian or brother!' he forced intently. 'Don't you understand, you little fool? There is a vast difference between chasing adventure, and risking your reputation. And for what? Another parlour game? One of your damned heroic adventures? If anyone else had recognised you … or seen you … the rest of your life would be…'

He paused to catch his breath as a shard of moonlight fell between them.

'It's no good,' he muttered, raking his hand through his hair, 'you infuriate me to the point of all distraction, and I cannot trust what I am saying. It's time you left, lest I do something we all regret.'

Chapter Fifteen

Six weeks, six days, and avoiding the viscount until the wedding

'Oh, my goodness! What did you say?' Sophie breathed, her eyes as round as saucers as they stared up at the semi-ellipse of grand houses on the Royal Crescent.

'I told him he was neither my guardian nor my brother, and how I spent my time was of no concern to him … which only made it a hundred times worse,' Phoebe replied, her cheeks reddening at the memory of the previous disastrous evening. 'I think we can safely say the viscount considers me the oddest, adventure-seeking harlot alive, with frogs' eggs for brains.'

Sophie started to gurgle with laughter.

'Well, odd adventure seeker I'll allow, but harlot and frogs' eggs is definitely a stretch!'

She eyed her sister curiously.

'But he must have said something else? Before he put you in his carriage?' She suppressed another laugh, likely at the thought of the infuriated viscount handing Phoebe into his crested carriage, clutching two halves of a dress and a widow's cap.

Phoebe closed her eyes and shuddered.

'He was in every way most solicitous,' she muttered.

'Oh well, I suppose that's good…' her sister began doubtfully.

'No! Not good!' Phoebe hissed. 'He is the most arrogant, condescending, obnoxious person I've ever met! His eyes…'

'Yes?' Sophie waited, watching Josephine and Matilda run down the crescent green, bonnet ribbons streaming.

'His eyes made every personal judgement it is possible to make! He followed me backstage, just waiting for an opportunity to confront me! How much he must have enjoyed extricating me, in my petticoats, from a dress fight… He even called me *Mrs Smith*…'

'He put two and two together when he saw you with Aurelia in the Carlisle box,' Sophie guessed, her eyes widening.

'He must have,' Phoebe groaned, wishing for the umpteenth time that morning that the ground would actually open up and swallow her whole.

'You should tell him the truth, then.' Sophie frowned. 'That you were there for Aurelia!'

'What? I may have frogs' eggs for brains, but I am no betrothal wrecker! … No, I must avoid him, at all costs – forever.'

Phoebe stared after Matilda and Josephine, trying to ignore the violent twist of emotions in her core. So much for adventures – all they'd brought was ignominy and embarrassment. Perhaps the most heroic thing she could do now was to get married, and spare her sisters any further possible disgrace.

'But there's still the Damerel dinner,' Sophie murmured. 'Thomas has given Aunt his permission for us to attend, on account of it being in Bath and a private family affair.'

Phoebe nodded, the viscount's parting words echoing in her head as the twist tightened.

'It's time you left, lest I do something we all regret.'

'And Aunt says she feels obliged to go,' Sophie continued 'on account of the viscount rescuing Matilda – and refusing a new suit…'

'Then we will go to the dinner, and I will behave just as I ought,' Phoebe returned, forcing a smile. 'And that will be the end of our obligations.'

'Do take care, Josephine, dear!' Aunt Higglestone called, waving a kerchief from where she stood just a few paces behind Phoebe and Sophie. 'We don't wish to be calling Dr Cox this evening!'

'A little light exertion will do her good, Aunt,' Sophie reassured, watching her younger sisters startle a flock of pigeons before continuing their chase. 'She's been bedridden long enough.'

'Oh, I do hope so,' her aunt agreed fervently. 'Speaking of health, Phoebe, dear, Thomas made an enquiry about *your* recuperation today. He also shared a few more details about your forthcoming nuptials!'

Sophie shot her silent sister a concerned glance.

'He has received another visit from the earl, and they've settled on a wedding at the end of May. Just think, dearest, you'll be a countess before the summer, and with all the fine dresses, jewels and horses any young lady could wish for. It is a triumph, indeed, and I know your dear Mama would have been so delighted for you! As I understand it, and on account of his age and health, the earl is going to request permission to wed quietly, and your brother has entrusted me with your honeymoon attire because…'

Their aunt rattled on, but Phoebe heard nothing past *the end of May*. Even by her own dazed calculations, that left little more than five weeks before her life was entirely over.

'Oh, look, Aunt. Josephine has dropped her shawl!' Sophie interjected suddenly. 'We'll go and retrieve it for her.'

She grabbed Phoebe's arm and pulled her over the lawn towards their carefree younger sisters.

'Look, I know it's not what you want, Phoebs,' she rushed as soon as they were out of earshot of their well-meaning relative. 'And Lord knows, it's not what you deserve. But all your efforts towards heroic adventures only seem to land you in trouble: duels, canals, mop-heads, acting debuts…'

Phoebe listened to her chatter on, wondering how to tell her that her terrible attempts at heroism were all that stood between her and the rest of her pitiful existence. That just as Sophie's life was beginning, hers was ending, and she'd never felt so suffocated.

She opened her mouth, but it felt as though the canal weeds had wound their fronds around her words too.

'Oh, look, Matilda has got her bonnet stuck in the tree!' Sophie sighed in exasperation. 'Honestly, you'd think they were still in the nursery!'

'I'm fine,' Phoebe managed finally, as they picked up their

pace. 'None of it is a surprise after all, and we both know Thomas won't be content until his Monstrous Marriage Master Plan is well and truly underway. My only consolation is that at least you, Jo and Matty will have more say.'

'Perhaps,' Sophie qualified, frowning. 'Though how much *real* choice any of us have with Thomas, is debatable. At least we know Lady Aurelia and the viscount are perfectly matched!' she added, with a rueful smile. 'They can be perfectly obnoxious together!'

Phoebe nodded as they reached the younger girls, who were attempting to dislodge the bonnet with old pine cones, but her thoughts were full of a disagreeable viscount, his fingers raking his perfect hair, staring at her as though she were a mud monster that had crawled out from the murky canal.

She closed her eyes and pulled off her own bonnet before handing it to Sophie.

'Here, hold this,' she instructed.

'What? No wait! Phoebe!' Sophie implored, but her sister was already swinging herself up into the lower branches.

'Five weeks,' Phoebe called. 'I need to rescue all the stuck bonnets I can find!'

'Yes! But not with half of Bath watching!' Sophie wailed, while their younger sisters danced with excitement.

But Phoebe was a million miles away. Viscount Damerel was the most infuriating, interfering gentleman, and he clearly thought her behaviour so reprehensible as to warrant the highest censure.

So, why did the thought of his marrying Aurelia make her feel so woefully bereft?

With a final effort, her fingers closed around the offending bonnet and, forcing a smile, she turned to wave it at the small crowd of nosy matrons and their delighted offspring at the bottom of the tree.

She could barely understand it at all.

Chapter Sixteen

Five weeks and still avoiding the viscount until the wedding

'I t is all the more reason why you must have the best mask!' Sophie insisted, tying the gold filigree mask around Phoebe's hair, and taking care to pull her coiled ringlets free of the black velvet ribbon.

Phoebe stared at her reflection, hardly recognising herself. She'd buckled under pressure and let Sophie dress her hair, while her aunt had marched her to Madame Paragon's a few days before.

'For we can hardly have a future countess going to a private family dinner in a mud-stained dress, now can we?'

Phoebe thought the canal water stains on her picnic dress hardly noticeable at all, but knew better than to refuse, and if an evening gown of pale blue silk net, with silk embroidery and a silk, satin trim felt a little extravagant, especially after recent events, she consoled herself with the thought that at least no one was going to fight her for it.

'And now you look like a *real* heroine!' Sophie concluded, standing back to admire her handiwork.

Phoebe pulled a face, but even she could see Sophie had outdone herself. She'd twisted and curled most of Phoebe's dark copper hair up into the latest fashion, as described in *La Belle Assemblée*, before carefully pulling a few strands free to accentuate her shapely face and neck. Her mask, Sophie's most recent acquisition from Madame Paragon, was shaped like an elegant golden butterfly and set with a thousand tiny rhinestones, which sparkled in the candlelight.

'You look most elegant, my dear,' her aunt smiled from the doorway, 'the earl should watch his step!'

'Perhaps he would, if he could see his own feet,' Phoebe muttered.

Sophie giggled as their aunt frowned enquiringly.

'Phoebe was just saying how much she loves her new dress!' Sophie covered, pulling on a pair of gloves to match her own new gown of cream satin, which Madame Paragon had edged in French lace.

Their aunt had spared no expense, overriding objections with the argument that their mama wouldn't want them to attend looking like country bumpkins.

'Bath society is much more relaxed than London, my dears, and of course, this is a private family dinner at the direct invitation of the captain, but you must behave with the utmost propriety. Do I make myself clear? We must give no rise for gossip!'

Phoebe felt Sophie eyeball her across the room, knowing full well she was thinking about the many different ways in which her behaviour had already given rise to so much gossip.

She nodded as sincerely as she could, certain that while Sophie might try to use the dinner to further her acquaintance with Captain Elliot, she was equally as determined to find the quietest corner and remain there.

She had no desire to see either Lady Aurelia or the viscount, or listen to any talk of betrothals, or fuel his impression that she was a disruptive country nobody whom he should have left to moulder at the side of the road. Furthermore, while she was dreading marriage to the earl, she was even less willing to bring her aunt, uncle, or the Fairfax family name into any further disrepute.

All of which left her fully resolved that this night would be the least heroic of her whole miserable existence.

Damerel Place turned out to be a large family townhouse in the Royal Crescent, and only a stone's throw from the Assembly Rooms.

'Trust the viscount's family to have one of the smartest houses in the row!' Sophie chattered, shuffling forward in her seat to get a better look at the looming Georgian townhouse, lit by an extravagant number of copper lanterns.

'Hush now, dear, it's not de rigueur to speak in such a way. One must merely remark how very *fine* it is, and then flick open one's fan like so, see?' Aunt Higglestone demonstrated with a twinkle in her eye.

Sophie giggled, while Phoebe remained silent. Somehow, actually seeing the viscount's townhouse brought back their last meeting as clearly as though it were yesterday. She could still see the derision in his eyes, still hear the contempt in his tone when he handed her into his chaise, and bid his driver deliver her home.

She closed her eyes and inhaled deeply. He was altogether the most obnoxious person of her acquaintance, and while he might have considerable reason to think her touched in the head, she hadn't invited him to be her hero. She tightened her mask, fixed her smile and followed her aunt and Sophie into the viscount's home.

The first thing to strike her was that Sophie's impression was quite accurate. Set over five floors with a cerulean ballroom, Bath-stone stairs and far too many mirrors and pillars to count, the viscount's townhouse was more accurately a town manor house.

The captain's *private dinner* also seemed to be a vast understatement in itself, for there were more than thirty guests, a gaming room, a ladies' retiring room, a dinner buffet that seemed to replenish itself and an impressive garden lit with a multitude of tiny candles.

'Of course, a Damerel dinner wouldn't just be dinner,' their aunt muttered, wide-eyed as she wandered off in search of a sherry.

'Oh, look! You'd think we were at an exotic palace!' Sophie exclaimed as they reached a set of French doors that led out onto a wide, rolling lawn, which boasted crowing peacocks and a miniature maze among other ornamental decorations.

'The peacocks?' Phoebe murmured, scanning the garden carefully.

They'd left their aunt at a card table, and their uncle

ensconced in a debate about the efficiencies of the new four-course crop-rotation system.

'No, the pastries…' Sophie glared. 'Of course, the peacocks! Have you ever seen peacocks at a dinner party before?'

'Oh, I've seen plenty of peacocks at a dinner party – peahens too, truth be known!' A masked lady interrupted as she waltzed up to them with all the confidence of a debutante on the verge of notable marital success.

Phoebe scowled harder than she ever had in her life.

Aurelia could wear all the laced masks and violet taffeta she liked; but there was no mistaking her duplicitous china-doll eyes. She swayed as she paused, red wine in hand, and laughed while Phoebe stared, searching for any sign of the girl she'd glimpsed in the theatre box.

There was none.

'I have nothing left to say to you, Aurelia,' she said, taking Sophie's arm.

It was the truth. She'd hidden the poultice inside a well-packed hat box, and dispatched it to Aurelia the following day.

'Ah, well, yes, with regard to that,' she smiled. 'As it turned out, it wasn't required after all, silly me!'

She paused to clamp a slim, gloved hand across her pretty mouth, her eyes dancing with mirth.

'I was also curious to discover that you'd elected to leave the theatre early,' she continued airily. 'The viscount did seem unusually abrupt when he returned, but then I discovered you'd disclosed your identity and as he really can't abide dishonourable behaviour of any kind…'

'I wonder then at his marrying you!' Sophie blazed protectively.

'Captain Elliot!' Phoebe greeted a newcomer forcefully. 'I would recognise your immaculate uniform anywhere. How are you?'

'Dearest Captain Elliot,' Aurelia simpered instantly. 'If you've come to claim my hand for a dance, you'll be sadly disappointed for my card is full until the quadrille, which you may have I suppose, though I shall have to disappoint others.'

She fluttered her fan with practised ease.

'There is dancing?' Sophie exclaimed as the masked captain bent low over Aurelia's hand. 'I'm liking this dinner more and more!'

Phoebe studied them both carefully. Even if Aurelia had decided she was no longer with child, it didn't mean the captain wasn't originally involved. And yet her instincts told her he was no more involved than she.

'Now that is a disappointment,' he returned gallantly, 'but perhaps one of the Misses Fairfax will oblige me with a waltz instead? For one can hardly attend a Damerel dinner dressed as a Romeo, and not hope for a dance with a Juliet after all.'

'Indeed!' Phoebe smiled, while Sophie positively beamed in his direction.

'I'm sure there are many young ladies here who would like to claim that namesake. But alas, you seemed to have foiled our efforts this evening! Aren't you at least supposed to *pretend* you don't know us? Or are our masks entirely wasted?'

'Not at all!' He winked, before leaning forward conspiratorially. 'Your aunt pointed you out, mostly out of sympathy for my nerves! Mama's friends are forever trying to matchmake me with their prodigiously boring daughters…'

He pretended to shudder, his eyes alight with humour, and

not for the first time Phoebe wondered at the twist of fate that had dealt two brothers such different personalities.

'Well, I think Sophie would be most happy to help you in your hour of need,' Phoebe smiled. 'While I have promised Aurelia a swift turn about the gardens.'

With a sudden burst of purpose, she ignored her sister's blushes, and propelled Aurelia out into the gardens.

'Really, Phoebe! I *am* promised for the next few dances as I said—'

'And I won't keep you from them,' Phoebe interrupted, the moment they were out of earshot. 'But I will say my piece and then we will be done.'

She turned to face Aurelia, never more serious in her life.

'We made a deal and I expect you to honour it! I thought we could be friends,' she continued, 'even had moments when I thought I could understand you – feel empathy for you. But real friends don't try to expose or undermine one another, especially those who have little enough control as it is.'

Aurelia waited, a gleam creeping into her eyes.

'You said once that we weren't that different, and I disagreed. Well, I take that back because you were right.' Phoebe scowled. 'We're both pawns in a gentlemen's game. Yet, unlike you, I don't trade my friends for a fallible king! So, I say again, we made a deal and I *expect* you to keep to it. Stay away from me and stay away from my sisters. I hope you understand that, if nothing else.'

There was a brief pause while Aurelia paled with anger.

'I never lied!' she retorted, her lips white. I thought I was with child, and now I find I am not. And we were never the same – you think that because you grew up fighting with brothers and falling out of trees, you have some greater claim to the notion of equality? This fight has been raging a lot longer than you or I, and at least I don't have double standards. I know all about the earl and trust me, I can't wait for that little event to unfold!'

Phoebe stared, wondering why she ever tried to help.

'*Why* are you like this?' she challenged after a beat. 'And who told you about the earl?'

Aurelia laughed again, but this time there was a definite edge.

'You country bumpkins are *so* ignorant! You wear such a ridiculous, hunted expression, anyone would guess at it. And besides, Viscount Damerel tells me *everything*. How we laughed when he relayed your duel with the highwayman, and your reluctance to return home to your brother…

'Tut-tut, Phoebe, I'd keep your *expectations* to yourself if I were you, unless you wish the whole of Bath to know how particularly you tried to escape your own *situation*!'

Then she turned and swept back inside, leaving Phoebe alone with the curious peacocks, and the distant strain of the violins, warming up to the waltz.

'What are you looking at?' Phoebe threw at the nearest bird, before picking up her skirts and heading out into the garden.

It wasn't long before the sweet-scented roses and climbing wisteria began to reach inside Phoebe's unsettled thoughts. Damerel Place was tiny compared to Knightswood, or even the viscount's country estate, but it had a soothing magic of its own, and soon she was far enough away from the house to think more clearly.

She already knew Aurelia didn't care for her, but to believe she'd taken against her because of her notions on equality? That the viscount had told her about the duel and Thomas's dressing down? What else may he have told her?

A strange and uncomfortable prickle reached up the back of her neck.

And why had Aurelia sought so hard to expose her when they both felt exactly the same frustrations, and were so blatantly fighting for the same thing?

She reached the southern-most garden wall, beyond the miniature maze and twinkling lanterns, before she allowed herself to pause. The spring night was scented with thyme and fresh honeysuckle, and she inhaled deeply, missing Knightswood more than ever. Which was when she noticed the swing, concealed inside an old magnolia tree, and far enough away for the sound of music to be almost drowned out by the churr of a dusk nightjar.

'Perfect,' she muttered, ducking beneath the low branches to reach the wide wooden seat.

Moments later, she was being lulled by its gentle rhythm and if it seemed unusual for a bachelor of the ton to possess such a distraction, her curiosity was swiftly replaced with a brief escape into memories of Knightswood and rides with Misty.

'It's been a few years since anyone has used it.'

Instantly, Phoebe executed a dismount that would have rivalled any of the village boys caught in the cider barn before harvest was done.

She spun, scanning the darkness, wondering if she'd finally taken leave of her senses.

'A dismount worthy of a circus acrobat, Miss Fairfax!' the

voice came again. 'Not that I'm surprised. I suppose I should be grateful we aren't near a sword – or a canal – or a stage!'

This time the voice was accompanied by the dusky figure of a masked highwayman, emerging from the aged and dense branches behind the swing.

Phoebe inhaled to steady herself. It wouldn't matter how many masquerade outfits he wore, she would know his sculpted cheekbones anywhere. She stared at his careless Corinthian locks, and lips already parted as though in readiness for their next caustic set down.

'Viscount Damerel tells me everything. How we laughed when he relayed your duel with the highwayman, and your reluctance to return home to your brother…'

A flare of fury tore through her.

'Thank you,' she forced, 'for your assistance at the theatre. I was meeting someone backstage and your … intervention was appreciated.'

The muscle in the viscount's cheek twitched, and for some inexplicable reason Phoebe caught her breath.

'You are most welcome,' he returned, taking a couple of steps forward and stilling the swing. 'It was fortuitous that I am a trustee of the theatre. But I must own to being somewhat perplexed as to why either a debutante – or even the widowed cousin of a famous actress – would be fighting over her own dress in her petticoats? I suppose I might have further questions about kissing officers in a private Assembly Room,' he continued, 'though I persuade myself I might understand the interest there…'

There was a strained silence during which Phoebe

wondered what the etiquette was when it came to landing the host of your first private dinner, another leveller.

Instead, she eyed him with contempt.

'Tell me,' she challenged after a beat. 'Do you enjoy other people's discomfort, or are you singling me out because you are labouring under some misguided notion that I actually need your help? I assure you, I have managed things quite well by myself for eighteen years. And, even though it is no business of yours, I kissed no one!'

'Well, that's a relief,' he replied evenly, the muscle in his cheek twitching again. 'On both counts.'

Phoebe clenched her fingers tightly. How could a man who'd done nothing but interfere and infuriate affect her so? It made no sense that she wished him a thousand miles away while nowhere else at all, and could only conclude that he vexed her to the edge of insanity.

'Who I kiss – *whether I kiss* – is entirely my business alone, as was my behaviour at the theatre, and at every other incident you've witnessed with extremely suspect timing. There were reasons, and they remain *my* reasons.'

He stepped forward then, soft shafts of moonlight falling across his face which, to her further annoyance, was clad in the best highwayman mask she'd ever seen, putting the sackcloth fraudster she'd sparred with to dire shame. She clamped her mouth closed lest it drop open. He really was the most irritatingly handsome man she'd ever set eyes upon.

'A highwayman?' she said scornfully to cover her hammering chest. 'I thought it was a masked dinner party, not a game of charades!'

There was a poignant silence while he leaned against the wizened trunk.

'Isn't it always a game of charades?' he returned languidly. 'And I suppose you could say I was somewhat *inspired by experience*.'

Phoebe bit her lip, a bubble of laughter threatening everything.

'Speaking of which, I trust you are fully recovered from your injury now?'

She gazed at him, recalling the moment he'd arrived at the roadside, like an incoming hero from one of Josephine's novels. Even then, his appearance had both infuriated and intrigued her, despite everything. Her stomach lurched, and suddenly she was back in the library again, with his fingers brushing the cotton bodice of her nightgown, his breath warm on her skin. A strange shiver stole through her as she forced herself to meet his gaze. His eyelids had slunk lazily, but his gold-flecked eyes had never gleamed brighter across the small clearing between them. She swallowed, certain he was recalling exactly the same moment.

Yet this man had all but insulted her in every way possible, before recounting the whole to a person who'd made it their sole business to undermine and discredit her.

'Quite recovered, thank you,' she returned, gathering her scattered thoughts. 'Now, if you'll—'

'Why are you out here?'

She paused as he sank down onto the swing seat, and for the first time she noticed his unsettled air.

'I … miss home,' she faltered, wondering how he'd react if

she were to tell him the truth about his fiancée. '…I can't breathe here.'

His gaze roamed from the top of her fashionably ringleted head to her silver-slippered feet, the air between them intensifying.

'I feel the same way,' he murmured, loosening his cravat. 'And for the record, I much prefer your … understated look.'

He muttered the last words in a way that conjured memories of all the moments he'd berated her in less than suitable attire – a borrowed nightgown, a soaked picnic dress, corset and petticoats – and this time there was no denying her flush.

She swallowed, searching for something to say.

'That is a highly improper thing to say,' she muttered finally.

'Since when did you care a jot about propriety?'

She looked up sharply and found his eyes had darkened in a way that wasn't in the least bit apologetic.

'You see, that is what intrigues me most about you,' he continued. 'You dress like a boy, you've more courage than most, you put the life of your sister before your own, and then you hide at a social dinner I would have thought you'd relish … given your impending nuptials.'

Phoebe flinched, her mind racing.

'That's *really* why you're here, isn't it?' he asked, standing abruptly and removing his mask. 'And it explains all the scrapes and adventuring, too. Because no matter how fearless you pretend to be, deep down … you're terrified.'

Phoebe stared into his accusing eyes, feeling as exposed as she had the night of the library.

Which meant what now? *More ridiculing? Something else to tell Aurelia?*

She caught her breath.

'I've said it before, but my behaviour is no business of yours!' she scowled. 'And just because there are some things I don't yet…'

Phoebe tailed off as the viscount stepped towards her, his eyes glinting in the lowlight.

And suddenly it was there, the very same draw she felt the first night; a visceral heat that reached between them, intensifying the closer they drew, fading out every sound and fogging every thought except this moment. It was intoxicating and breathtaking and addictive all at once.

'Why society mothers don't tell their daughters more, I will never understand,' he whispered when he reached her, picking a stray magnolia petal from her hair. 'There are so many things I would like to tell you … to show you … given the chance.'

He spoke huskily, as though caught in the slew of a dream as his fingers dropped to the top of her bodice, and gently lingered across her warm, exposed skin as he pressed closer, until she could feel every hard line of his taut body.

Briefly she closed her eyes, listening to the thump of his chest, before summoning the willpower to pull away, reminding herself he was the same arrogant, promised viscount that had riled and thwarted her from the day they met.

She drew a ragged breath.

'Yes, I'm sure that would be most *entertaining*,' she flared in a way that left him in no doubt as to whom she was referring.

His expression hardened abruptly.

'I have never betrayed your confidence,' he blazed, 'except in frank admiration of a young woman who appeared unafraid of anything. If I spoke too freely, it's because I've never met anyone quite like you!'

For a moment there was a poignant silence, when all Phoebe could hear were the evening crickets echoing the thump of her heart.

'You must know,' he added, his voice dropping again, 'that ever since that night in my library you have … plagued me. You have stolen my peace in ways I cannot explain… I thought I had known every feeling there is to know, that no one could surprise me, but … I cannot help but believe that deep down, you know I am lost.'

His tone was more accusing than that of a lover, and yet it felt as though every blossom-strewn branch stilled to listen. Phoebe hardly dared breathe, so aware that she must be dreaming, that the most vexing man of her existence couldn't be standing before her now, saying these things. And yet, it was his dark face that inclined towards her, and his lips that chased tiny, burning kisses down her neck in a way that made the glade spin like a top.

'Tell me,' he whispered hoarsely, when he came up for air, 'tell me that you feel the same way? Tell me you think of nothing else? You must know, from the past few weeks, that I cannot stay away from you.'

Phoebe exhaled raggedly, every chance meeting and scathing judgement suddenly taking on new meaning. Could it really have been masking something else entirely?

He was so close she could count each of his eyelashes, while his eyes lingered on hers, almost as though he was scared to look away. She inhaled unsteadily, conscious of the oddest fluttering in the pit of her stomach, and suddenly she realised she was *so close* to tipping point – that it was happening again – whatever happened in his library.

Phoebe fought to order her thoughts. The viscount had been nothing but arrogant and interfering since the day they'd met, but he also made her feel more alive than anyone else she knew. And right now, if she didn't do something, she would do *everything*, and that would be the biggest scandal of all her born days.

She squeezed her eyes shut and forced herself to think of Aurelia.

'I suspect you are being missed,' she forced coldly, turning before she could change her mind.

'Wait!' he entreated hoarsely, his warm breath on her neck as he slid his hands around her waist, drawing her back. 'Don't leave, say something…'

She inhaled, every disloyal limb burning to stay and yet somehow, she found the will to tear away and pelt across the dusky gardens towards the lights of Damerel Place.

'Miss Fairfax, is that you scaring the peacocks?'

Phoebe slowed as two figures loomed out of the darkness – the captain with one of his friends, a stockier soldier with a long moustache, coiled dark hair and gentle eyes.

She inhaled shakily, genuinely relieved to see a friendly face, and tried to assemble her scattered thoughts.

'Miss Phoebe Fairfax, please may I present to you Lieutenant Kapoor of the East India Company: a friend, a crack shot, and one of the best physicians I know.'

The captain threw his arm around his friend, who shrugged

him off with a swift glance. Phoebe smiled politely, pretending not to notice.

'Captain Elliot, Lieutenant Kapoor, it's a pleasure to meet you,' she nodded, bobbing a swift curtsey.

'As it is you, Miss Fairfax, a delight!' Lieutenant Kapoor returned, bowing low.

She liked him instantly.

'Are you in Bath for long?' she rushed, conscious of the silence behind her.

'I'm fortunate enough to be staying here at Damerel Place, at the viscount's invitation,' Lieutenant Kapoor replied. 'Until the regiment moves on, that is. Then where the regiment goes, I go, too.'

He looked across at the captain and smiled, and for some reason, he looked faintly apologetic.

Phoebe nodded, conscious her pulse was still racing.

'And from whom do you run, Miss Fairfax?' Captain Elliot grinned.

'Surely no adversary is too great for our intrepid, pirating adventurer?' He turned to warn off the darkness with dramatic flourish and was rewarded with a screech from the nearest peacock, making them all laugh.

'I wish I had half the fortitude you imagine,' Phoebe exhaled.

The captain threw her a brief, quizzical look just as two more silhouettes loomed out of the darkness towards them.

'Oh, there you are! I've been looking everywhere!' Sophie began to remonstrate before she spied her sister's company.

'Oh! Captain Elliot, do excuse me for interrupting,' she exclaimed, flushing prettily. 'I did so enjoy our dance earlier.

'Phoebe, where have you been? Aunt is going frantic trying to find you! I tried the buffet and card rooms but you were nowhere to be seen, so I thought—'

'The Earl of Cumberland is here, Miss Fairfax!'

Phoebe started as Aurelia emerged from the semi-gloom, a triumphant expression on her face.

'He's talking to your delightful aunt, who has just launched into *quite* the explanation for your attendance here this evening. Of course, the earl is an old family friend of the Damerels, so his attendance at a private family dinner is hardly a surprise,' she added, her eyes glittering.

'And, I do believe he's mentioned a dance…?'

She paused to tinkle with laughter, as everyone turned to Phoebe. Phoebe forced a smile, though a strange chill was reaching through her.

The earl shunned the season and socialising – it was his reason for a no-fuss wedding – so why would he choose to be here tonight? And why was the universe insistent on moving in such tiny circles?

She swallowed, inordinately grateful for both her mask and the night.

'Now, I must return,' Aurelia added, bestowing her most dazzling smile on the captain, 'for I'm promised to the viscount for a dance, and in truth, we make such a handsome couple – do we not?'

'Indeed, you do!' the captain replied, though his tone was noticeably cooler.

Satisfied, Aurelia spun on her satin heels, and disappeared back towards the lilting music, leaving Phoebe to stare after her, suppressing a rise of emotion she couldn't even begin to understand.

'So modest,' Sophie muttered beneath her breath.

'Are you feeling quite well, Miss Fairfax?' the captain added with a slight frown. 'Do you wish to sit down? Or shall I procure a glass of water, perhaps?'

'How kind you are, Captain Damerel!' Sophie beamed, 'but you should know my sister has the constitution of an ox! Do let's hurry, dearest,' she added, slipping her arm through Phoebe's, who'd fallen as silent as the night around them. 'Aunt bid me not to keep the earl waiting.'

'Then we must bid you both adieu,' the captain returned gallantly, 'and assure you of our service, whenever it may be of assistance!'

Phoebe nodded, with the faintest of smiles, before heading towards the house.

Chapter Seventeen

Five weeks and avoiding the earl until the wedding

There was no avoiding the earl. Apart from the fact that every pair of eyes seemed to be on the unexpected guest, he was also the only one not wearing any kind of mask.

'Ironic when he stands most to benefit,' Phoebe muttered to herself.

'Pardon?' Sophie whispered.

Phoebe shook her head.

'He didn't expect to find us here,' Sophie added as they threaded around the dancing, 'on account of us not being properly out. But Aunt explained why Thomas permitted it, and he seems content. He's a friend of the viscount's mother I think.'

Phoebe looked across at the viscount's mama, a dazzling creature in green velvet and white ostrich feathers, holding court with Marchioness Carlisle and other matrons, and wondered why she hadn't considered the earl's attendance a possibility before. He might dislike socialising but he was also an unmarried, wealthy member of the ton, well known to most of the scheming and ambitious mamas here. Briefly, she scanned their sycophantic faces, willing any of their pale daughters to take her place anytime soon.

'I did try to escape to warn you,' Sophie continued in a low voice, 'but then aunt insisted on introducing herself, and explaining everything, until everyone was quite muddled and then the earl said he would see you if you were here...'

Phoebe nodded, forcing her damp slippers forward, her recent escapades fanning through her head like pages from a book: escaping Knightswood, fighting the highwayman, fighting the viscount, escaping to Bath, fighting Aurelia, fighting herself...

She had done little else but try to fight or escape, yet none of it had been enough; and now she was staring directly at her future, who appeared to be sporting the most ridiculous shirt points, a gold-thread frock coat bursting at its seams, and a wig, which looked as though it wanted to run as much as she did. And despite all of this, a small herd of hopeful mamas and their daughters were gathered around his eminent person and her flustered aunt, who was doing her best to waylay them.

'Why Thomas hasn't deflected him onto someone more willing, I'll never know,' Sophie whispered, side-eyeing her sister anxiously.

Phoebe thought of her brother's incandescent rage the day she'd returned with the viscount.

'Do you understand the disquiet you've caused? Let alone how I have burned the midnight oil trying to fathom how to tell the earl

199

that his betrothed has seen fit to run away on the common stage, dressed in her brother's clothes!'

She swallowed. Time was running out, and despite all her efforts, none of her escapades had felt truly noble, at all.

'We can all be heroic in big and small ways, loud and quiet, if we wish.'

A ghost of a smile flitted across her face as she squeezed Sophie's arm.

Perhaps it wasn't entirely too late.

'He may have tried,' she returned with lightness that belied the stone in her chest. 'But the reality is I have always been betrothed to the earl, and Thomas is merely following Papa's wishes.'

Sophie frowned, but then their flustered aunt was upon them, with the earl in tow.

'Ah, there you are, my dears! We thought you must be admiring the viscount's many works of art for some are quite breathtaking, are they not, Mr Higglestone?' She beamed at her long-suffering husband before continuing, without drawing breath. 'The Earl of Cumberland was just enquiring after your health, dear Phoebe, following your riding fall a few weeks ago?'

She nodded so vigorously, she put Phoebe in mind of one of the laying hens at home.

'And your uncle and I were just saying how much the Bath air has improved your shoulder and your sister's lungs, too, weren't we, dear?'

Uncle Higglestone downed his brandy without comment.

'But you can see this for yourself of course, Your Lordship!

Doesn't Miss Fairfax look quite the picture of vitality and health?'

Phoebe avoided Sophie's gaze, certain she'd heard the estate manager say the very same when Thomas made enquiries of the deer herd.

'Thank you, Aunt, I do feel most recovered, thanks to your care. Good evening, Your Lordship.'

Phoebe sunk into a low, dutiful curtsey, conscious that the mamas trailing the earl were watching with both interest and suspicion.

'Miss Fairfax and … the younger Miss Fairfax,' the earl nodded, waving a port that almost matched the colour of his cheeks. 'It is most excellent news that you are recovered. Indeed, I have just come from Knightswood Manor, where your brother assured me all Fairfaxes descend from good, healthy stock!'

Phoebe reddened as the earl descended into a belly rumble that put his frock coat under even more pressure. She could just imagine Thomas tripping over himself to assure the earl of such a thing when he heard of her injury. Perhaps this visit was a surprise inspection to reassure himself that he wasn't being shortchanged.

'In truth, Your Lordship, I'm sure my aunt has much to do with my recovery,' Phoebe returned evenly, 'she has been most attentive.'

'Oh dearest, that is too kind, I—'

'Youth forgives everything,' the earl interrupted, tossing back the remainder of his port, 'I've often considered its benefits are wasted on the young, who do not appreciate them at all! Though I hear you've also been taking the waters? Tell me, how do you find them?'

Phoebe glanced at her crestfallen aunt and felt a sudden flare of protectiveness.

'In truth, Your Lordship, all I can taste is mud!'

Matilda's words were out before Phoebe could stop them, and at precisely the same moment two things happened. The first was that all the listening mamas gasped in unison, and the second was that a tall, elegant figure stepped in beside her aunt, distracting everyone.

'It's a new expression among the young set, my lord,' Viscount Damerel interjected smoothly. 'Mud as in *mudicinal*, which no one can dispute. It is the sulphur, I am told.'

'Oh … I see,' the earl conceded slowly, with a frown. 'Well, I'll take your word for it, Damerel.'

He reached out to take another port from a passing footman.

'I don't usually dance, Miss Fairfax,' he continued condescendingly, 'but as this is a *private* gathering, you may do me the honour, and then escort me to the card room.'

'As you please, sir,' Phoebe replied, every feeling revolting at the thought of dancing with an overstuffed pheasant.

'I believe a quadrille is starting now, that will do,' he added, tossing back the contents of the glass.

Phoebe raised her eyes to the viscount. His face was shuttered, his manner composed, and there was no evidence of the man she'd glimpsed beneath the magnolia tree.

Had he meant any of it? Or had he just been entertaining himself the way he'd entertained Aurelia?

She flushed dully.

What did any of it matter, anyway?

It seemed as though the whole world turned to watch her dance with the most coveted, yet ridiculous, suitor in the room. And to make matters worse, the earl's dancing turned out to be a form of mincing, crossed with a few half-remembered steps from his youth. Yet every way he turned, the ambitious mamas simpered and smiled, his birthright exonerating all crimes.

Phoebe fixed her gaze over his rounded shoulder, so conscious of Aurelia and the viscount dancing only a few paces away. They were indeed the most handsome couple in the room; matched in every way, and now it seemed their dancing was perfectly timed too. She painted her face with a smile and tried to ignore Aurelia's sidelong glances; but the earl's unsteady progress, and insistence on humming aloud, ensured no one was looking anywhere else. She lowered her gaze, feeling as conspicuous as he looked, and burning with humiliation that this ridiculous person was soon to assume control of her life. Then the music moved on, heralding a brief change in partner, and she looked up to find herself directly opposite Captain Elliot.

Phoebe smiled wanly, never more grateful to see his warm eyes.

'Don't look so hopeless,' he whispered as they stepped together, their hands creating an arch above their heads. 'You know, we aren't so different, you and I.'

She smiled benignly, conscious that the viscount and Aurelia were close by.

'Trying to freeze time, before life catches up,' he whispered as they stepped together again.

She glanced up at him, their brief interlude in the garden

with Dr Kapoor flitting through her thoughts, and suddenly, she just *knew* he couldn't be responsible for Aurelia's situation. She'd glimpsed the secret behind his dancing eyes, and if she wasn't much mistaken, that secret had much more to do with a Lieutenant of the East India Company, than the daughter of Marchioness Carlisle.

Phoebe swallowed, recalling the warmth between them and Dr Kapoor's wary smile. It was so far removed from her knowledge of accepted social unions, and yet she was sure she was correct, in the same way she was sure he'd glimpsed her inner turmoil. Her lips parted to remind him that, as a gentleman, he had so many more avenues for escape than she, but he was already gone – leaving a glacial highwayman in his place.

Phoebe inhaled tightly.

'I cannot help but believe that deep down, you know I am lost.'

His words hung on the air between them as she focused on his cravat, its folds as precise as ever. Then the dance brought them together, and his warm fingers interlaced hers briefly, sending a shiver that divided and chased across the entirety of her tense body.

'I apologise for my earlier attentions, Miss Fairfax,' he murmured. 'I see now that they were entirely inappropriate. And while I cannot bring myself to regret them, I hope in time'—his gaze flickered past hers momentarily—'that you will learn to … forgive them.'

She stole a glance up, a million thoughts racing, but then he too was gone, leaving the earl in his place, puffed-faced and purple.

Phoebe danced on, feeling oddly breathless, and never

more grateful than when the last few notes of the dance spilled out over the floor. She sank into a curtsey, conscious that the rest of the guests were watching as the earl proffered his arm in a way that made his favour decidedly clear.

'Please do excuse me, my lord,' she murmured, 'I am a little overcome … and in need of some air.'

The words tumbled out of their accord, and if the earl was surprised by her sudden indisposition, he was just as swiftly distracted by the herd of ambitious mamas the moment she turned.

'Be my guest,' she whispered, as she fled the room.

Phoebe took the wide Bath-stone steps two at a time, only slowing when she'd climbed three stairwells, and the noise of the music had receded to a distant blur. Then, finally, she allowed herself to step off the plum-velvet carpet and into a shadowy corridor lined with oil paintings. She exhaled heavily, recalling the night she'd been surrounded by the viscount's family portraits in Ebcott Place, and how it had been the start of something she barely understood at all.

Slowly, she stepped along the corridor, savouring its quiet solitude after the scrutiny of the dance. The first two portraits were of the viscount's mother and grandmother, the next were a series of mini paintings of his deceased father, surrounded by horses and dogs, and finally there was a portrait of the viscount with his siblings, in the gardens of Damerel Place.

Phoebe stared, trying to match the relaxed young gentleman in the portrait with the proud highwayman she'd left downstairs. He was standing behind his brother, who was seated beneath a flowering magnolia tree, while a young child with golden curls played at their feet.

'Which explains the swing,' she muttered to herself, peering closer. There was no mistake, it was the same lonely swing she'd discovered in the garden that evening, and the child looked no older than three or four years of age.

For a few moments she stared at their same intelligent brow, quizzical eyes, and impossibly high cheekbones – before a muffled cough suddenly disturbed the quiet.

Startled, she peered down through the silent murky corridor, her chest thumping. The last thing she needed was to be discovered by one of the servants, or even the viscount himself. He'd already insulted her this evening – she could only imagine his reaction, or the story he might tell Aurelia, if he believed her snooping in private family quarters. The thought was beyond mortifying, so she did the only thing she could think of doing, and slipped inside the nearest room.

Phoebe closed the door softly and waited. The room appeared to be a family bedchamber and particularly warm, and for a few moments she was content to hide and gather her thoughts. It was only when it had been quiet for some time, that she heard the cough again, and this time it was much closer. Carefully, she peered around a small entrance hall to glimpse a well-stoked fireplace, a small four-poster bed, an armoire, and a dresser. It was clearly a child's bedchamber and, frowning, she ran her gaze from the thick eiderdown, to the roaring fireplace, to the tightly closed window on the opposite wall.

'Are you looking for something to steal?'

Phoebe caught her breath as she spied a head full of golden spiral curls, just visible above the eiderdown.

'Perhaps a little time,' she smiled ruefully. 'I don't suppose you have any of that lying around here, do you?'

Two dancing blue eyes joined the golden spiral curls.

'I have too much of it in this bedroom,' the child grumbled, before coughing again in a way that stirred old memories for Phoebe.

In a heartbeat, she was beside her, sitting her up and rubbing her back in a way that always helped Josephine. However, this child was much younger, eight or nine years at most, and the cough showed little sign of abating.

Alarmed, Phoebe looked round for any of the tonics or tinctures she'd used with Josephine over the years, but her bedside glass was empty, and the child was already gulping for breath.

'Do you have any medicine? Can I call for your nurse?' Phoebe hushed, recognising the warning signs of a lung seizure.

But the child only clung to her, and struggled for breath in a way that filled Phoebe with mounting fear. She looked into her face; at her reddened cheeks, laboured breath, and scared eyes, and knew she had to act. Her sister had suffered with bronchospasms long enough for her to know how swiftly she could deteriorate.

Swiftly she scanned the room again, looking for anything with which she could improvise, and found herself staring through the window at the spring sky. In a blink, she was seven years old again, and watching Harriet hold Josephine close to the nursery window, praying the moorland air would work its magic. As it had, so many times. She glanced down at the child and knew there was no time to waste. This may not be Knightswood, and she wasn't their dear old nurse, but the principle had to be the same.

Jumping to her feet, Phoebe ran across the room, and tried to force open the old window but it refused to budge. She whirled frantically, looking for anything that might help, until her gaze landed on the fire poker. Without hesitating, she snatched it up and drove it into the window with all her strength. There was a moment's silence, before it fractured like a giant spider's web and then it fell away, letting a stream of fresh air fill the room.

'Come on!' she exclaimed, running back to the bed, and scooping up the semi-conscious child.

She wheezed something unintelligible, her lips already blue-grey, and Phoebe's alarm intensified. She'd watched Josephine suffer too many times not to know the signs of a severe attack, and this child was so young. Swiftly, she ran towards the window, and turned her towards the evening air.

'Harriet used to help my sister in this way,' she whispered, 'and it always worked. Just keep breathing.'

Her soothing tone was so at odds with the fear threading her veins, as she listened to the child dragging in each hoarse breath, before expelling it on a rattling wheeze. She pushed her closer to the fresh air, rubbing her back and willing her lungs to ease. Josephine had rarely suffered so acutely, and certainly not for a long while. And suddenly, all of Phoebe's own troubles seemed so insignificant as to barely warrant a second thought. How she could even think herself stifled, or in want of adventure, when a young life could dangle so precariously, was beyond her comprehension. All that mattered was this moment, and each breath she managed to preserve. Silently, she waited and counted, watching the hollow at the base of the child's neck depress with effort until, finally, just when she was beginning to think it might all be in vain, the little girl inhaled deeply, and a tide of colour flushed her face.

'You can have … some of mine … if you like?' the child whispered tearfully, finally able to finish her earlier thought.

A flood of relief filled Phoebe's limbs as she smiled down at the little girl, who seemed entirely oblivious to her predicament.

'I'll let you in on a secret,' Phoebe whispered, taking care to keep her in the fresh air. 'I would turn back the hands on our nursery clock, when I didn't want to go to bed!'

At this the child exhaled such a gurgle of laughter, that Phoebe worried she might actually set her off again.

'What is the meaning of this?'

The arctic voice startled them both into silence, before Phoebe lifted her gaze to find the viscount regarding her stonily.

'Why are you up here? With Florence?' he barked, striding across the room until he towered over them both.

'Alex! Alex!' Florence bubbled happily, stretching out her arms as though she hadn't just narrowly escaped a violent lung seizure.

'Alex is my big brother!' she confided. 'Look, Alex … a pretty thief came … and smashed my window…!' She grinned as though that covered everything.

It took all of Phoebe's reserve not to roll her eyes as the viscount bent to scoop Florence up, and even more so when the ungrateful creature proceeded to throw herself around his neck, and proclaim him the best brother in the whole wide world.

Instead, she inhaled deeply, and resigned herself to the fact that this was probably not going to all end well at all for her.

'I apologise for the window,' she began, 'but when I heard Florence…'

'This is not the first time I've discovered you somewhere you really shouldn't be, Miss Fairfax!' the viscount interrupted in a searing tone. 'You have clearly endangered my sister, and damaged my property! Might I remind you, this is my private home—'

'Dr Kapoor!' Florence squealed, just as a large flare of indignation tore through Phoebe. 'I had a cough, but then a thief broke the window, and saved me!'

To Phoebe's great surprise, Captain Elliot's friend, Lieutenant Kapoor, appeared in the doorway and was across the room in a few swift steps.

'Hush now, Florence, we must remain calm if this is true,' he murmured. 'Miss Fairfax?'

He smiled kindly while Phoebe flushed, vacillating between the shame of discovery in the viscount's private quarters, and the downright injustice of his wrath.

'There was no tonic, honey, ginger, anything!' she garbled in a rush. 'Even laudanum – much as I detest it – would have been a help! I had no choice but to break the window!'

Phoebe caught her breath, aware it sounded lunatic even to her own seasoned ears, before looking up into the viscount's face. His jade eyes had never glittered so coldly, and all at once she knew it wouldn't matter what she said.

'You had no choice but to expose my sister to the cold night air, which could have killed her?' he replied crushingly.

'Yes... No! It wasn't like that!' Phoebe fired, unable to believe she'd ever wondered if she'd misjudged him. 'I have a ... sister with the same condition.' She exhaled, the events of the evening finally threatening to topple her. 'Cold air can exacerbate the problem, but it can also help!'

'With respect, Viscount Damerel,' Doctor Kapoor frowned, 'Miss Fairfax was not wrong to act as she did. There is much research to suggest that altering the air temp—'

'I don't care about your damned research!' the viscount snapped, rounding on Dr Kapoor. 'I brought Florence back to Bath as you suggested, and not one of your measures have improved her seizures!'

Phoebe stared, suddenly recalling the viscount's *urgent family business* at The Swan Inn, and then his mention of the same when she arrived in Bath. Could it have all been to do with Florence's condition?

'Again, with respect, sir,' Dr Kapoor tried valiantly, 'we've yet to implement any of my measures. For example, my research indicates eucalyptus, ginger, and garlic can all have a positive—'

'Not now! I must remove Florence from this draught,' the viscount cut in abruptly. 'Dr Kapoor, please escort Miss Fairfax back to her party immediately, I am sure the earl will have missed her.'

Then he turned and strode from the room, as though the moment beneath the magnolia never happened at all.

Chapter Eighteen

Four weeks, six days, and lying to Sophie until the wedding

'I'm just saying it was unlike you, that's all.'

'Well, perhaps family dinners aren't my thing!' Phoebe scowled. 'Though I think Josephine may have been right – about adventures,' she added, thinking of all that had taken place recently.

It was a slow-growing realisation; she hadn't had any of the noble adventures she'd dreamed about, but the past few weeks had been filled with more mishaps, falls from grace, and small triumphs than she'd ever had in her life.

'What's that?'

'It doesn't matter ... and anyway I attended, didn't I?' she amended wearily, picking up her bookish sister's latest read, *A Midsummer Night's Dream*. 'At least Titania had an excuse,' she muttered to herself.

'Yes, well, that's just it, you attended the dinner, but you didn't actually *attend* the dinner!' Sophie frowned. 'You spent half the night out in the garden with the peacocks, and then when you did finally join us for two minutes, you left in such an abrupt manner, Aunt assumed the salmon had given you the bellyache! Finally, when you returned – a whole hour later – it was in the company of the captain's friend, and even though I'd trust Elliot with my life I'm not sure—'

'*Dr Kapoor* was escorting me back … wait, *Elliot*?'

'Yes, Captain Elliot Damerel.' Sophie shrugged. 'I heard Doctor Kapoor address him directly last night, and he told me he only invited his closest friends to call him by his Christian name. It was a clear invitation, don't you think?'

Phoebe stared at Sophie's delighted face, and thought no such thing. She exhaled under her breath. Perhaps it was kinder to let her believe she and the captain had an understanding, that waned of its own accord.

'Perhaps so.' She smiled faintly. 'But be careful, you wouldn't want Aunt to think you were being indiscreet or encouraging his attentions without *an understanding*.'

'Of course not!' Sophie protested, flushing. 'That is to say, there is nothing to encourage, we're just friends. But, oh, Phoebe, isn't he quite the handsomest gentleman?'

Phoebe pictured the viscount's masked face in the shadows beneath the magnolia tree, and felt the strangest rush.

Could a man be beautiful? In a galleried sort of way?

She looked up to find Sophie staring at her.

'He was the most dashing officer there,' she compromised. 'And one of the kindest, too.'

'Of course, you also missed the viscount and Lady Aurelia's official betrothal announcement,' Sophie added, pinning a ringlet adroitly.

Phoebe looked down at her hands, feeling the same hollow flutter as when her aunt described the announcement as *a most proper affair, with just the right amount of pretty language and champagne*.

Yet moments before he'd kissed her beneath the magnolia. And moments afterwards, he'd been ready to call the constable. She swallowed again. She'd suspected the viscount was trifling, and now she was certain of it.

'I'm sure it was perfectly arranged,' she returned tightly.

'Well, I thought the earl was in … good form,' Sophie tried valiantly. 'He only danced with you! Aunt says all the mamas were talking about it, and how yours will be the match of the season when the news is official.'

Phoebe pictured the purple-faced earl's tight frock coat, and ridiculous shirt points, and refrained from saying anything. Being seen with the earl in company had only made her world shrink further. Yet perhaps she was never intended to be anything more than his wife, onion-scented or not.

'I've heard the earl's estate in Cumberland is five times the size of Knightswood,' Sophie chattered on, while colour-coordinating her stockings. 'Plus, he has houses in London, Bath, and all over the place! You need not see each other from one season to the next if you don't wish it, except perhaps on birthdays and at Christmas…'

She looked up, a sudden wobble in her voice.

'Oh, Phoebe, what of birthdays and Christmas?! How are you to leave us at all? What if Josephine has one of her seizures, or Matilda falls out of a tree, or the twins hide a box of frogs in my bed or—'

'Hush now.' Phoebe chuckled, crossing the room and

pulling her sister into a tight hug. 'You're a Fairfax, remember? No tree is too high, no pudding too large!'

Sophie gurgled in the most unladylike manner, before nodding.

'I know, and I know Josephine was right, too: being heroic really *isn't* about running away to join the theatre or pinking unimpressive highwaymen, is it?'

'More's the pity.' Phoebe sighed, rolling her eyes.

'It's in the decisions we make, and the way we treat others.'

Phoebe nodded, reaching out to squeeze Sophie's hand.

'And I always knew we'd end up leaving Knightswood and starting our own homes and families,' Sophie continued tearfully. 'It's just I thought I'd feel older, readier. But now, I can't help but think that when one of us leaves, things will never be the same again.'

Phoebe pulled her close again, a sudden, hard lump in her throat.

'I don't know what the future holds, Sophie,' she returned, 'but I can tell you that wherever we may be, we will always have each other. And nothing, and no one, can ever change that.'

Sophie smiled wanly, burying her head in Phoebe's shoulder just as Matilda hurtled into the room and threw herself on the bed.

'I fell off the wall, Josephine has the cough, and Cook has just made the most *divine* batch of shortbread… And who can't change what?' she demanded, yawing and rolling over to reveal three warm shortbread in her hand. 'I've already smuggled one in to Jo. Aunt said best not to give her anything until she stopped coughing, but I figured – who would want to be coughing *and* hungry?'

There was a moment's silence before her sisters burst into laughter.

'Besides, aren't they *delicious, delightful* and…'

Matilda paused to look at her sisters expectantly.

'*Delectably, deliriously* good?' Phoebe grinned, snagging the biggest piece.

Sophie giggled, earning herself a pillow swat.

'Show off!' Matilda pronounced, rolling her eyes.

'Oh … and Fred is downstairs!'

Then she grinned and scoffed the rest of her shortbread, while her sisters took off at speed.

Chapter Nineteen

Four weeks, six days, and lying to Fred until the wedding

'To celebrate our last exam, we took an eight-oar rowboat down to Sandford, and returned by Iffley Lock.' Fred grinned at his sisters. 'Sanderson – he was stroke of the head boat – pushed her out of the lock as quickly as possible and then we all rowed for England. It was capital sport!'

'Did you win?' Sophie exclaimed, clapping her hands together.

'We did in the end!' He beamed. 'We were in hot pursuit under the bridge, and our bow was struck several times—'

'Struck?' Phoebe echoed blankly. 'As in hit?'

'More *bumped*.' He shrugged, with a sheepish smile. 'It's all in the rules, I assure you! Anyway, we inched over just in time, hoisted our flag and celebrated with a picnic at Nuneham. Was almost as good as the Hexworthy race, Phoebs!'

'It sounds it!' Phoebe grinned, inwardly aching at how easy

it was for her brother to have as many adventures as he liked without so much as a by-your-leave.

'So, what of you all? Have you been enjoying Bath? Been to the Assembly Rooms, the theatre, seen any ancient sights, perhaps?'

Phoebe inhaled while Sophie nearly choked on a fresh piece of shortbread.

'I'm sure Aunt Higglestone will have ensured you've seen more ancient ruins and sights than I saw the whole time I was in Athens!' He laughed good-naturedly. 'Am I right?'

'Foolish boy!' their aunt reprimanded indulgently.

'Well, there have been *a few* ancient sights,' Phoebe laboured, making Sophie snort again.

'Actually, we haven't seen that many ruins or sights at all!' Josephine complained, wrapped up in her aunt's favourite bluebell coverlet with a dog-eared copy of *Pride and Prejudice* on her lap. 'Aunt is determined to cure my cough with the waters first.'

She rolled her eyes, but had to give in to a cough instead, the effort of controlling it showing on her thin face. Phoebe frowned, Josephine still hadn't wholly recovered from her chill at the picnic, and she was more convinced than ever that the laudanum was doing more harm than good.

'Though Aunt has spoiled us in many other ways,' she soothed, passing Josephine a glass of water.

'Dresses, picnics … even a masked dinner! Though it was more of a dance and buffet really,' Sophie added, wrinkling her nose. 'It was at Damerel Place – the viscount's Bath home?'

'And Thomas permitted that?' Fred quizzed, genuinely surprised.

'It was a private affair, just family … apparently,' Sophie clarified, 'and we were only permitted as a thank you. In truth, it wasn't the disagreeable viscount who invited us, but the delightful captain instead. With whom I danced the cotillion!' she concluded rapturously.

'Viscount Damerel, disagreeable?' Fred quizzed, frowning. 'The same Viscount Damerel who was up at Oxford with Thomas? He was a capital fellow back then, impressive oarsman with a devilish right hook, if I remember rightly,' he mused.

Phoebe thought back to her own devilish right hook the night in his library, and bit her lip.

'I daresay there's more to being agreeable than having moderately above-average boating and boxing skills,' she suggested.

'Ah, but who are we to judge, dear!' Aunt Higglestone admonished. 'He is a rather stern gentleman at times, to be sure. But it was kind of his brother, the captain, to invite us, especially after *the unfortunate incident* at Sydney Park!'

Fred looked enquiringly at Phoebe, who developed a sudden interest in her embroidery.

'It was truly an honour to be treated like old friends!' Aunt Higglestone continued, beaming. 'I'm not sure what we did to warrant such consideration, but your uncle and I were most flattered – were we not, dearest?'

Uncle Higglestone managed to convey the extent of his appreciation in two small grunts and a shake of his daily newspaper, while Phoebe drew a steadying breath.

She was quite determined not to think of the viscount, if she could help it. In truth, their last parting had been so fraught, she'd quite made up her mind never to think of him again.

'I think you may all be labouring under a further illusion when it comes to Captain Elliot Damerel.' Fred frowned, while Phoebe began to wonder if she'd looked forward to her brother's visit a little too much. 'He's a nice enough fellow, but not his brother's influence in any way! He was always one of the quiet ones, and his brother bought his officer ranking long before he finished Oxford. There was some kind of hush-up, which seemed odd to me as he didn't seem the type to attract a scandal. Still ... one never can tell with some fellows.'

'You knew there was a scandal, but failed to find out what it was?' Sophie asked in a pained tone.

Phoebe conjured an image of Captain Elliot's kindly face and dancing eyes.

'We aren't so different, you and I.'

He was absolutely right: neither of them were comfortable with the role their birth had mapped out for them. Dr Kapoor's wary glance rose to the forefront of her mind – that he and the captain shared something more than friendship she was certain, and while she might not know its full extent, she was aware that polite society would be damning.

She wracked her memory, trying to recall something one of her governesses had said about ancient civilisations and tolerance. At the time she thought it a curious statement, but now she realised her governess had understood the weakness of their society – that one restrictive mould could exclude people like the captain, and even herself.

Instantly, she felt a rush of empathy and warmth for the soldier, surviving life with his dancing eyes and dazzling smile. It was just a well-rehearsed act, for the people that demanded it.

'Captain Elliot is the very definition of a gentleman,' Phoebe replied quietly. 'Indeed, sometimes I wonder at he and the viscount being related, at all.'

'Well, they've got the same chin,' Matilda pronounced, wrinkling her nose.

They all laughed, though Phoebe was conscious of Sophie's glance.

'I'll call on the Damerels, anyway, if they're in town.' Fred shrugged, flicking a fleck of dust from his sleeve. 'As I will the earl, too, of course. Thomas mentioned the wedding date has been fixed now, even if the old dog hasn't actually covered his proposal yet! Congratulations, Phoebe, you're going to be the toast of the season!'

Phoebe raised her eyes to her brother, and for the first time in her life, forced a smile.

'Truly,' she observed. 'I'm having fits of the vapours just thinking about it.'

Chapter Twenty

Four weeks, five days, and trying not to lie to anyone until the wedding

Phoebe could not rid herself of the notion that by the time she found herself at the top of an aisle, beside the onion-scented earl, she would consider any one of her Bath mishaps high adventure indeed.

'Which only goes to prove that the perception of adventure is entirely defined by the bleakness of your life,' she muttered, leaning forward to pat Bluebell's damp neck.

She closed her eyes and inhaled her fresh scent, trying not to think of the fact that she'd disobeyed both Thomas and her aunt in order to take an early morning hack, entirely unaccompanied. And yet, she was feeling freer than she had in weeks, as well as sincerely grateful to Fred, who'd inadvertently distracted their aunt from her usual hawk-eyed vigilance.

She relaxed into Bluebell's stride and allowed her mind to wander, aware that above all things, she'd reached a point when she couldn't pretend anymore.

She'd pretended to Thomas, to Aurelia, to the viscount, to Sophie, to Fred – and worst of all, she'd even pretended to herself. She'd pretended the ticking clock wouldn't matter if she had but a few heroic tales to take with her. But it had always mattered, as it continued to matter, and worst of all she'd proven to be the poorest heroine in the entire history of heroism: naive, ill-judged, and downright gullible.

She flushed as she recalled the unimpressive highwayman, the parasol duel, the near kiss with the mop-head, the fairy snuff, the disastrous picnic ride, and finally, the moment Sophie's dress had ripped entirely in two, backstage at Bath's Theatre Royal. Her sister still hadn't forgiven her, while the disagreeable viscount thought her a foolish country bumpkin who not only possessed dubious morals, but also endangered the lives of children.

And now there was to be no more pretending, no more fighting, and no more fleeing. She was quite simply the Right Honourable Miss Phoebe Fairfax, awaiting the announcement of her betrothal to the Earl of Cumberland. It was a good match – the match of the season, they said.

Yet she'd never felt more like taking off through the sleeping city, and never looking back.

'For surely, there is far more risk in marrying someone so violently purple, than there ever can be in riding you,' Phoebe murmured, leaning forward to pat her dawn partner again.

She was headed to Bath's Prior Park, long recommended by

the captain, and this morning the entire city seemed to be hers. Phoebe exhaled slowly as she rode, savouring the quiet streets, the distinct toll of the hour by the Abbey Bell, the bleary-eyed baker and a barefoot boy pushing a barrel full of oranges. Instinctively, she pushed her hand into her riding skirt, and threw him the remainder of her coin, before encouraging Bluebell into a gentle trot. Soon enough, the air filled with the thud of hooves on dewy earth, a comforting sound that enveloped her thoughts until Prior Park's entrance rose up to meet them.

She passed through the impressive, gated entrance quietly and took a moment to absorb her new surroundings. Prior Park was twice as beautiful as the captain had promised, and its vast carpet of wild garlic quite breathtaking. Carefully, she followed its undulating dance around a large, silent lake, holding Bluebell in check, before finally letting her have her head. Then, the carpet spun into an ivory blur and all the trying events of the past few weeks receded inside a few short, golden moments – only for her thoughts to return like shadows when they reached the elegant Palladian Bridge.

Phoebe exhaled as she slowed Bluebell to a trot. She still had no real idea why Aurelia had taken against her so vehemently, and now she and the viscount would marry. They deserved one another, as Sophie would say, and yet the thought disturbed her more than she could understand.

Sophie was another matter, altogether. Phoebe had never known her heart quite so openly engaged, yet she was equally certain the captain's heart was not free.

Then there was the viscount himself. She clenched the reins

briefly. How such an arrogant, opinionated gentleman who, despite having *no desire to be either her guardian or brother*, had managed to vex and thwart every adventure she'd attempted to have, was a mystery of epic proportions. He claimed she'd stolen his peace and that he was lost, yet he was the one who'd interfered in everything from the moment of their meeting at The Swan Inn. And finally there was the night of Florence's attack when he couldn't have been any clearer, so why then was her head determined to replay every look and word exchanged, until she no longer knew what to think?

She gazed thoughtfully at the bridge's beautiful Venetian roof. It was serene and silent, and she would have been quite content to linger awhile, if it wasn't for the sound of another rider, approaching from the lakeside. Cursing, she urged Bluebell on, well aware that the last thing she needed was for a report of this morning's indiscretion to reach the ears of her aunt, or brother.

'Miss Fairfax!'

She caught her breath as his voice reached through the chill of the morning, certain her mind had to be playing tricks.

No one human being could have as much terrible timing.

'Or should I address you as Mrs Mary Smith at this hour of the morning?'

Phoebe slowed as the viscount emerged from the lakeside path and trotted up to the bridge. He was astride a spirited chestnut, and his proud demeanour gave no indication as to his thoughts. She exhaled raggedly, conscious of a pained mix of emotions that seemed neither joy nor dread, and yet both simultaneously.

What were the chances of his choosing this place to ride at this hour of the day? She swallowed hard and yet, some tiny unheroic part of her, deep down inside, was unreasonably happy to see him, too.

'My name is Phoebe Fairfax, sir,' she returned coldly, gathering her reins. 'As you well know. Now, if you will excuse me—'

'Why do you ride at this hour? Without a chaperone? It is not safe.'

She paused.

Was the infuriating viscount, who made a lover's proclamation right before threatening to call the constable and becoming engaged to another, really assuming the right to question her decisions, again?

She shifted in her saddle, trying to maintain some semblance of calm.

'Truly, sir, save your attentions for your fiancée, who I'm sure will welcome them. I am well used to taking care of myself, and my wellbeing has never been your charge…'

'I beg to differ!' he returned, unflinchingly. 'Time after time, I have found myself in a position where ignoring your wellbeing would have put you at risk of considerable peril.'

Phoebe eyed the glowering viscount, certain she was starting to glower herself.

'On the contrary, sir, I can handle myself and always have done,' she reiterated stiffly.

The viscount urged his chestnut forward and paused only when they were face to face.

'Your assertions might bear some credence at Knightswood,' he challenged, 'but on the common road, at the

Royal Theatre, *in a public park*, your ability to find yourself in the most ridiculous and reprehensible of situations is beyond—'

'Everything I've done, I've done for reasons known only to myself and my sisters! Private reasons!' Phoebe interrupted furiously. 'I never asked for your interference, and I'm absolutely certain these last few weeks have been curtailed further by it, sir! Now if you have quite finished advising me on the improper nature of my behaviour, might I suggest you turn your attentions to your own, which I might hazard to suggest has been *less than virtuous* for a gentleman on the verge of marriage!'

They regarded each other furiously. The viscount's face was shuttered, the flinching muscle in his cheek his only visible movement, and the air between them so laden with confused thoughts, Phoebe was unsure if they were fighting anymore.

'Thank you … for your observations. I am quite aware my behaviour has been vastly less than what it ought to have been.'

He spoke quite deliberately, his eyes so narrow she could barely make out their colour at all.

'I assure you, I intend … wish to … make reparations.'

'Good, well, do excuse me if I don't stand by and watch!'

Without waiting, Phoebe urged Bluebell into a sprint up the rolling park lawn, and into a peaceful woodland glade beyond. She could barely think straight, let alone understand why he felt it necessary to tell her how he planned to make reparations to Aurelia. Well, he could do as he wished, but she didn't have to know. That much she could control.

She galloped until the woodland glade surrounded them

and then finally, slowed to a walk. Thankfully, there was no sound of pursuit, and exhaling heavily, she let Bluebell choose her own path among the closely knitted trees surrounded by buttercups and more wild garlic. The spring woodland was an instant balm to her furious thoughts, and she rode in the tranquil morning light until her chest stopped hammering, and her breath calmed. It was only when she began pondering whether she ought to start making her way back, that she heard the voices.

Low, urgent voices.

Frowning, she slid from Bluebell's back and climbed a small bank to spy the ivy-clad roof of an old summer house through the branches of a thick peony bush.

'You know how careful we've always been, but there are whispers – and they're not the sort to just disappear, especially with you know who around...'

'But surely she wouldn't wish to marry into scandal?' a softer voice returned.

'Perhaps not, but she might seek control through it – I'm certain she wants Florence and me out of the way when she moves in, for a start.'

Phoebe caught her breath in disbelief.

'Has anyone *said* anything, Elliot?' the softer voice came again. 'Might you be imagining some of the suspicion? You know how I feel, I love you and won't give you up on a maybe...'

Everything went quiet, and Phoebe felt a strange prickling heat spread upwards from the nape of her neck. She was certain it was the captain and Dr Kapoor, and she would hazard a guess she knew who they were talking about, too.

Was this the real reason she'd run into the viscount? Was he actually looking for his brother?

Phoebe swallowed. She knew she was intruding, but the intensity of their discussion was intoxicating. She'd guessed the captain and Dr Kapoor were more than friends, but that they considered themselves *in love*? And yet it made so much sense, too. It even explained Aurelia's reaction when she'd asked if the captain could be responsible for her situation. She knew, too. And the captain knew she knew.

Silently, Phoebe peered closer through the branches and suddenly they were there, beneath the open facade of the summerhouse, a kiss finishing their conversation. A rush of blood stole through her. She knew she shouldn't linger, but somehow it took her back to the magnolia tree, to the moment the viscount had almost kissed her – to the way she'd so wanted him to.

'Phoebe!'

A third voice suddenly split the still of the woodland, driving the two men apart, while Phoebe spun in a panic. She was astride Bluebell in a heartbeat, and then cantering through the trees until they melted into wide grassy lawns, where finally, she started to laugh. So much for a quiet dawn ride. Prior Park appeared to be almost as popular as a Sydney Gardens picnic.

'Phoebe!'

Her name rang out again, and this time it was accompanied by an approaching figure on horseback that filled her heart with misgiving. Muttering pithily about a universe that refused to give her any peace, Phoebe drew a deep breath and slowed to a walk.

'What in the devil's name do you think you're doing?' Fred demanded as he caught up, his fine bay making light work of the distance between them. 'I saw you leave this morning and thought I might have to call the constable!'

'Join the queue!' Phoebe replied.

'What do you mean?! What are you doing here, Phoebs?' he ploughed on without waiting for an answer. 'It's risky even for you. And riding, too? Isn't that against the rules? I swear if I hadn't seen a barrel-boy on the way, I'd be at Bath races by now and have washed my hands of you!'

She gazed at her happy, carefree brother, and never felt more envious.

'What's it like, Fred?' she asked after a beat. 'To be able to choose what you do, and when and with whom you do it?'

He stared at her suspiciously.

'Well, it's not quite…' he began before tailing off and exhaling. 'Lord, Phoebs, I know this arrangement with the earl isn't what you dreamed of when we were younger, but this marriage will mean your security. It's how things work for you girls. Plus, if you don't marry the earl, Thomas will feel he's failed both our father and our sisters. Your marriage sets the bar for you all!'

'I'm sure Thomas isn't averse to having a countess in the family, either,' Phoebe muttered as she encouraged Bluebell back towards the bridge.

'No, but it was one of Papa's last wishes, and as I understand it, you've not shown any inclination elsewhere?'

'I've not had the chance,' she protested. 'I haven't even had a season! Though if a season means Sophie endlessly ringleting my hair, I suppose even a purple earl can hold appeal!' she added, rolling her eyes.

Fred chuckled.

'I can't imagine you ever enjoying a regular season, either!' He grinned. 'All that primping and parading, you'd be bored by the end of the first waltz – and jumping into the nearest canal!'

'It wasn't quite like that,' Phoebe returned indignantly.

'So I understand. And it sounds like Matilda was lucky you were there,' he conceded. 'Clearly, we owe Viscount Damerel a debt of thanks, too.'

Briefly, she closed her eyes and pictured the viscount standing on the canal side: hair soaked, shirt glued to his chest, perfect eyebrows forked in disdain. It was chased by another image of him beneath the magnolia, standing so close she could feel every beat of his heart; before that, too, morphed into a darker image, his face shadowed by anger, accusing her of endangering his little sister. Finally, there was his admission on the bridge, that he was seeking reparations with Aurelia, that everything he'd said and done beneath the magnolia had been less than virtuous behaviour, nothing more.

Something twisted deep inside.

'We owe the viscount nothing!' she forced. 'Any debt has been more than settled, and he has more pressing matters on his mind, now that he is betrothed.'

She caught her breath, aware Fred was perplexed.

'Lord, Phoebs … at least you know your fate could be worse – imagine marrying someone you *really* disliked, like the viscount? Now there's an adventure you wouldn't want!'

He tailed off into nervous laughter, while Phoebe tried to

empty her thoughts of the viscount's dark silhouette: schooled face, gold-flecked eyes gleaming with intent. Fred knew her better than anyone, but even he would be scandalised if he knew the full extent of what had passed between them.

'What a fate, indeed!' she exhaled, urging Bluebell to a gallop.

Chapter Twenty-One

Four weeks, five days, and lying to Thomas until the wedding

'Good morning, Alfred… Phoebe!'

Phoebe straightened the moment she heard Thomas's authoritative tone, and turned her gaze slowly towards their aunt's pretty breakfast room. Sure enough, their eldest brother was standing between the lemon damask chaise longue and matching curtains, eyeing her muddied riding habit with something between forbearance and disdain.

She clenched her fingers tightly. Of all the people she least wished to see, after spending much of the ride thinking of the person she should least wish to marry, Thomas had to be at the very top.

'Thomas!' Phoebe returned, glaringly aware of his spotless frock coat and pantaloons. 'Fred didn't say you were coming.'

She swung a gritty smile back at Fred, who was opening and closing his mouth like one of Edward's toads.

'Indeed, I didn't *know* Thomas was joining us!' Fred

recovered, striding across the room. 'But they do say May is the month the fashionable set decamp to Bath… Or were the stakes a little deep at Whites last night?'

Thomas broke into a rare smile as his younger brother shook his hand, giving Phoebe a chance to prop herself up on her aunt's sturdiest chair.

'Thank you, Alfred, but as I am neither fashionable nor afraid of faro, your theories are wasted on me. I'm actually in town on business, and pleased to find you both together, if a little less so to know the nature of your diversion.'

'Aunt knew nothing!' Phoebe returned in a flash, determined to avoid any repercussions. 'And Fred merely followed to ensure my safe return from the park – I've missed the moor,' she added, on a quieter note.

'I'm pleased to hear Bath has had a positive effect on your health,' he returned, unusually buoyant. 'That was its purpose, after all. But as for missing the moor, well, you will need to develop some fortitude on that front, for I've come to confirm details of your happy news!'

He smiled then, and Phoebe realised she'd never really seen him smile properly, at least not in her direction. She stared, feeling the dread she'd been suppressing at her very core start to seep into her veins.

'Details?' she murmured, conscious of Fred's glance.

'Yes, the Earl of Cumberland and I enjoyed a very beneficial meeting last week, during which we agreed your dowry, your guest list and your personal effects. Everything will be small and in accordance with the earl's wishes for a low-key affair – he has little taste for society these days – but properly managed. Your betrothal will be placed in the *Bath Chronicle* and the *London Gazette*, as well as announced formally, and your wedding will take place at the end of the month. With regard to the formal announcement, and for the sake of ease, I have agreed to a swift presentation at the next Bath Assembly Ball.' He paused. 'May I be the first to offer you my felicitations, dear sister. I think Father would be most pleased indeed.'

Thomas's face then lit up with satisfaction, while Phoebe's stomach fell like a stone into her boots.

'But that's barely three weeks away,' she whispered, 'a *whole week* less … than I thought.'

'Indeed! Well, the earl was very generous in his praise of you after the Damerel dinner, and when you get to his age, there is little reason to wait, after all. He's in need of a son to inherit his title, as soon as possible of course, and I've assured him you are from excellent Fairfax stock!

Do not let Papa down on this, Phoebe. You are to be a countess, and your sisters will rely on you for introductions and husbands. Do I make myself clear? It is time for you to do your duty.'

Phoebe stared dully at her eldest brother, wishing with all her heart that she were Fred, standing by awkwardly, searching for words to make it better.

But, of course, he couldn't, Thomas was her legal guardian, and she was but a pawn in the world of men until she grew old and useless.

'Can I return to Knightswood, until the day?' she asked quietly, suddenly wanting nothing more than to ride on the moor, while she still could.

'I think not,' Thomas returned bluntly. 'I've made

arrangements for you and Sophie to attend the Assembly Ball next week in honour of the new King George, where you shall both be presented. I understand most of the haute ton will be there, and I will require you, Alfred, to ensure the Assembly Room patronages talk of no one else.'

'Capital!' Fred smiled nervously. 'There's nothing I enjoy more than spending time with ambitious mamas! By the time I'm done, not one of them will be in any doubt about the vivacious new countess who will be eclipsing their dull daughters in Almack's before the month is out!'

He threw Phoebe an anxious smile.

'You'll do no such thing,' Thomas returned, flicking an imaginary speck of dust from his sleeve. 'You will restrict your conversation to the quiet propriety of Phoebe's upbringing, and the earl's preference for an unaffected young lady who is not prone to fainting, dramas, or distraction by the politics of the day! Breeding, duty, and family commitment is all he requires, so there will be no more climbing trees, wild swimming, or indeed, riding at dawn! The earl wishes for a quiet life with his new bride, and that is what he shall get. Our family name depends upon it. I trust this is all understood, Phoebe?'

There was a brief silence while Phoebe recalled the morning she left Knightswood in Fred's clothing, never more certain that there was time for everything.

'Indeed, brother,' she returned icily. 'After all, you have been the very model of brotherly virtue, since you inherited our father's title.'

The words were out before she could stop them and, briefly, it seemed as though Fred shrank a little.

Thomas's eyes bulged.

'I thought I'd made myself perfectly clear, Phoebe,' he returned, 'but let me spell it out for you, anyway. You *will* marry the earl and you *will* be the obedient wife he wants and you *will* be grateful for it. My conduct, or the conduct of any of your brothers, is no matter for you. You're my sister and my ward, and this match was our father's dying wish, so for once in your life, you *will* obey me!'

He ground the words out as though engraving them, while a wave of wrath rose within Phoebe. Their father was a quiet, bookish man who'd shown little interest in society or its rules. Why he'd left such a wish in his will, she would never understand, and yet now it was her obligation for life – because of an old promise between two men who didn't even know her.

'Have no fear, brother,' she seethed, 'I will marry the earl, and do all that is required of me in the name of duty, but do not mistake it for obedience! I will do it to honour Father's promise – never for you!'

Then she swept from the room with a grace that belied her turmoil, leaving her brothers in silent awe.

Chapter Twenty-Two

Three weeks and lying to everyone until the wedding

'I'm almost grateful we weren't presented at the beginning of the season now,' Phoebe murmured, swirling her glass of steaming water. 'All the primping and preening, and dos and don'ts, just for an Assembly Ball in honour of the new King George – it's enough to give anyone the headache!'

'Almost as much as the gossip in the Pump Room!' Sophie added, gazing up at the statue of Beau Nash.

'Or the *mud water*!' Matilda interjected.

'Or the goddess Minerva!' Josephine added thoughtfully.

They all looked quizzically at their most bookish sister.

'I read *something* about there being an ancient Temple to the Roman goddess in these parts,' she clarified, 'possibly even beneath our feet!'

'You think the goddess Minerva is slowly poisoning us?' Matilda scowled, staring into her cloudy glass. 'Perhaps she disapproves of Phoebe's wedding as well!'

'Matilda!' Sophie hushed, glancing around.

'What? Harriet said the Roman goddesses loved blood sacrifices!' Matilda protested.

'That may be, but I'd hazard they also know what *secret* means!' Sophie retorted.

'Blood sacrifices apart, I'm very happy you're here today.' Phoebe smiled at Josephine, changing the subject. 'We'd all but given up hope of you being allowed.'

'Aunt gave me strict instructions not to cough!' Josephine rolled her eyes. 'Which is a lot trickier than it sounds.'

Phoebe nodded, eyeing her carefully. Josephine still hadn't recovered fully, and she couldn't help but wonder whether her sister should be out at all.

'I'll make you a honey tonic later,' she promised.

'When you're a countess, you'll be too important to make honey tonics!' Josephine replied, her eyes bruised with exhaustion.

Phoebe smiled to cover a dart of fear; it was true: no one knew her sister's affliction the way she did.

'I'll still have Sophie,' Josephine soothed, as if she could read Phoebe's mind, 'and we can write down all your top-secret tonics and tinctures before you leave, so we'll have plenty of remedies to try if we need them.'

'Well, I'll drink poisoned water to that,' Phoebe rallied. 'And who's to say you won't all be able to come and stay with me? I have it on excellent authority that the earl has several huge houses, and I think we should put them all to good use!'

'He might not like that!' Matilda mused. 'But, as a countess you can probably do exactly as you please – perhaps even chop off people's heads!'

'Matilda!' Sophie protested, while Phoebe and Josephine started to laugh.

'Who's losing their head? And for what crime?' a jovial voice interrupted, making them all look up.

'The earl – if he won't have us to stay!' Matilda returned, with a scowl.

'How lovely to see you, Captain Elliot!' Sophie exclaimed swiftly.

Phoebe looked at the captain in his spotless military uniform; his medals gleaming and his fair hair groomed into the latest fashion. He was a respected, upstanding officer – a veteran of Waterloo, no less – and yet he hid a secret that could change everything in a heartbeat. She might not know how two gentlemen could love one another, but a discreet enquiry had confirmed that the most severe penalty awaited, should such a relationship ever be discovered.

'Captain Elliot!' She smiled at him warmly.

He bent over her hand with his usual flourish, and yet she could sense a slight wariness, too. In a rush, she realised he must have heard Fred shout her name in the park, that he was wondering whether she knew his secret and would keep it, too. She met his gaze, certain there was a brief acknowledgement, before Matilda gasped.

'Of course! The captain can shoot the earl in a duel if he refuses to let us stay!' she exclaimed. 'Captain, please shoot the earl, then we can all move in permanently – Phoebe can look after Josephine, Sophie can design pelisses, and I…'

They all waited, their expressions ranging from delight to abject horror.

'And I can become a pirate!' she finished, triumphantly.

'Anyway, no one need be in the doldrums anymore because I have fixed it all!'

'Does Miss Sophie have aspirations in the … er … ladies' fashion industry?' Captain Elliot enquired, eyes dancing.

'Not yet, but she should!' Matilda grinned, attracting the disapproval of several mamas whose own delicate offspring were behaving with the utmost propriety. 'She is forever sketching the things, and Lord knows she talks about fashion enough!'

'That is quite enough, Matilda!' Aunt Higglestone exclaimed, bustling up next to them. 'I do apologise, Captain Elliot. Matilda is a very spirited child, with a lot of spirited ideas.'

'Not at all, Mrs Higglestone,' the captain replied gamely. 'A young lady with both spirit and ideas is very special indeed! Consider me at your disposal, General Matilda, your word is my command!'

Then he bowed as an unapologetic Matilda was whisked away, to endure one of Aunt Higglestone's longer monologues on appropriate conversational topics in the Pump Room.

'*One really should restrict oneself to the weather, and the health of the person with whom one is conversing,*' Josephine parroted with a giggle.

'Don't you start, Josephine Fairfax!' Sophie declared. 'It's bad enough the captain thinks we have one shameless villain in the family!'

'I would be disappointed if there weren't more!' The captain winked, making Sophie flush.

'It really is lovely to see you this morning, captain!' Phoebe insisted, wondering again if she was doing her sister any favours by withholding the truth.

He'd clearly perfected the art of distraction, perhaps with too little consideration for the effect of his attentions. She could only hope his unit would be recalled soon, and his absence would prove a gentle let down.

'How are you finding the waters?' she added.

'The waters, I confess, are the least of the attractions this morning,' he smiled.

'You're such an incorrigible flatterer, Captain Elliot.' Sophie giggled, tapping his forearm with her new French lace fan.

'Oh, the captain is certainly a flatterer!' a musical voice trilled. 'A flatterer and a jester, are you not, *sweet* Captain Elliot, no matter what idle gossipers might say.'

Phoebe frowned as Aurelia paused next to the captain.

'And Captain Elliot Damerel always keeps his admirers close to his heart, don't you, *dear* captain?' she added with a tinkling laugh. 'All *sorts* of admirers.'

'It is the best and most noble place to keep them!' Phoebe injected swiftly, aware the captain had gone unusually quiet.

'Indeed,' he nodded gratefully. 'A gentleman never divulges anyone's confidence. It would be most … dishonourable.' He bowed sombrely. 'Now, if you'll excuse me.'

'Lady Aurelia! How are you?' Sophie muttered, as the captain took his leave.

'Oh, I'm positively radiant!' Aurelia smiled archly, lifting her hand in a way that invited everyone to admire the emerald stone on her engagement finger.

'I am somewhat accustomed to the idea of being *promised* to the viscount, so our betrothal isn't exactly news. And we aren't to marry until my twenty-first birthday, of course, but he has been most attentive since the announcement.' She turned to Phoebe. 'Still, you know all about that, don't you, Phoebe? Now that your own special announcement is on the horizon?'

Her voice had softened, but there was no mistaking the subtle crow.

'Indeed,' Phoebe replied coldly. 'And I am most grateful I've not had to rely on the confidence of others to make it thus far.'

Aurelia stared for a second, before smiling slowly, showing her pearly white teeth.

'What a strange creature you are,' she murmured. 'I do hope you revise your manners once you're married, for the earl will surely expect his countess to behave better than a common actress!'

'Indeed, well I hope you revise your tongue when you're married, for a countess will surely expect a viscountess to show more respect!' Phoebe retorted.

'Phoebe,' Sophie whispered as Aurelia whitened, before reaching for the arm of a gentleman in conversation behind her.

It was already too late when Phoebe realised it was the viscount.

'Did you hear, Alexander?' Aurelia quizzed. 'Miss Fairfax believes I should curtsey and simper on account of her forthcoming nuptials.'

The viscount stared briefly, before appearing to collect himself.

'Those are the rules, Aurelia,' he replied abruptly. 'I

understand we will be addressing you as Countess before the month is out, Miss Fairfax. May I offer you my felicitations.' He nodded, avoiding her gaze. 'And now, if you will excuse me…'

Phoebe nodded, her chest hollowing as the viscount bowed and walked away, as indifferent as the day they met.

'These notorious rakes of the haute ton!' Aurelia sighed. 'It is such a skill to *retain* their attention – thankfully that is a role for which I've been preparing my whole life.'

Phoebe wondered if she was imagining the relief in her voice.

'What a sad prospect,' she replied, after a beat. 'For a girl to be prepared for life solely on the basis of the husband she will attract and marry? Far better she is prepared to think for herself, for the gentlemen I know rarely think beyond their own situation.'

'Oh, I am all in favour of thinking for oneself, as I'm sure you'll agree!' Aurelia retorted. 'But I'm also a realist. Society works a certain way, and we cannot change it. Any talk or behaviour to the contrary just makes a man vexed and, as we know, a vexed man is … unforgiving.'

She levelled her gaze straight at Phoebe, triumph in her eyes.

'I do not accept that the only way forward is deception,' Phoebe returned sharply. 'If we do not try to influence things for the better, how can we look for change? We will go on living this same meaningless existence—'

'It isn't meaningless if we're exactly where we wish to be, living exactly how we wish to live! Have I not explained this already?'

'All you have explained is a willingness to expose others to ridicule and danger!' Phoebe replied, her anger flaring. 'Because the hard, inescapable truth is, you're as trapped as the rest of us!'

She watched Aurelia's smile die with satisfaction.

'From the moment we met, you've done nothing but scheme and deride and undermine, and while I may not understand the extent of your disdain, I do know this – the one thing you long for, the thing that evades you during the day, and keeps you awake through the night, is the same for you as it is for all of us – your freedom!'

'No!' Aurelia hissed, making several mamas in the vicinity look up with interest. 'I've never wanted anything more than my birthright,' she defended furiously. 'In exchange, I will do those things that are required of a society wife – and in between, I will live my life exactly how I choose.

I fail to see how I could be freer!'

'Playing dubious parlour games? Spooking horses? Relying on strangers to help you with *spots of bother*?' Phoebe challenged, shrugging off Sophie's warning hand. 'Oh, yes, I can see why those adventures would capture any heroine's imagination! Tell me, when was the last time you made a *real* decision?'

'I have as much freedom as I want!' Aurelia fired back. 'If I wish to … race phaetons at dawn, I can and I will!'

'Done!' Phoebe glowered.

'Phoebe?' Sophie enquired nervously.

'Name the day!' Aurelia growled.

'A race to the death!' Josephine nodded approvingly, her eyes shining.

'Phoebe, I really think…' Sophie tried again.

'Sunday. Name the route!' Phoebe demanded.

'Pulteney Bridge, Great Pulteney Street, Sydney Gardens – finish at the Sydney Hotel,' Aurelia reeled off without drawing breath. 'A dawn meet and a fifty-pound stake, unless you wish to apologise! You forget, there is more than one way to win!'

Then she swept away, leaving Phoebe to Sophie's wide-eyed despair.

'Oh, Phoebe.' She shook her head. 'What if Thomas hears of it? Or the earl?!'

'They won't,' Phoebe seethed, lifting her chin. 'Besides, you heard Aurelia: it's a matter of honour now. She issued a challenge, and I can't not meet it.'

'When will you see that you don't have to *act* like a man, to know you are as courageous as one?' Sophie despaired. 'Especially when the stakes are so high? Aurelia's parents are members of the haute ton, with connections enough to hush anything up. But you? If this comes out, Thomas will cut you off – or worse! You're risking everything for someone who could fit all they know about heroism into a snuffbox! You must apologise, before it's too late.'

Chapter Twenty-Three

Two weeks, six days, and lying to herself until the wedding

'All I'm saying is that it's still not too late,' Sophie whispered, passing Phoebe another cool, wrung out cloth.

'You could write to her, say you never intended to offend, and that you both have extremely good reasons to avoid this madness. It's not as though you even own a phaeton for goodness' sake…'

They both paused as Josephine descended into a severe coughing fit that made her grip the coverlet until her knuckles whitened.

'Can you pass the honey and ginger?' Phoebe frowned, counting under her breath. 'Also, open the window and ask Cook for some wild garlic leaves … and, I think, send for Dr Kapoor. We need a second opinion this time.'

She gazed at Josephine's pale face, at the bluish tinge around her lips, and the cold beads of sweat around her hairline. She'd managed so many of Josephine's lung seizures, but this one had been brewing since the picnic, and her fever was more stubborn than any Phoebe had seen in a long while.

'What about Dr Cox?' Sophie frowned. 'He knows Josephine.'

'Dr insulate-everything-that-moves? No, I think we need fresh thinking. Could you write a note to Captain Elliot, perhaps? Ask him to contact Dr Kapoor, urgently? They're … good friends I believe.'

'Yes, of course.' Sophie's tired eyes lit up at the thought of having a legitimate reason to dash the captain a note at midnight. 'I'll go this minute… But Phoebe, please consider what I've been saying. Our presentation is at the Assembly Ball the night before the race. You should be waking up to flowers and congratulations, not a race to the death! Just imagine Thomas's wrath if he finds out. It's the very worst timing.'

Phoebe held the glass of tonic against Josephine's dry and cracked lips, before looking up.

'I imagine any wrath on Thomas's part will be entirely connected to whether or not I can still make the wedding,' she muttered, raising her eyebrows.

'Phoebe…'

'Dr Kapoor, Sophie,' Phoebe insisted. 'And anyway,' she added with a faint smile, 'I came to Bath seeking adventure; what better way to leave it than with a race in the name of freedom? Perhaps, one day, I might even consider myself heroic!'

'But you already are,' Sophie sighed, closing the door behind her.

Dr Kapoor came before dawn, and if Phoebe had suspicions as to how he was able to attend so swiftly, she kept them to herself. Josephine's breathing had worsened, and one look at Dr Kapoor's countenance was enough to know he was worried.

'Has she had consumption? Or pneumonia?' he asked rapidly, listening to her chest through a piece of apparatus that looked a lot like one of Uncle Higglestone's pipes.

'Consumption, when she was perhaps six years of age?' Phoebe murmured, holding her sister's limp hand. 'My memory of that time is sketchy, though I do recall her going to Brighton for a time to convalesce.'

Dr Kapoor nodded, examining Josephine's bloodshot eyes and counting her pulse.

'Your sister's shortness of breath has quite possibly been exacerbated by the fever, so we are battling both, so to speak.'

Phone nodded anxiously.

'But I do believe if we ease her breathing, her body can fight the fever. I see you have already opened a window,' he observed. 'And as you already know, I believe changing the air temperature can sometimes ease the lungs…'

She nodded again, suddenly bereft of words as she conjured a memory of Florence, struggling for breath.

'Fear makes mortals of us all, does it not, Miss Fairfax?' he murmured.

She raised her eyes to his, wondering if he was talking of Florence, or his own predicament, as she replayed the viscount's incandescent rage. Could it have been fuelled by her rejection in the garden? Or his own disbelief that he'd ever admired her?

'Have you tried steam to ease the laboured breathing? And does your aunt have anything like *Datura Stramonium* in the garden?'

Phoebe blinked at the doctor's gentle face, his dark eyes brimming with concern.

'Thorn apple,' he clarified. 'I would rather burn eucalyptus leaves, but I haven't seen too many eucalyptus trees in Bath.'

Phoebe smiled wanly.

'I don't know, but I know someone who will,' she returned, already halfway to the door.

Much to Phoebe's relief, Dr Kapoor remained until morning. Twice, they lifted Josephine from her bed to the open window, where she could gasp for air between coughing spasms and moments of lucidity, and once Phoebe thought they'd lost her completely.

The prescribed thorn apple turned out to be a weed Uncle Higglestone pulled from his peony borders and, without uttering a word, he pulled on his boots and procured more than enough for Dr Kapoor to burn for a week.

Slowly, it filled the room with a sweet, pungent scent that eased Josephine's fits.

'It relaxes the muscular fibres of the bronchia,' Dr Kapoor explained.

'You know how I feel, I love you and won't give you up on a maybe...'

She watched as the gentle doctor tended her sister, quite convinced that not only was he one of the most gifted doctors she'd ever known, but that he was also a good and kind man who deserved to live the life he wanted.

'Trying to freeze time … before life catches up.'

Did he fear it would, in the end?

Josephine's fever refused to abate for a further two days, and while Phoebe and Sophie had nursed their sister through episodes before, they both knew it was more serious this time.

'So much for Bath's healing waters!' Sophie scowled, sponging Josephine's listless arms again. 'The air and waters have done nothing for her! I think we should take her home.'

Phoebe agreed, but she also knew Thomas would insist she remain in Bath for her presentation and betrothal announcement, which would mean separation from Josephine at her most fragile. This she couldn't allow, and by the time her sister's delirium and breathing finally subsided, Phoebe felt she would willingly agree to a thousand weddings, if it meant her dearest bookish sister was spared any further illness.

'Stay close by, keep her warm and elevated and burn plenty of Datura Stramonium. I will call on the patient daily to check her progress.'

Dr Kapoor had proven to be as good as his word, supporting them all through the worst of Josephine's fever until the days and nights started to separate again, which had also hurried the approach of her betrothal announcement. And while her aunt could talk only of the Assembly Ball, Phoebe's thoughts were consumed by the phaeton race that followed.

Where one obtained a high-perch phaeton at very short notice was her most pressing challenge. There was no chance of appealing to Fred as he'd only blurt it to Thomas, and then she'd find herself garrisoned in some remote turret of

Knightswood. Which left one distinct option – and it was this idea that occupied her thoughts until she finally felt confident enough to leave Josephine in her aunt's hands, and retire to her own bedchamber.

6th May 1820

Dear Captain Damerel,

I trust this letter finds you and your family in good health?

I wanted to write to express my sincere gratitude for your assistance earlier this week.

Doctor Kapoor's knowledgeable counsel proved a critical turning point in Josephine's recovery, and my sisters and I cannot thank you enough for your prompt action.

It is therefore with some regret, that I must appeal to your generosity once again.

For reasons I cannot divulge, I find myself in need of a high-perch phaeton and pair this forthcoming Sunday morning. The phaeton needs to be in good repair, and the horses fresh, and I will, of course, have them returned to you long before your household is risen.

I understand you may not keep such equipage yourself, but wonder if you might have use of the stable at Damerel Place and therefore be able to borrow them…?

Phoebe paused, biting the end of her quill. It was one thing asking the captain for help, quite another to ask him to appropriate his brother's horses. And yet, there was nothing to be done, who else could she ask?

I cannot write more detail here, only assure you my intention is not to race to the coast and stowaway on the first pirate ship I find – though I'm sure you'll understand why such a life might appeal just now!

I thank you for your utmost discretion in this matter, and remain your faithful servant,

Miss Phoebe Fairfax

A response came within the hour.

Dear Miss Fairfax

I thank you for your letter.

First and foremost, I am most relieved to read Miss Josephine is making a good recovery, and have no doubt it is the result of the excellent care provided by yourselves, and my good friend, Dr Kapoor.

On the question of a phaeton and pair, please rest your concerns. I can procure and bring both to Wood Lodge just before dawn on Sunday. My brother keeps a good stable, and as long as we ensure their safe return before breakfast, no one shall be the wiser.

I must also confess to your hour of need coinciding with one of my own. However, I have given the matter a great deal of thought, and hope I do not prevail upon your good nature in so much as to offer a compromise, which may assist us both greatly in the future.

I believe you understand the nature of the esteem in which I hold Doctor Kapoor, and that others might not share the same understanding.

Furthermore, it has come to my attention that certain rumours are circulating among members of the ton that could damage, not only the career of both my esteemed friend and myself but also, the reputation of those around us. Indeed, such are the nature of these rumours, that I am left little choice but to refute them in the only way remaining – to marry.

While this may seem rash, I can assure you I have contemplated this course for some time, and would not unburden myself, except I am persuaded you are also in need of a friend.

It is with this in mind, that I venture to suggest that we assist one other. I cannot promise wealth, but I can promise you as much freedom as you wish, within the safe confines of my name. I also believe our natures to be entirely complementary, which would bode well for future companionship.

If you find yourself in agreement, please pack a light trousseau, and bring it on Sunday morning. We shall leave for the border the moment you have concluded your prior engagement – that's the Scottish border, and nothing to do with pirate ships which, I'm persuaded, would bring a whole new set of challenges!

Lastly, I must ask you not to share the contents of this letter whatever your decision, and to consign it to the fire, once read.

Your ever faithful friend,
Captain Elliot Damerel, Esq.

Phoebe sat beside the fire, staring at the captain's ornate lettering. He had such a handsome hand, one that captured his personality perfectly, with swirls and loops that echoed his sunny smile. Yet, as she knew only too well, appearances could be very deceiving. And now this – less a marriage of convenience, than one of escape. The captain may have worded his concerns lightly, but they both knew either the gallows or transportation could await, should his relationship be discovered.

A cold fear crept through her as she weighed up her choices.

Refusing the captain's proposal would save her family from social disgrace, yet she would have to live with whatever fate befell him and Dr Kapoor. Accepting would not only hurt her family, Sophie especially, but also create the very scandal she'd been seeking to avoid – while the viscount....

Phoebe's mind overflowed with images of the viscount, from the highwayman duel, to the library, to the picnic, to the way his dark eyes had glinted with a thousand fallen stars beneath the magnolia tree, to his rage in Florence's bedchamber, and then finally to his cold indifference at Prior Park and Pump Room.

She'd never known such an infuriating, arrogant, changeable man in all her life, so why she was even considering his view mystified her. Except that conjuring his face, and the moments they'd shared, sparked the most confused jumble of feelings in her core – a jumble that only seemed to worsen the longer she dwelt on them.

She scowled and forced his face from her mind. Perhaps you didn't have to like people to care for their view; perhaps it was all some strange fixation that would pass once she married.

Married.

And what of Papa's wish that she marry the earl? Could she live with her own family disgrace, to save the captain and Dr Kapoor from the gallows?

Did she have any choice?

Phoebe's head spun with too many questions she suspected had nothing at all to do with being heroic, and everything to do with being the worst kind of coward imaginable.

'Which perhaps, after all, is all I am,' she whispered before tossing the captain's letter onto the fire, where it flared momentarily, before crumbling to ash.

Chapter Twenty-Four

Two weeks and one royal presentation until the wedding

It turned out that considering an Assembly Ball presentation, a betrothal announcement, a dawn phaeton race and an elopement to the Scottish border, all within the same twenty-four-hour period, was enough to give anyone the headache, let alone the least heroic of them all.

'I have no idea why the captain should write to you, unless it was to offer his felicitations which, of course, I would understand as he is proper above all things.' Sophie frowned over a luncheon of sandwiches and cake. Carefully, she sliced off the crust of her sandwich and popped it in her mouth. 'I was the one to write the letter of urgency when Josephine had her excessively dramatic moment,' she continued, 'and I maintain, the only reason Dr Kapoor came so quickly – quite apart from his hippo… Hippo…'

'Don't recall a hippo?' Matilda interjected through a mouthful of almond cake.

'Hush, dear, don't speak of hippos with your mouth full,' Aunt Higglestone admonished.

'Oh, Lord…'

'Sophie!' her aunt warned.

'Don't recall any of those, either,' Matilda added, eye-spying her sister through a napkin ring.

'I was just trying to think of that promise doctors make?'

'The Hippocratic oath,' their uncle supplied, behind an article about nectar-rich honeysuckle.

'That's it!' Sophie exclaimed, stabbing another sandwich. 'That's what the captain called it. All doctors have to swear an oath, which obliges them to save lives, even in the middle of the night!' She sliced another crust off her sandwich and popped it into her mouth.

'How tiresome for doctors!' Josephine chimed, her hollowed eyes dancing.

Phoebe smiled to cover her anxiety. The idea of leaving Josephine while she was still in recovery was only outweighed by the fact that the captain would be far more understanding than the earl, if she needed to return.

'He wrote only to pass on his felicitations ahead of tonight's announcement,' she mumbled, over a pastry broken into so many pieces that no one noticed she hadn't eaten a crumb.

Briefly, she imagined her betrothal announcement at the Ball and closed her eyes. All those congratulations to get through, all that scrutiny by ambitious mamas, only to sneak out at dawn for a race of honour, followed by an elopement scandal that Thomas would never forgive.

She still couldn't believe she'd made up her mind to accept, and yet what real choice did she have? The captain and Dr

Kapoor were in grave danger, and she would never forgive herself if something happened and she could have prevented it.

'Is that all?' Sophie jibed, prodding her sister in the ribs, before selecting a thin slice of fruit cake. 'I was merely asking because I couldn't see the letter when I looked in your dressing table.'

'Sophie!' Phoebe exclaimed, while Josephine and Matilda fell about laughing.

'Sophie, dearest, it really isn't polite to look for or read Phoebe's letters without her permission,' their aunt reprimanded, fanning herself. 'And in truth, I'm sure both of you have a few other matters to consider just now, such as your formal presentation in a few hours? Oh, my dears, whatever would your dear mama and papa say if they were here? Your uncle and I are so proud of you!'

She beamed then, before turning her misty-eyed gaze on her husband, who grunted his assent, having moved onto a literary discussion on the benefits of hive-keeping.

Phoebe inhaled deeply, certain that whatever their dear parents might have said on the matter, would have been entirely retracted come morning.

Phoebe stared at her reflection in the Higglestone's coach window, barely recalling the tree-climbing, adventure-bound girl she'd left behind in Devon.

Instead, she looked every inch a young society debutante on the cusp of marital success. Her dress was in the very latest fashion; an ivory gown with a silk net overlay and a satin trim embroidered with tiny trailing rosebuds, while its puffed sleeves and whole skirt had just the right amount of fullness.

It was altogether a very romantic affair and even she had to admit that with her hair twisted up in the cover-style of *La Belle Assemblée*, no one would think her the least bit capable of brandishing a parasol as a sword. She turned to Sophie, a Pre-Raphaelite vision in white, and sparkling at the prospect of having her own presentation brought forward by a year.

'I suppose having an *almost countess* in the family brings its privileges,' she whispered, adjusting one of Phoebe's cascading ringlets. 'You look beautiful this evening, Phoebs,' she added, pulling her sister into a brief hug. 'I'm so proud to call you my sister.'

Phoebe returned the gesture, blinking fiercely. This was the night that would change everything and set her on a path from which there would be no return. Once she left town in the company of Captain Elliot, she would be considered compromised by most of the polite world, and her marriage would merely save her sisters from similar ruin.

She held Sophie a moment longer, knowing her plan was also going to create a rift that even time would struggle to heal. She was certain her sister's real affections were not engaged for the captain, and yet she also knew her elopement to the border would feel a bitter disloyalty. She could only hope that, in time, Sophie would understand.

'Now, then, my dears,' their aunt began, seated opposite, 'while this isn't St James's Palace, it *is* the Upper Assembly Ballroom, and from what I understand, King George likes to enjoy himself at these affairs. Your presentation is a little late in the season, but he has made an exception given Phoebe's imminent marriage to the earl. He will likely say little during your actual presentation, but if he does, just smile and offer polite commentary about the local sights, or waters. And for goodness' sake, let there be no mention of mud! If the conversation falters, you can always offer a short compliment about Brighton Pavilion.'

'We've never been!' Sophie objected.

'Neither have we, my dear, and by all accounts, it's quite monstrous, but you mustn't say that to the king! Now, then, let us make haste. Your uncle is to wait with your brothers, and you are to be presented as soon as the Ball gets underway. You really are quite privileged, my dears.'

Phoebe followed their aunt through the Assembly Ball crush, which was no surprise given the imminent arrival of His Majesty, wondering how Sophie could look so serene. Briefly, she wondered if anyone would miss her if she escaped into one of the quieter rooms for a while, but every way she turned there was another ambitious mama and her dutiful daughter or son, wishing her well.

Finally, Thomas and Fred loomed into view in the corner of the ballroom, engaged in conversation with Uncle Higglestone. Thomas stepped forward to greet them, a smug smile pinned to his face, and her spirits sank even lower.

'Ah, there she is, the young lady of the hour!' he pronounced, holding a brandy glass aloft. 'I must admit to having doubts you would ever know your duty, Phoebe, but tonight you exceed even my expectations. You look quite the dazzling debutante!'

He smiled then, his teeth glinting in the candlelight.

'Like a countess to be!' her uncle added in a rare moment of presence, taking two glasses of champagne from a passing footman.

'Indeed she does, Mr Higglestone!' Her aunt beamed, accepting one of the proffered glasses. 'I was only saying so this morning – Phoebe has just the right fortitude and spirit for life as a countess. I'm sure her dear mama would have—'

'That's the herald!' Fred interrupted, flashing Phoebe a glance of intense sympathy. 'I think His Majesty may have arrived!'

'Oh, my dears, oh my dears,' Aunt Higglestone mumbled, fanning herself with a new lilac broderie fan, purchased especially for the occasion.

Phoebe could never understand how anything with so many holes could provide any useful service, but forced a smile as Sophie slipped her arm through her own. She squeezed it momentarily, conscious this moment was as important to her sister, as it was doom-laden for her.

'Viscount Damerel, Captain Elliot Damerel…' proclaimed the Assembly Room announcer. 'The Marchioness Carlisle and Lady Aurelia Carlisle.'

'Witness the predators stalking their prey!' Sophie whispered, beaming in the captain's direction.

Fred smirked, but Phoebe's thoughts were elsewhere entirely, consumed by the viscount's glance through the crowds, his eyes dark, his face devoid of warmth, just as it had been at Prior Park. A dull flush crept across her cheeks as she pulled her gaze away, only to lock eyes with the captain, his usual carefree manner replaced with something far more sombre. He nodded briefly, before following his brother into the main Assembly Room.

'No Doctor Kapoor?' Sophie mumbled, confused by the captain's brief acknowledgement. 'Do you think he has been called up by his regiment? Perhaps the captain has received news, too…?' Her voice trailed off uncertainly as the marchioness and Aurelia paused beside them.

'Mrs Higglestaff, and the *lively* MissesFairfaxes!' the marchioness pronounced, her vulturous gaze running over their debutante dresses. 'How lovely it is to see you all, but then, one is rarely allowed to miss you… I see you've been keeping Madame Paragon busy, and French silk is always *such* a gamble. Do enjoy your evening!'

'Thank you … it's Higgle*stone*,' their aunt murmured faintly as the marchioness moved on.

'I trust you're in fine spirits, Miss Fairfax.' Aurelia paused behind the marchioness, her china-doll eyes gleaming. 'It could be a long night!'

'Indeed, I am!' Phoebe forced brightly. 'There's nothing I like so well as an evening of adventure, especially if it brings forth a victory.'

A strange smile played around Aurelia's lips.

'One can hardly be ignorant of your impending announcement, Miss Fairfax – and it's such a relief your brother can finally consider your papa's gambling debt settled, too!'

Phoebe paused, feeling as though the room had suddenly shrunk a little.

'Oh! Don't tell me *you didn't know*?' Aurelia exclaimed artlessly. 'I thought someone must have told you by now?

After all, it has been an open secret among the ton these past twenty years…'

A dull pulse began to thud in Phoebe's ears as Aurelia shook out her fan, and tittered.

'I believe you were a stake in faro, or some such thing?'

'That's impossible!' Sophie replied scornfully. 'Papa didn't gamble!'

'Oh, I'm talking about long before you were born, when he and my mother were betrothed.'

This time both sisters paused.

'La! Does no one tell you poor country mice anything?' Aurelia purred. 'Well, you see, your papa and my mother were quite the love match – quite unbelievable, isn't it – until my grandparents put an end to it. And by all accounts, your papa was as much a gambling man as any, if not worse. He and the earl considered themselves true *Corinthians*, my mother says, living life to every excess including gambling for the highest stakes! It's why your papa married an heiress and retired to the country – he had no choice. But not before he gambled away the hand of his first-born daughter to his best friend, the earl, should he ever choose to marry. Looks like the earl decided it was time to call in his oldest debt!'

There was a moment's shocked silence, while Aurelia glittered with triumph. Then she swept away, leaving Phoebe to stare after her, entirely bereft of words.

'Take no notice,' Sophie whispered fiercely, 'she's provoking you ahead of the race, nothing more.'

Phoebe nodded, wanting to believe Sophie with all her heart and yet knowing, *somehow*, that every word Aurelia had spoken was true.

Apart from anything else, it made so much sense: Papa's dying wish, Thomas's insistence she honour it, the earl's ease with the arrangement – he had owned her all her life, after all – and the looks of sympathy she'd detected among senior members of the ton, too, those old enough to recall the rash promise of a young gambling rake.

Nausea climbed into her throat as she acknowledged Papa's will had contained not so much a dying wish, as an old gambling record. She was a debt recovered, no more.

Could anyone be any less heroic in their whole life?

'He's here, he's here.'

A mutter of excitement filled the air as four footmen, clad in gold-embossed violet, entered the lobby. Phoebe swallowed, her scattered thoughts overwhelmed by the fuss around her.

'It's time, my dears.' Aunt Higglestone bustled forward, entirely oblivious to the drama that had just played out.

'Remember, heads up, eyes down, speak only when spoken to and no mention of mud!'

Phoebe soon discovered that being presented to the king was rather akin to having a tooth drawn. There was a great deal of agonised waiting, for a short consultation that delivered immediate relief once it was all over.

And King George IV was the most ostentatious person Phoebe had ever encountered in her life. Tall, rotund, and with his silver locks brushed into a style of which Beau Brummell himself would have been proud, he oozed charm, fine jewels and an old rakish demeanour that made Phoebe feel distinctly grateful for his short dialogue, which comprised four words only.

'*Ah, the Fairfax girl!*'

Which left her in no doubt whatsoever that the king was *also* aware of past events that had brought her whole sorry existence to this point. And it was this burning thought that ensured she escaped his interest as swiftly as possible, and watched Sophie's far more graceful presentation from a quiet corner of the Upper Assembly Room.

'You're in luck today,' a voice murmured behind her. 'I've heard the king is still in a temper with Princess Caroline, and isn't in the mood for long interviews.'

Phoebe inhaled silently, and kept her eyes trained forward.

'He looks as though he's in mourning,' she managed, despite the twist in her core.

The viscount stepped out of the shadows, downing the rest of his brandy.

'Those aren't mourning clothes. Beau Brummell told him he looked better in dark colours, and he hasn't worn anything else since. As I was saying, he detests Princess Caroline, offered her everything so she would stay out of the country. But she's returned, anyway… One would hope marriage would result in a rather less fractious state of affairs.'

Phoebe's eyes flickered up to meet the viscount's intense stare.

'I'm aware their marriage isn't exactly a love match,' she returned.

A small satirical smile played across his lips, gold flecks glinting in the low light.

'Does such a thing exist within the confines of Almack's and the Pump Room?' he quizzed.

She stared at his unflinching expression before pulling her gaze back to Sophie, who was conversing quite comfortably with His Majesty. In the same breath, she caught sight of the Earl of Cumberland, clad in striped pantaloons, and a grotesque mustard waistcoat, on the opposite side of the room.

'It would appear not.' She exhaled. 'One can hardly blame Princess Caroline for pursuing some happiness of her own.'

'And what of *your* happiness, Miss Fairfax?'

She glanced up and it was there, weighing the air between them, a draw so strong she wanted nothing more than to ignore the world and everyone else in it.

But what good were brief, fractured thoughts that couldn't be expressed or acted upon? They meant nothing, trapped in time forever, like his fevered declaration beneath the magnolia tree.

Was he thinking about that, too?

'I've been meaning to apologise,' he muttered in a low voice, 'for my behaviour… It was unforgivable.'

Phoebe stared, wondering for which part he was apologising.

'I wouldn't call it—' she started.

'It was unforgivable,' he repeated. 'Dr Kapoor has made it abundantly clear that you saved Florence's life that night, and I should have thanked you – wholeheartedly – not berated you. By some small way of recompense, I have offered to fund his research into Asthma Therapy, if the army will agree to a period of leave.'

'I… Thank you!' Phoebe flushed in genuine shock. 'That

means a great deal, and I'm sure Dr Kapoor is honoured,' she added, wondering if the viscount was also aware of the rumours about the doctor and his brother.

'If I may be permitted any defence, Miss Fairfax, it is only that I am somewhat coloured by experience. We have come close to losing Florence through lung afflictions so many times, I have become somewhat overprotective. But then it is in my nature, you see. When I care, I care too much.'

Phoebe nodded, a strange sensation threading through her tense limbs.

Of course she understood, didn't she have the same instinctive fire when Matilda slipped into the canal at Sydney Park, when Josephine was struggling to breathe, or even when she herself was preparing to bruise Sophie's heart?

It was love – wrongly guided at times – but love all the same.

'So, I mean it when I say I am indebted to you, Miss Fairfax. And while I will not plague you with unwanted attentions again, my services remain yours to call upon – whenever they are needed.'

She caught her breath and all at once they were back in the garden, gold flecks burning, lips shaping words she longed to believe with all her heart.

And yet she was bound by the reckless promise of a dead man, and he to the most duplicitous girl of her aquaintance. He was in no position to offer anything, and suddenly she could no longer bite her tongue.

'How can I believe anything you say? One moment you're making the wildest proclamations, the next you're treating me like a common criminal! You interfere, judge, tell me I'm all manner of disrespectful things and then claim I've stolen your peace? And all before behaving as though we're veritable strangers again! You are the most confusing person I've ever known!'

'I found you in your corset and petticoats, backstage at the Theatre Royal! With a powdered wig upon your head!' the viscount returned, tautly.

'That was my hair!'

'Really! What of fighting a highwayman in your brother's breeches? Dangling after one of Elliot's unit? Riding under the influence of noxious substances or engaging in a common brawl with a bevy of actresses – all while secretly engaged to the Earl of Cumberland! – and *I'm* the confusing one? I may not have always behaved perfectly, Miss Fairfax, but I hope I have, at least, behaved with honour!'

His face was etched in shadows, as though his words were costing him deeply. Phoebe drew a deep breath, her head swimming with the many times in which the viscount's behaviour hadn't been in the least bit honourable and furious that she couldn't even begin to defend her own.

'I thank you for your offer, sir,' she returned in a clipped tone, forcing her gaze across the room at the ridiculous earl. 'But I find myself quite content.'

It was, without any doubt, the biggest untruth she'd ever told.

He scowled then, the muscle in his cheek working overtime, just as they were interrupted.

'There you are!' Aurelia exclaimed with a rehearsed giggle, slipping her arm through his.

It was a gesture that conveyed everything, and the viscount's face shuttered instantly.

'Congratulations, Miss Fairfax, on finally being able to attend balls and soirées, without fear of forcible ejection by the society mamas,' Aurelia tittered. 'Though I do suspect you enjoy all the drama!'

She took a sip of her sweet-scented negus, before wobbling slightly.

'Are you feeling quite well, Lady Carlisle?' Phoebe returned pointedly.

'Oh, I've never felt better.' She giggled again, leaning into the viscount who straightened instantly. 'And I'm sure Alexander will escort me for some air in a moment. We've set our wedding date, have you heard?'

Phoebe shot a glance at the viscount's heavily veiled eyes and, while she knew it to be inevitable, an unexpected dart buried itself somewhere between her corset and bones.

'My congratulations to you both, I'm sure you will complement each other exceptionally well,' she managed, before executing the briefest of curtsies. 'Do excuse me.'

It turned out that negus was excellent at taking the edge off everything, which was just as well as the earl chose to claim her hand for the next two dances. He was already alarmingly purple, and just when she thought several of his gold filigree, waistcoat buttons must forcibly eject themselves from his straining person, a voice intervened with all the timing of a real hero.

'Excuse me, sir, but I do believe Miss Fairfax promised the waltz to me. I humbly beg your pardon for depriving you of such a fair partner, but if rumours are correct you will have a great many dances to look forward to, while I shall likely die alone in my barracks, with only the rats for company.'

'Poppycock!' the earl huffed, before passing Phoebe's hand over, and making for the nearest tray of brandy.

The captain executed one of his most flamboyant bows, while Phoebe smiled with gratitude. He really was the most amiable, ridiculous gentleman, and she hoped her nerves weren't as visible as they felt.

'Good evening, Miss Fairfax,' Captain Elliot murmured, raising her hand to his lips. 'Might I be so bold as to venture that you look quite enchanting tonight – I do believe I may be forced to elope with you.'

His last words were uttered so faintly that only Phoebe could hear them as he led her through the lilting music. She swallowed, a faint flush spilling across her cheeks.

'Appearances can be quite deceptive, sir,' she murmured, 'you might learn to regret such a rash action.'

'And yet my instincts tell me otherwise,' he returned, raising his eyebrows in a way that reminded her only of the viscount.

She caught her breath, just as she became aware of Sophie's stare across the floor. It was a look that reached into her bones, and silently she berated herself, willing the musicians to finish. It was enough that she was stealing away with the captain at dawn, the last thing she wanted was to create any memories that rubbed salt in the wound.

As they waltzed through the steps, Phoebe thought briefly of the letters she'd written and entrusted to Josephine's care earlier, begging her confidence until the appointed hour the following day. Thomas, her aunt and uncle, Sophie, Matilda, and even the earl had one. Each charted a very swift love affair with Captain Elliot that had proven impossible to resist, despite her approaching nuptials. Each entreated the recipient to forgive her, and to know she'd acted as rationally as love had allowed. They were the only words she could find to explain what she already knew to be inexplicable, and in the end there was only one person remaining.

Papa.

She could tell herself there was honour in saving the captain and Dr Kapoor, even that her sisters would understand in time, but there was no escaping the damage to Papa's memory. A debt was a matter of honour, and a debt unpaid was a scandal that could affect them all.

Yet the captain hadn't exaggerated about the growing rumours, either. She'd already noticed the stares and whispers of a particular group of society mamas. They were the patrons and rule makers, the matrons who could make or break a debutante in a breath, while their husbands ran the banks, the army, and the courts. There would be little mercy for someone like the captain, despite his family name, and Phoebe was sure Aurelia had helped stir suspicions.

'Oh, the captain is certainly a flatterer! A flatterer and a jester, are you not, sweet Captain Elliot, no matter what idle gossipers might say.'

It would be just like Aurelia to think she could get rid of family members she disliked, particularly if they knew too much about her own misdoings.

Phoebe inhaled deeply, the captain's only hope was to convince the gossips that theirs was a true love match, while hers was that they would be forgiven – in the end.

Finally, the waltz slowed, and the room hushed as the king got to his feet.

'Much as I dislike to interrupt merriment of any kind.' He paused to acknowledge some polite laughter. 'It falls to me to share some *celebratory* news with you all.'

Phoebe glanced up at the captain, whose face shuttered as he bowed and offered his arm. She took it, and let him escort her back to Thomas, with dread coiling in the pit of her stomach.

'It pleases me greatly to announce there is to be a wedding – at last – in the House of Cumberland!' King George continued.

He paused to raise his glass, as the earl rose from his seat.

'It is not every day that such an *old* '—he paused for laughter—'and distinguished house chooses to venture into the state of matrimony – and while it has taken you far too long, Clarence, I'm sure everyone here will join me in wishing you great joy and many offspring!'

The room erupted into a blur of spontaneous clapping, while Phoebe accepted the felicitations of those nearest with a dazed nod.

Clarence? Why, above all things, was she surprised that this was how she'd hear the earl's first name? And why wasn't she surprised that it suited his purple face so very well?

'Where was your name?' Sophie demanded, in thinly veiled annoyance.

Her words echoed as Phoebe glimpsed her entire life reflected in the sea of jubilant faces surrounding her. Had it really all been leading to this? A wedding announcement that didn't even include her name? It was laughable – almost.

273

The earl raised his glass, not even looking in her direction, as those nearest him clustered around, eager to be the first to offer their congratulations.

And all the while, the viscount just watched from the shadows.

'Congratulations, my dear, the Countess of Cumberland to be!' Her aunt fussed as a wall of society matrons closed in, claiming their right to inspect the match of the season.

'Now, the announcement wasn't all that terrible, was it?'

'It wasn't, Aunt,' she agreed, with a hollow smile. 'It really was *quite* unremarkable.'

Two weeks and two moments of real note.

By the time carriages were called, Phoebe had danced a great many dances with a great many more titled gentlemen than she cared to know. And it struck her, as she waltzed beneath the extravagant candelabras, that there were only two moments of real note in any girl's life. The first was her birth and the second was her wedding. At both these moments, females were afforded a degree of importance – the former because she might actually be a man, and the second because she was marrying one.

And even though she was escaping one *marriage de convenience*, she was well aware it was only into a less constrained one. Phoebe thought of the captain's smart military coat, with its brass buttons and medals polished until they gleamed, just like him. He'd polished himself brightly to make sure no one saw beneath his sunny disposition – to protect himself – and now he would be as imprisoned as she.

The viscount's proud face followed swiftly, his gold-flecked eyes narrowing while her stomach coiled and chest ached for no reason she could understand at all. She swallowed, reminding herself to smile as the earl's chaise rattled past their coach window. His family coat of arms gleamed with an archaic right, projecting the sort of confidence that could only be gleaned though a thousand years of approval.

Could she really hope to run from it?

'Well, I can't say I've ever felt prouder!' her aunt gushed again, as soon as they were settled. 'A presentation and betrothal announcement by King George himself! I'm not sure even your uncle really expected that, did you, dear?'

Uncle Higglestone grunted his surprise into his faithful copy of the *Bath Chronicle and Weekly Gazette*, and for once Phoebe was grateful for his lack of interest. She already knew her dawn race and elopement would cast her out from polite society, but her aunt's pride only made her impending fall from grace even worse.

'I still think the king could have mentioned Phoebe by name,' Sophie murmured. 'I mean, the earl could be marrying his favourite horse, for all anyone knows!'

'Hush now, dear, we must remember it is the earl's name that matters most in this matter. While the Fairfaxes are a distinguished family of the ton, the House of Cumberland can trace its roots back to William the Conqueror!'

Phoebe glanced at Sophie, who seemed a little quiet. She was still conscious of her sister's watchful gaze during her waltz with the captain and longed to tell her the truth, yet to do so would mean trusting her with a fragile plan that could result in the captain's arrest, should it become widely known.

She laced her fingers tightly, the thought of hurting her sister was suffocating, and yet it was far better she found out with everyone else. She could only hope Sophie ensured news of her elopement *did* reach the ears of a certain earl – and that it persuaded him to wash his hands of all Fairfaxes forever.

'Are you okay?' Sophie whispered, reaching out to hold her hand.

'I am now,' Phoebe returned, savouring her warmth.

Chapter Twenty-Five

One week, six days, and one dawn flight until the wedding

A veil of darkness shrouded Bath's pretty skyline as Phoebe rose and gazed from her bedchamber window. Reluctantly, she turned to eye her small trousseau of essentials, unable to help comparing it to the portmanteau she'd packed when heading to London nearly three months before. A rueful smile passed across her lips as she conjured Effie's and Flora's faces. What would they say if they could see their *poor gentl'man* now? Preparing for a dawn phaeton race, and scandalous elopement, no more than three hours after a betrothal announcement by King George himself? It was a lot even by her standards, yet by the time the viscount's phaeton appeared at the top of the hill, like a ghostly apparition, she was ready.

Silently, she crept through the still house, brushing each of her sisters' bedchamber doors with her fingertips as she passed. There was a muffled cough when she reached

Josephine's door and, momentarily, she hesitated. Her quietest sister had looked so pale when she took the letters yet there was no more time, someone would hear if Josephine worsened – they had to.

She forced herself on before she could change her mind, down the modest stairwell and along her aunt's quiet mahogany hall, pausing only to gaze at a miniature portrait of her youthful mama and papa. They were picnicking amid a carpet of bluebells in Knightswood's grounds, and briefly she stared, wondering if they'd ever discussed Papa's debt.

Would they understand her course now? Or think her foolish for embarking on the most foolhardy escapade of her life?

'A young lady needs a certain air of fragility about her person – not ruddy cheeks and splinters.'

Didn't they know looks could be deceiving?

She dragged her gaze from theirs, before picking up a cherry-velvet ribbon on the hall table. It was one of Matilda's favourites and somehow, the stretch of soft material gave her a surge of strength. Of all her sisters, Matilda would understand best.

'Captain, please shoot the earl, then we can all move in permanently!'

She tucked it inside her riding habit as she made her way to the door.

'We can all be heroic in big and small ways, loud and quiet, if we so wish,' Josephine echoed.

'Lord, Phoebs, I agree we deserve to have as many adventures as our brothers,' Sophie added.

'Perhaps one day, you won't all think me the very poorest heroine of them all,' Phoebe whispered, blinking fiercely.

Then she turned the key and slipped out into the waiting dawn.

Captain Elliot Damerel was as good as his word, and if the sight of the viscount's high-perch phaeton and noble greys forced her stomach into her boots, the presence of the captain provided a balance of relief.

'I was worried you might change your mind,' he murmured, striding forward to take her trousseau.

She gazed up into his anxious chestnut eyes, and wondered again at the twist of fate that had brought their lives to this dawn crossroads, at the top of a quiet hill, in Bath.

'A Fairfax never changes her mind!' she rallied, with effort.

He nodded, and for the first time she realised it was already far worse for him.

He was in love with someone he could never have.

'I will expect nothing from you,' she reassured, feeling a rise of heat across her face. 'Your life can continue as it always has – I will consider myself a … companion only.'

His relief was palpable as he caught her hand and raised it to his lips.

'As I will make no demands of you,' he promised, reading her mind. 'Though I cannot offer my whole heart, I do care for you, Phoebe, and I will do everything in my power to make your life as comfortable as possible.'

Phoebe exhaled, both relieved and oddly hollowed by his words.

'There are so many things I would like to tell you … to show you.'

She closed her eyes as the viscount's face swam before her eyes and she knew now she was destined never to know to what he had been referring.

'Dr Kapoor?' she enquired.

'Will remain here until he is recalled to the regiment,' the captain returned, a shadow darkening his face. 'His continued presence will assist in quelling the rumours.'

Phoebe nodded.

'I think, once we send news of our wedding, we would also do well to rejoin the regiment. My commanding officer is a generous sort of fellow, and will likely overlook the scandal if I accept a tour abroad. You will be quite safe with me, Phoebe. And, once things have died down here, we will return and live quietly. I'm sure my brother will assist us as much as he can.'

She forced a smile as he handed her into the high-perch phaeton, and rounded the equipage to climb up. To his credit, he sounded almost confident, yet as he encouraged the spirited horses forward, Phoebe was far less certain. Despite the captain's optimism, they both knew there was a strong chance the king would declare them exiles, and then anyone with any care for their own social standing would give them as wide a berth as possible.

'I won't pry into the nature of your engagement this morning,' he murmured, as the greys made light work of Bath's quiet roads. 'Only bid you to take care. I'll be at the corner of Pulteney Street in an hour's time. From there we can drive straight to the Great North Road, and change horses at the first coaching inn. I'll send word to Alexander then, too. Unless … you're tempted to leave now?' he finished, on a wistful note.

'I am,' Phoebe conceded, sensing how much he needed to be away. 'But Aurelia's challenge is a matter of honour, and I can't leave town without meeting her.'

'That, I understand.' He nodded.

Phoebe exhaled, there was only so much dishonour one family name could take.

Silently, she ran through the race route: *Pulteney Bridge, Great Pulteney Street and around Sydney Gardens. Finish at the Sydney Hotel.* The viscount's phaeton and greys, racing against the viscount's betrothed. How the haute ton would enjoy the scandal if they knew.

'I'll meet you on the bridge in one hour,' she promised. 'They seem fresh,' she added, as the viscount's horses strained against the captain's careful rein.

'They're high spirited, and need only the lightest touch,' he said. 'I won't insult you by asking if you can handle them,' he added, with a rueful smile.

'It's the sort of question that got me into this situation in the first place!' she retorted, before they both started to laugh, and by the time the Gothic facade of Bath Abbey rose up before them, Phoebe was feeling much more herself.

'Pulteney Bridge in one hour,' the captain repeated, as he handed over the reins and climbed down.

'What will you do?' she asked, sensing the greys' eagerness to be off.

'What does anyone do, in a beautiful city, at four-thirty in the morning?' he returned with a brief return of his dancing eyes.

'Oh!' Phoebe breathed. 'Then please, pass on my best regards and bid him … take care of my sisters.'

'You can depend on it.' The captain bowed.

Then she lowered the reins, and let the greys spring forward.

The drive to Pulteney Bridge was shorter than Phoebe anticipated, and surprisingly pleasant, too. There was something calming about having the streets of Bath to herself at this hour, and the viscount's horses seemed to share her brief sense of escape; tossing back their manes, picking up their hooves, and pulling her effortlessly towards the bridge, while echoes of her argument with Aurelia reached out of every house she passed.

Phoebe scowled. She hadn't exactly spared her words, but then Aurelia had been determined to ruin her from the moment they met. Briefly, she racked her brain, thinking over every meeting and conversation from the Assembly Room, to the picnic, to the theatre, to Aurelia's frequent interruptions whenever she happened to be conversing with the viscount…

She caught her breath, the Bath-stone buildings suddenly merging.

'I have never betrayed your confidence except in frank admiration of a young woman who appeared unafraid of anything. If I spoke too freely, it's because I've never met anyone quite like you.'

They were the viscount's words, spoken beneath the magnolia tree, the night of the masked ball. She hadn't made much of them then, but could he have *somehow* given Aurelia a different impression?

Her chest thumped as the start of the bridge rose into view, revealing a pretty white phaeton and pair of chestnuts, tossing their heads impatiently. Their driver glanced back, a dark scowl twisting her china-doll face and Phoebe's suspicions doubled.

'Oh, how droll you are… I can almost see why the viscount finds you so entertaining!'

Phoebe inhaled raggedly. Surely she was just the hare-brained simpleton he found fighting a highwayman on a country road, *nothing more*?

And yet, what did any of it matter now, anyway?

The race was on.

Chapter Twenty-Six

One week, six days, and a race of honour until the wedding

'Are those not Alexander's horses? And phaeton, too?' Aurelia demanded, her eyes narrowing.

Phoebe felt a brief moment of satisfaction. Let Aurelia think what she wanted, she could hardly expect Phoebe to borrow a farm gig, when everyone knew she owned one of the fastest lightweight phaetons in Bath.

'The Damerels are generous!' she nodded coldly.

'A race, in the name of freedom, reliant on a borrowed phaeton?' Aurelia muttered scornfully.

'A race, in the name of freedom, won on a borrowed phaeton!' Phoebe retorted.

Aurelia stared, before turning her horses about.

'It's no matter to me, anyway. Let's get this done. I have a wedding-dress fitting this morning…'

'Wait,' Phoebe demanded, as she drew alongside Aurelia's

lightly sprung equipage. 'Tell me, why did you *really* want to meet me?'

Aurelia stared for a second before tipping her head back and laughing.

'La, what a simpleton you are!' She exhaled when she could, a curious smile spreading across her face. 'You know, I've endured stories about you all my life. Your papa's exploits, his charms, his loss of fortune, his fall from grace, and of course, my personal favourite, his swift marriage to the rich heiress, which broke my mother's heart. So, when Alexander mentioned his chance encounter with one of their offspring on the Bristol Road – fighting a highwayman, no less! – and how he'd never met a pluckier or more courageous girl...' She paused, her eyes glinting as Phoebe felt the last piece of the jigsaw fall into place. 'Well, you can imagine his tale, while *excessively diverting*, didn't exactly fill me with the same excitement.'

'You see, I know your kind, Phoebe. You're as able as any gentleman, but are denied the same education. So instead, you read a few pamphlets, listen to a few speeches, and think yourself the first feminist in Regency England! Well, trust me, you aren't! We *all* want more! But when the rules are set, we have to win by wit and stealth instead.'

'Rules are only set if you allow them to be!' Phoebe threw in, conscious the horses were straining. 'And change doesn't come from hiding the fact we're just as curious and capable as our brothers. I've said it before, we want the same things! And you can't hold me responsible for something that happened to your mother thirty years ago.'

Aurelia rolled her eyes.

'Don't worry, I'm not *that* churlish!' she scoffed. 'But I did promise myself I would *never* let any man affect me in the same way.'

Phoebe stared as a strange smile crept across Aurelia's face.

'Don't think I haven't seen the way you are with the viscount, your eyes as round as the moon. You're in love with him! It's as plain as a pikestaff! And in truth, I care not, because it only proves that for all your silly talk of adventuring and equality you're no better than any of us! At least I'm honest – I'm a lady in a gentleman's world, playing the game a whole lot better than you!'

Phoebe stared, white-lipped. 'Well, I'd rather try and change the world, than hold myself in so low a regard that I must pay an actress for help – all while hoping drink and snuff get there first!' she accused.

It was a wild guess, but entirely correct, judging by the look on Aurelia's face.

'As for the rest, let's let the race decide, shall we?'

'With pleasure!' Aurelia snapped, her chestnuts springing forward.

Seconds later, both phaetons were bolting along the bridge at breakneck speed, their surroundings already a blur. Instinctively, Phoebe leaned low over the reins and whispered to her team.

'Nice and steady!' she encouraged the greys, watching the way they flicked their ears in response. She gritted her teeth, she was an experienced horsewoman, but even she was in awe of the way they seemed to understand. Effortlessly, they flew over the bridge and into Great Pulteney Street, a long avenue with impressive townhouses, pediments and Corinthian pilasters – and if she was vaguely aware of movement behind the occasional window, she was way past caring.

'Keep a firm hand, don't let them have their heads too soon…'

She could almost hear Fred's voice as she kept the lightest touch on her team, keeping them in check as Aurelia overtook with a triumphant glance. She drew a steadying breath, there were still the Sydney Gardens to navigate, and she had no wish to lose a wheel, or lame a horse.

Carefully, she adjusted the reins and focused on the road ahead, the argument echoing through her head. How dare Aurelia suggest she held any kind of torch for the viscount; it was inconceivable, and beyond comprehension. She'd done nothing but detest him since the very first day they met, and he'd proceeded to interfere and irritate beyond all reason.

'You're in love with him! It's as plain as a pikestaff! And in truth, I care not, because it only proves that for all your silly talk of adventuring and equality you're no better than any of us…'

The words dug under her skin as Aurelia leaned forward and, with a sudden flash, lay a whip about her horses' sweaty flanks. They responded immediately, lengthening their lead, while Phoebe inhaled sharply and held the greys firm.

'I have never betrayed your confidence except in frank admiration of a young woman who appeared unafraid of anything.'

She'd assumed he'd been mocking her, but what if he was actually being honest?

Phoebe swallowed, memories of their many encounters fluttering through her head, like pages from a book she hadn't read carefully enough. Blood surged to her temples. She'd been so riled by the viscount's continued interference that she hadn't stopped to consider if he'd been sincere at any point.

She'd been aware of the friction between them, of some inexplicable draw, but real care or feelings?

'When I care, I care too much.'

Squeezing the reins, she turned into Sydney Road, which ran the perimeter of the pleasure gardens. This morning, they were glistening in the dawn sun, and Phoebe felt the greys leap forward enthusiastically.

'Steady,' she muttered beneath her breath.

Aurelia was a fair distance ahead now, her fair hair streaming out beneath her riding hat.

'More tortoise, less hare,' Phoebe added, wishing Josephine was there to share her moment of inspiration.

The greys flicked their ears as though in understanding, which was also precisely the moment she became aware that someone was in pursuit.

Scowling, she craned her neck to spot not one, but two figures, riding as though their lives depended on it, and a flare of anger tore through her as she recognised her eldest brother's inelegant seat.

'Of all the pompous, overbearing brothers in the world!' she groaned, shaking out her reins. 'Forget the tortoise, it's hare-time!'

The greys seemed only too delighted to forget a fable they'd never read, and given a long rein at last, leapt forward with new energy.

'You really are magnificent creatures,' she murmured as the distance between herself and Aurelia closed dramatically. Within moments, she was close enough to see the gleam in her opponent's eyes whenever she glanced back, yet their pursuers were gaining, too.

'If Thomas catches us, it will be game over and no mistake,' she whispered into the horses' sensitive ears. 'I'll have to marry the earl, the captain will be arrested, and you two will have to take Aurelia shopping every day!'

Their ears twitched again, and even though there were tiny specks of foam on their flanks, they lengthened their stride, narrowing the gap again.

'Thank you,' Phoebe whispered gratefully.

It was just as they rounded the top of the gardens that Phoebe finally drew adjacent to Aurelia, and one glance was enough to see her chestnuts were tiring. There was foam around their mouths and bridle bits, while one seemed to have developed an uneven stride.

'Your mare!' Phoebe yelled, all thoughts of the race receding. 'Slacken your pace, you'll injure her!' she warned.

Aurelia's only response was to extend her whip with a loud crack that reverberated through Phoebe's bones. Scowling deeply, she whispered to the greys again and with a final effort, they pulled forward in front of Aurelia's gleaming white phaeton. But Phoebe felt no jubilation, her only consideration was for Aurelia's struggling mare. She knew only too well there was a breaking point with horses, and if Aurelia pushed her team too far, they might not finish the race at all.

Rapidly, she racked her brains as one of the smaller entrances to the Sydney Gardens appeared just ahead. There was no way Aurelia would throw the race for a horse, and if she stopped, Aurelia would consider she'd won. But the narrower side path would force them both to slow their horses through the gardens to the Sydney Hotel finish line – if the angle of the entrance didn't overturn them first.

Summoning all her courage, she took the greys wide.

'Last one to the hotel forfeits fifty pounds!' she yelled back, before beginning to turn.

All her focus was on holding the greys steady, yet as she swung through the gates with barely an inch to spare, she could sense the panic on Aurelia's face, and the shock on her brother's too, just a short distance behind.

'Almost as well as a man, wouldn't you say, Thomas?' she muttered, holding her team tight as they thundered down the side path.

It was only when she dared breathe again, that a sickening crunch filled the air. Instantly, she knew it was the sound of metal meeting stone, and a shudder passed through her as she glanced back. Aurelia's phaeton had become irretrievably embroiled with one of the park's metal gateposts and, as she jumped down and sprinted to the healthy mare's head, Phoebe saw exactly what she intended to do. She may have spared the injured mare a laming, but Aurelia would never let a wrecked phaeton stand in her way. She was going to complete the race on horseback.

Gritting her teeth, Phoebe pulled in her reins, and then she, too, was jumping down from her perch, and running to her team. They whinnied and stamped in confusion, but there was no time to lose. Aurelia was already on a bench, and preparing to climb, bareback, onto her good mare, while Phoebe's brothers were just visible beyond the entrance.

From this vantage she could see the expressions on their faces, and it was all the motivation she needed. Swiftly, she loosened the freshest grey, who whinnied in excitement as Phoebe tucked up her skirts. Then, with one swift jump, she was astride his back. It was a manoeuvre that had earned her many a scolding at Knightswood, and briefly, she hoped Thomas was watching.

'Too late,' Aurelia shouted as she galloped past, her riding habit billowing out behind her like a cloak.

'Phoebe, I order you to stop!' Thomas bellowed.

'Oh, go to the devil!' Phoebe yelled, squeezing tightly and leaning low over the grey's ears.

He was warm, but not spent, and moments later, they were chasing Aurelia along the canal path and towards a small ornamental bridge. Phoebe hadn't ridden bareback in a while, and as she yanked off her restrictive skirt, she was grateful she'd had the forethought to wear pantalettes underneath.

'I think we may need a diversion,' she muttered, tossing the skirt to one side as they galloped over a bridge, conscious her brothers were only seconds behind.

Veering away from the main path, Phoebe guided her willing grey along the scenic canal route and soon enough, they were passing the exact spot where Matilda had fallen. She inhaled as a memory darted though her.

'What is perhaps less understandable, is your theft of a horse while under the influence, again…'

She flushed, despite everything. Could she really believe such a man actually cared for her? And could she really have cared for him too, all along?

It was just a few words, unravelling weeks of confusion. Yet in this much, Aurelia seemed to be right, and now Phoebe was going to marry his brother.

Because of a world built by men.

She closed her eyes briefly. She could still do one heroic thing before it all caught up.

Leaning low, she and the grey thundered up the bank overlooking the canal. The grass was dewy, but her ride nimble, and soon enough they were winding past the low-hanging apple tree, and onto the bridle path that had witnessed her fall from grace so many weeks before. And if it felt like fate had played a hand in bringing her back, she wasted no time dwelling on it. Instead, she only patted the grey's flank, as a faint shout went up behind them.

'I'd say they've lost our trail,' she said triumphantly, 'and now we stand a chance!'

She urged the grey forward again, and this time she held nothing back. They had precious seconds to make up, and it seemed as though they grew wings along the beaten track, until the bushes disappeared and they were, finally, sprinting across the main lawn with the Temple of Minerva on the right, and the familiar facade of the Sydney Hotel straight ahead.

Which was when she noticed two new important things.

The first was Aurelia, forcing her exhausted horse across the middle of the dewy lawn, a look of grim intent pinned to her face, and the second was two figures, stripped to their waists, in front of the hotel.

A dart of fear reached through Phoebe, as she urged her loyal grey into one final sprint.

Had her brothers got there before her? Had the law caught up with Captain Elliot before they'd had a chance to escape? How could she stop them?

It was only as they flew up the final rise, with Phoebe fully contemplating throwing herself at her husband-to-be with violent protestations of love, that the identity of the figures became clear.

And her fear sharpened.

The duellist's faces were stony, their bodies tense, and their arms rigid with concentration. A hundred different scenarios jettisoned through Phoebe's head yet there was no time to think; it was all her fault, and somehow she had to stop them.

'Wait! Please wait!' she yelled, swinging her leg over her mare's sweaty back and dropping to the ground as they reached the crest of the lawn.

Then she was aware of the captain looking up, the ground flying beneath her, and of the viscount, cursing profanely, as he threw his blade down.

Before a bruising impact, a strained shout, and everything went black.

Chapter Twenty-Seven

One week, six days, and a few home truths until the wedding

'Of all the courageous, *hare-brained simpletons*!' the viscount thundered.

His voice was disembodied, somewhere just out of sight.

'Elliot, send for Dr Kapoor now!'

'This is your fault entirely!' the captain accused. 'She was simply trying to break us up…'

'Alexander! What on earth are you doing here?' Aurelia gasped. 'I have never had such an awful ride in my life, this mare is pigeon-livered! The race wasn't fair from the start…'

'Race? What race?'

'What have you done to my sister, sir, and where is the rest of her riding attire?' Thomas fumed. 'The Earl of Cumberland will have something to say to this…'

'The Earl of Cumberland is a gobble-cock and is welcome to call me out if he so wishes!' the viscount fired.

'There is no need to inform the earl, Thomas,' Fred

reasoned. 'Let's get Phoebe home and hush up this whole damned affair.'

'No one is going anywhere, least of all Phoebe!' the viscount countered. 'And is that one of my greys?'

'Well, there's no need to shout about it,' Aurelia objected, mulishly. 'I'm sure we can all hear you very well. And why are *you* here, Alexander? Elliot?'

Phoebe inched her eyes open to find a scene of such huge comical proportions that a bubble of laughter escaped her, despite the throb at the back of her head.

'It's not funny!' Aurelia hissed. You're the cause of so much trouble, Phoebe Fairfax, just like your father before you…'

'Enough!' the viscount roared, and to Phoebe's utter shock, Aurelia fell silent.

Phoebe blinked, trying to stop the world from spinning, and found herself in a somewhat curious position. Her head was cushioned by the viscount's shirt, the captain was chafing her hand, and the remainder of the small crowd were gathered around her with faces worthy of a state funeral.

Another bubble of laughter threatened.

'Is my sister injured?' Thomas demanded, peering closer, with all the concern of a banker watching his investment wobble.

Phoebe fought to sit up, unsure if it was the blow to her head, or the viscount's golden chest against which she rested that was making her feel faint.

'I assure you, I am perfectly well,' she managed, relieved to discover that despite a volcanic headache she was still, somehow, in one piece.

'That's more luck than judgement, you little fool!' the

viscount returned roughly. 'What have I told you about getting involved with duels?'

Then he was kneeling beside her, and gazing with such tenderness, that for a moment she was entirely bereft of words. She'd spent so long convincing herself that the viscount was an arrogant rake of the first order, that his only interest was in vexing a girl who seemed to attract drama and trouble wherever she went, that she'd been blind to everything.

Yet it was right there in his jewelled eyes, a glint that was both fear and care, and something else, too; something that had been there from the very first night in the library.

The oddest sensation slid down Phoebe's spine, just as the captain's broad hand covered her own.

'We're still leaving the moment Dr Kapoor has seen her.'

He spoke stiffly, and Phoebe knew then that this was the reason he and the viscount had been fighting.

'Good riddance!' Aurelia snapped, hobbling over to the hotel steps with the heel of her riding boot in one hand. 'Has *anyone* noticed the state of my habit?'

Phoebe looked up and was delighted to note that Aurelia's lilac riding habit was indeed splattered from head to foot with thick mud.

'You owe me fifty pounds,' she added serenely.

Fred whistled.

'You ladies don't go in for low stakes, do you?' he observed.

'Phoebe is going nowhere!' Thomas addressed the captain directly. 'And you, sir, will meet me for this … insult!'

His tone was ugly, and his uncompromising expression one Phoebe knew well.

'My brother will do no such thing,' the viscount returned, snatching up his sword. 'If anyone gets to murder him, it will be me!'

'Thank you,' the captain murmured, 'I think.'

Phoebe exhaled in exasperation before pushing them all away, and clambering to her feet.

'Cover yourself, sister!' Thomas barked furiously. 'You are in company!'

The park spun out like a maypole as, bemused, Phoebe looked down at what was left of her riding habit. Her short jacket barely reached the waist of her exposed pantalettes and briefly, she marvelled at their unblemished white, before drawing a breath.

'Firstly, no one is murdering anyone on *my* behalf,' she began, grateful for the captain's steadying hand. 'Though if you all choose to murder one another for other reasons, I'm sure I wish you well in your endeavours.'

She drew another deep breath, relieved to find the world slowly steadying.

'Secondly, the captain and I *are* leaving together.'

A murmur of dissent went up immediately, to which Phoebe held up a hand.

'Thirdly, none of you will stop us because the morning is advancing, and this race will be the scandal of the season, *involving all of you*, unless you let us go.'

'Damn the scandal! Why Elliot?' the viscount interrupted in a low, raw tone she'd not heard before.

It was the moment she'd been dreading most as she turned back to face him. Lying to her brothers about the captain was one thing, lying to the viscount about her true feelings quite another. She caught her breath as a strange weakness melted through her. He was all golden skin and tousled hair, while his dark eyes were unexpectedly vulnerable.

'I … love Elliot … and he … he loves me,' she forced, watching a shadow of pain flicker across his face, and somehow find its way into her chest, too.

She clenched her jaw, forcing herself to hold his gaze.

'Phoebe, this is ridiculous!' Thomas expostulated. 'You are to marry the earl in a week! Or have you forgotten Papa's dying wish?'

'It wasn't his dying wish!' Phoebe rounded on her brother furiously. 'And I'll wager you've always known it. It was a gambling debt! Left over from when he was young and reckless! Tell me, what kind of gentleman would gamble the hand of his first-born daughter in marriage? And what kind of brother would not want to find a way to undo it?! Except it suited you, didn't it? You only ever wanted Knightswood, not the family that went with it!'

There was silence, as a range of expressions from fury to smug satisfaction registered around the small group.

'Is this true, Thomas?' Fred asked, the first to find his tongue.

'No! Of course—'

'Well, the gambling part is,' Aurelia interjected, sliding up behind the viscount and pushing her arm through his.

'Which is why you were fighting *so* heroically to stop the captain, wasn't it, Alexander? The Damerels have no desire to be associated with scandal. And a true gentleman *always* honours his debts.'

She paused to sigh in self-satisfaction at Thomas.

'No, that is not the reason, and Phoebe cannot marry Elliot!' the viscount hissed, shaking Aurelia off and taking a step forward, every line of his upper body taut in the dawn sun.

'Miss Fairfax is engaged to the earl, Elliot! Why now?' he challenged.

'You know how love is, brother,' the captain returned warily. 'It has a habit of surprising you.'

A noise, much like a strangled growl, ripped from the viscount's throat as he reached a punishing blow directly to his brother's nose.

'Stop!' Phoebe cried as the captain staggered back, and the viscount made to follow.

'Affecting though this display of brotherly love is,' Thomas interjected coldly, 'might I remind you Phoebe is *my* sister and *my* ward. There may be little care among you for family honour, but while there's the slightest chance of retrieving—'

Yet whatever Thomas was going to say was drowned out by a thunder of hooves, approaching at speed.

Phoebe looked up in disbelief, wondering what other possible drama could unfold in Sydney Gardens on this bright spring morning. Yet the messenger was swift enough for them all to fall silent as he dismounted, ignored their varying states of muddy undress, and made straight for Thomas.

Phoebe stared as she caught sight of her aunt's scrawl on the letter in his hand.

How had she known where to find them?

Josephine had had the strictest instructions not to deliver the letters until she and the captain were miles away.

And then she just knew. The realisation fanned through her,

like a heat and a chill all at once, before Thomas uttered the words she dreaded most.

'It's Josephine, Phoebe,' he confirmed acerbically. 'I trust you have no objection to accompanying me now.'

The journey back to Wood Lodge felt a hundred times longer than any Phoebe had ever undertaken before. And all she could think was that she'd left her sister when she needed her most, when nothing, not even her papa's debt to the earl, came close to mattering as much.

Silently, she accepted Thomas's furious tirade that she was the most selfish and disgraceful sister alive, but her thoughts were elsewhere entirely, thinking back over the past few weeks and the way Josephine had slowly deteriorated.

'*The air and waters have done nothing for her! I think we should take her home.*'

Sophie had said it, and Phoebe had been so wrapped up in her own problems she hadn't done anything about it – and now, she might be too late altogether.

Guilt bled through her as she recalled her sister's cough when she'd left the house earlier that morning. Her aunt's letter had outlined Josephine's feverish condition, and said that Dr Kapoor was already in attendance, but Phoebe also knew her sister was much weaker than before.

How could she have left her at all?

She raced up the stairwell in her riding jacket and pantalettes, taking the steps two at a time, until a figure appeared in the shadows at the top.

'Phoebe!'

She pulled up at the betrayal in her sister's tone.

'Or should I call you, Mrs Captain Damerel?'

'Sophie…' she began, faltering. She had so much explaining to do, but it would have to wait for now. 'Read me all the lectures you want afterwards, but for now, please, let me come to Jo.'

Whether it was the plea in her voice, or their sister's condition, Sophie let her pass.

She entered Josephine's bedchamber quietly. It was already thick with the scent of thorn apple, and she was propped up against numerous pillows with Dr Kapoor in calm attendance, but one glance was enough for Phoebe to know the seriousness of the situation. Her sister's skin looked translucent in the late morning light, while her breath was shallow and laboured. Phoebe flew to her side, noticing the empty laudanum bottle on the bedside table as she took her pale hand.

'How has it come to this so swiftly?' she asked Dr Kapoor, yanking off her muddied jacket. 'I overheard a cough early this morning, but she otherwise seemed settled.'

Dr Kapoor looked up, while Sophie scowled from the doorway.

'In my limited experience, lung spasms are more severe in those who are being treated with laudanum,' he returned quietly. He nodded towards the offending bottle. 'While it is a favoured remedy among many of the medical profession, my personal research has discovered it to be of dubious benefit. It will calm symptoms, but also weaken a patient over time.'

Phoebe stared, feeling all the tiny hairs across the backs of her arms and neck start to strain.

Hadn't she suspected as much? Her guilt intensified, tenfold.

'It has poisoned her?' she whispered, her thoughts woolly and dazed.

'I believe so,' Dr Kapoor nodded, 'but it doesn't explain this lung spasm, which could have been caused by anything, of course.'

He looked at her, his midnight eyes meeting her frank blue ones, acknowledging they both knew *exactly* what had caused this latest attack.

Phoebe took her sister's hand, icy fear trickling down her spine as she thought back to the evening before, when she'd given Josephine her letters and begged her confidence until the agreed hour. She'd had given it readily, eager to please, and now Phoebe's foolish thoughtlessness had cost her dearly. How would she ever forgive herself? Nothing was worth the loss of such a beloved sister.

'Jo … I'm here now,' she whispered hoarsely. 'I'm so … sorry,' she added, her words turning to stones in her throat, 'but I'm here now.'

She looked down at Josephine's pinched, unconscious face, and felt each wracking breath as though it were her own. She couldn't die, not at sixteen, with her whole life ahead of her. She would take a thousand unwelcome betrothals before that.

'We'll go *home*, Jo!' Phoebe whispered, her voice catching. 'Home to Knightswood and the moor. I'll speak to Thomas and make it happen, I promise. I'm here now, and never going away again… Please Jo … just stay.'

Chapter Twenty-Eight

Knightswood Manor, four weeks later

Tufts of cotton grass danced in the breeze, their ivory blooms swaying above the moorland gorse as Phoebe leaned forward to pat Misty's dappled neck.

'You're right,' she whispered as Misty whinnied impatiently, 'it's far too long since we've been to the woods. You watch the path and I'll listen for warblers, it'll be just like old times.'

Phoebe urged her forward, letting her choose her path through the prickly gorse and marshy soil, while she filled her lungs with the heather-sweet air.

'You'll always be the lady of us,' she murmured.

The day hadn't yet arrived, and shadows of night lingered over the hills, creating the sleepy, misted world she'd missed so much.

'How about we take our old trail, so we're back in time for breakfast?' she suggested, as they reached the edge of the trees.

'We'll keep a close eye on the sun,' she added, 'you know how fractious Sophie gets if we're late.'

Misty whinnied while she exhaled. Sophie had only just begun talking to her again, and she'd no desire to upset her further.

Quietly, they followed the glistening river into the woods, Misty's hooves treading the mossy trail with practised ease until they reached the river stepping stones, where Phoebe drew to a standstill. She paused, letting echoes of her childhood reach out from the rippling, moorland water. They were carefree, sunlit days, unlike the journey home four weeks before, when a coldness had entered her heart. And day by day, hour by hour, ever since, it had been thawing.

They'd come so close to losing Josephine. If she closed her eyes, she could still see her sister's blue lips, still feel the cost of each laboured, wracking breath – yet somehow, they'd made it home, and the moment they turned into Knightswood's gates, Josephine seemed to breathe more easily.

Then, armed only with Dr Kapoor's medicinal brew, and fresh moorland air, she and Sophie had nursed their sister through the worst of her delirium. It was different this time. She didn't regain consciousness for days, and at one point seemed to lack the strength to return at all. But they refused to give up and slowly the midnight fevers and choking fits lessened, until finally, she opened her eyes.

'There, Misty, all is well now, she is recovered,' Phoebe whispered, as much to reassure herself as anything else.

If only the same could be said of her own heart.

She swallowed, thinking of the long nights Sophie had

remained silent, refusing to talk to her at all, before her inevitable fury.

'Of all the gentlemen in Bath, you had to choose the one I cared about, and make me feel a complete fool... It doesn't matter that you aren't married now, you were going to be, and that changes everything... You aren't the sister I thought you were!'

The words were etched into Phoebe's heart, and even though gossip about her intended elopement had helped to quell the rumours about the captain, there had been plenty more about herself. Approval of the family rested on a knife edge, and it had been deemed best they all withdrew, the captain went abroad, and Dr Kapoor continued with his research at Oxford. All of which had left a strange wariness between the sisters that had eased gradually into a sombre acceptance.

'Careful, Misty, the ground is a little uneven here,' she murmured, as her pony stepped into the fresh spring river.

It hadn't taken long for news of her scandalous race, and intended elopement, to reach the earl's ears, and his rebuke echoed as Misty leaned low to take a drink.

'I'd rather write off Fairfax's debt altogether than marry a hoydenish miss without a shred of propriety or family honour!'

Which had given rise to the first unexpected thing. Thomas hadn't banished her to one of Knightswood's leaky turrets.

This was a much happier outcome than she'd dared hope for, and while he still read her a long lecture on the unfortunate fate that befell sisters who chose to ignore those who knew better, he'd also given her the estate books and accounts, together with a short note about how he hadn't expected to be a guardian at thirty.

It felt like the closest thing to an apology.

Since then, she'd discovered she'd quite a talent when it came to managing the estate, and had already made several suggestions for improvements, including running water to all the bedchambers, which Thomas had agreed to consider. He'd also agreed to her overseeing Matilda's studies, which she ensured included plenty of time for tree-climbing, and treasure-hunting.

And so the days passed. News from Bath was slow and intermittent, which they all welcomed, and yet also gave rise to the second unexpected thing: the viscount and Aurelia didn't marry.

'It's just us and the woodland fae, isn't it, Misty?' Phoebe murmured, the ancient oaks reaching over their heads to create a natural canopy.

And in that moment, enclosed in the heart of the woods, she could have believed in a little magic. Because she didn't really trust her eyes when she glimpsed a distant figure coming toward her, a figure on a familiar grey, with a proud seat and dark, tousled hair. She drew to a halt, unwilling to tread further and watch the apparition melt away with the night shadows. Except it didn't. It continued getting closer, until she could see the light in his jewelled eyes.

'It's really you?' she whispered, as he stopped and dismounted.

Phoebe swallowed, suddenly aware of the pounding inside her chest reaching over the dawn song around them. She'd tried to picture the viscount's face so many times these past weeks, but never could outside her dreams, when he came to her in the kind of intimacy that left her breathless and bereft when she woke.

Yet this was no dream; he was right here, standing before her, extending his hand – and then, she too was in the stream, standing closer than was good for either of them.

'Sophie said I could find you here.' His voice caught as his eyes held hers.

'I thought you'd gone to London…'

'I'm staying nearby, and couldn't…'

They trailed off as their voices overlapped, and for the first time Phoebe noticed his loose shirt, unkempt hair and boots speckled with moorland moss. He'd never looked less perfect. She gazed at him, noting the way the light caught his dark eyelashes, accentuating their curve, and the golden hue of his skin inside the open collar of his shirt. She swallowed, conscious of a rush of something as he smiled, stealing words.

'Well, I might have,' he murmured, 'had it not been for someone who insists on proving me wrong – about everything.'

She smiled faintly.

'I thought I was a *hare-brained simpleton* who needs to rethink her expectations?'

He cursed softly, before catching her hand and raising it to his lips, kissing it with the kind of fervour she thought belonged only to novels.

'I am the biggest simpleton for ever saying it!' he groaned. 'And while you *will* need some driving tuition before you go near my greys again…'

His eyes danced as Phoebe bit her lip.

'Upon my family's honour, I've never known a girl as headstrong, stubborn, reckless, and hopelessly courageous as you,' he murmured. 'You *are* a heroine in every way.'

She looked up in astonishment, unsure how to receive compliments from a man who'd only ever laboured her shortcomings.

He was so close now she could feel his breath on her cheek, his heat blurring her thoughts, and suddenly she realised she wanted him too close, this arrogant viscount who'd done nothing but infuriate and interfere since the day they met.

'What of Aurelia?' she whispered, her name feeling awkward in the space between them.

He drew a breath.

'That betrothal was arranged when we were each in the cradle. I never relished the prospect, but was prepared to honour it until Elliot told me her part in your escapades. Since then, the Marquis and Marchioness of Carlisle have called off the engagement. They were quite willing, after I pointed out the perils of their only daughter concluding her first season amid a cloud of rumours involving dubious actresses and snuff! As I understand it, she may well be the new countess before the year is out, anyway.'

A slow smile spread across Phoebe's face.

'If anyone was ever born to it,' she murmured, raising her eyebrows.

'She will make a much better countess than you,' he agreed.

'Oh, yes?' Phoebe parried. 'And why is that? Apart from the fact I'm not fit to grace polite circles as a general rule?'

'On the contrary,' he smiled, gold flecks glistening, 'it's just I believe you would make a much better viscountess.'

There was a brief silence when a lone blackbird warbled softly.

'But I punched you!' she whispered, her thoughts in glorious disarray. 'And broke your window ... and stole your precious greys ... and nearly married your brother!'

'Greys aside, your crimes have only worsened my affliction,' he whispered, gently tucking back a tendril of her hair.

'But I promised Matilda I'd never marry,' she breathed, 'unless it was to a pirate – or a schoolmaster with an extensive library of heroic novels.'

He smiled and took her hands.

'I may not be a pirate or a schoolmaster, but I can help with a school.'

Phoebe stared.

'Ebcott Place?' he added. 'Somewhere girls like Josephine and Florence can learn, unhindered, because they have the best doctor in residence.'

'Doctor Kapoor?' Phoebe asked in wonder.

'Doctor Kapoor can't conduct research at Oxford forever.' He smiled. 'Elliot can visit when he's on leave, and General Matilda, of course, can keep us all in line.'

He caught his breath then, the sun just melting through the trees.

'I meant what I said at Damerel Place,' he whispered. 'You've stolen my peace, and I cannot sleep or *breathe* without you... Rescue me, Phoebe? You'll have all the adventure you want – providing it doesn't involve running away with my brother.'

There was a moment's quiet, when the blackbird warbled again.

'Well then...' she replied with a gentle smile, 'it's probably the most *heroic* thing I can do.'

Glossary

Adventuress – Regency slang for prostitute.

Bit of muslin – Regency slang for prostitute.

Cheltenham Tragedy – Regency slang for making a big deal out of something or blow a situation out of proportion.

Deuced – refers to rolling a two in dice, which is the lowest possible score one might get. In this way the word is used to refer to things of less-than-ideal luck and has the same meaning as 'damned' or 'cursed'.

Foozler – Regency slang for one who does things clumsily, a bungler.

Gobble-cock – Regency slang for turkey.

Gundigut – a Regency insult, meaning a fat, pursy fellow.

Hexworthy Races – traditional moorland races where thoroughbreds and not so thoroughbreds raced side by side.

Hornswoggler – Regency slang for a fraud or cheat.

Hoydenish – saucy, boisterous or carefree behaviour.

La – Regency exclamation or equivalent of 'like/totally', often overused as a verbal crutch by young women.

Lawks – vulgar Regency exclamation.

Miss Sarah Siddons (1755–1831) – British actress and tragic heroine, daughter of English Theatre's Roger Kemble and Sarah Ward. Would have been sixty-five years old when Phoebe crossed her path. Sarah was the eldest of thirteen children, so Phoebe could have passed as a younger widowed cousin (with the assistance of spectacles and powdered hair).

Ninnyhammer – Regency slang for a person who is stupid or foolish.

Pigeon-livered – Regency slang for cowardly.

Salmagundi – a Regency dish of chopped meat, anchovies, eggs, onion, and seasoning.

Short-drawers – short Regency underwear (unlike long-drawers) for gentlemen, much like boxer shorts today.

Questions And Commands – a popular game in British households in the seventeenth and eighteenth centuries, the precursor to Truth or Dare.

ONE MORE CHAPTER

YOUR NUMBER ONE STOP

FOR PAGETURNING BOOKS

The author and One More Chapter would like to thank everyone who contributed to the publication of this story...

Analytics
James Brackin
Abigail Fryer

Audio
Fionnuala Barrett
Ciara Briggs

Contracts
Laura Amos
Laura Evans

Design
Lucy Bennett
Fiona Greenway
Liane Payne
Dean Russell

Digital Sales
Lydia Grainge
Hannah Lismore
Emily Scorer

Editorial
Janet Marie Adkins
Kara Daniel
Arsalan Isa
Charlotte Ledger
Lydia Mason
Ajebowale Roberts
Jennie Rothwell
Caroline Scott-Bowden
Emily Thomas

Harper360
Emily Gerbner
Jean Marie Kelly
emma sullivan
Sophia Wilhelm

International Sales
Peter Borcsok
Ruth Burrow

Marketing & Publicity
Chloe Cummings
Emma Petfield

Operations
Melissa Okusanya
Hannah Stamp

Production
Denis Manson
Simon Moore
Francesca Tuzzeo

Rights
Helena Font Brillas
Ashton Mucha
Zoe Shine
Aisling Smythe

The HarperCollins Distribution Team

The HarperCollins Finance & Royalties Team

The HarperCollins Legal Team

The HarperCollins Technology Team

Trade Marketing
Ben Hurd

UK Sales
Laura Carpenter
Isabel Coburn
Jay Cochrane
Sabina Lewis
Holly Martin
Harriet Williams
Leah Woods

And every other essential link in the chain from delivery drivers to booksellers to librarians and beyond!